THE INSIDE MAN

A Levi Yoder Thriller

M.A. ROTHMAN

Primordial Press

Copyright © 2019 Michael A. Rothman

Cover Art by M.S. Corley

This is a work of fiction. Names, characters, businesses, places, events, locales, and incidents are either the products of the author's imagination or used in a fictitious manner. Any resemblance to actual persons, living or dead, or actual events is purely coincidental.

All rights reserved.

ISBN-13: 9781092279550

ALSO BY M.A. ROTHMAN

Technothrillers: (Thrillers with science / Hard-Science Fiction)
- Primordial Threat
- Freedom's Last Gasp
- Darwin's Cipher

Levi Yoder Thrillers:
- Perimeter
- The Inside Man
- Never Again

Epic Fantasy / Dystopian:
- Dispocalypse

- Agent of Prophecy
- Heirs of Prophecy
- Tools of Prophecy
- Lords of Prophecy

For the innocent victims, may you find peace.

CONTENTS

US Senate Testimony by Tim Ballard	1
Chapter 1	3
Chapter 2	23
Chapter 3	40
Chapter 4	56
Chapter 5	69
Chapter 6	84
Chapter 7	97
Chapter 8	112
Chapter 9	130
Chapter 10	143
Chapter 11	151
Chapter 12	164
Chapter 13	174
Chapter 14	182
Chapter 15	191
Chapter 16	207
Chapter 17	222
Chapter 18	241
Chapter 19	255
Chapter 20	265
Chapter 21	274
Chapter 22	289
Preview of Never Again	299
Author's Note	317
Addendum	319
About the Author	327

This page purposefully left blank.

US SENATE TESTIMONY BY TIM BALLARD

March 6th, 2019
Testifying: Tim Ballard
Senate Committee on the Judiciary

…

Human trafficking is real, it's tragic, and I am grateful this Committee is willing to learn more and to understand more about this horrific practice…

…

At the DHS, I spent 12 years as a special agent and undercover operator for Homeland Security Investigations. For 10 of those years, I was combating sex trafficking on the southern border and became one of the country's foremost experts on the issue of trafficking through years of undercover work, research and investigation.

…

Part of the job ... is to recognize and fight human trafficking. To understand just a little about the issue it is important to understand that there are an estimated 40 million modern-day slaves worldwide with children making up an estimated 10 million of these victims.[1]

...

The US is also one of the wealthiest nations in the world, creating fertile ground for child traffickers who are trying to get their product to this lucrative illicit market.

The State Department has reported that roughly 17,500 people are smuggled into the United States annually, many of which are women and children that are forced into the commercial sex trade.[2] About 10,000 children a year suffer the horrors of commercial sexual exploitation in the United States.[3]

---

1. *Guardian*, Feb 25, 2019
2. Trafficking in Persons Report, US Dept of State, June 14, 2004
3. *Indianapolis Star*, Feb. 1, 2018

CHAPTER ONE

"Pizza delivery."

The familiar voice broadcast through a hidden speaker in the small security office. A yellow LED on one of the security consoles flashed, indicating someone had sent an "open" command to the front gate.

Yoshi Watanabe checked the surveillance monitors that overlooked the sprawling apartment complex. One of the video feeds showed the north security gate sliding open, allowing the Domino's delivery person onto the property.

There was nothing unusual about a pizza delivery. Ten p.m. was a little later than normal, but not overly late, and Yoshi recognized the delivery man's voice—he'd heard the same voice several times a week for nearly a year. But this time, there was something about the way the driver had spoken that caught his attention.

Had the man's voice quavered just a bit?

The hairs on the back of Yoshi's neck stood on end.

He scooted his chair closer to the monitors and scanned the images for the delivery car. There were nearly two dozen different motion-activated video cameras dotted throughout the property, but it took only moments to find the Honda with a Domino's emblem on its side, parked in front of Building 3. There was no one in the driver's seat, yet a plume of exhaust came from the back of it.

Yoshi shook his head. "That's how you get your stuff stolen."

But then he spotted a gray blob lying next to the car. He zoomed in several times, and the gray blob suddenly turned into a person with bright-red hair.

It was the Domino's delivery guy. No doubt about it.

His heart racing, Yoshi flipped through Building 3's other cameras. He caught a man wearing a ski mask racing from one of the apartments, a child's limp body draped over his shoulder.

He checked the feed: first floor. And the man had run out of the third apartment from the end.

Yoshi's breath caught in his throat.

Apartment 1C.

That wasn't just any child. That was the granddaughter of Shinzo Tanaka, the leader of one of Japan's largest crime syndicates.

"No!" he yelled impotently at the screen, waking the other security guard.

"What? Who?" The bewildered guard was still blinking the sleep out of his eyes as Yoshi raced from the security office.

Sprinting across the courtyard toward the security gate, Yoshi grimaced when he heard the two-ton gate begin to move. He arrived in time to see the back of a late-model Honda fishtailing away from the apartment complex, the exit gate yawning open behind it.

THE INSIDE MAN

Gritting his teeth, Yoshi spun on his heel and raced toward Building 3.

He was greeted by one of the security guards. "Yoshi? What's going—"

"Shut up and call the police. There's been a kidnapping! Building 3, apartment 1C."

A chill raced up the middle of Yoshi's back. If they had gotten away with the child ... what had they done to her mother?

~

Ryuki Watanabe took the first available flight to Tokyo after his brother, Yoshi, called with the news. Ryuki had been instrumental in getting Yoshi placed at the apartment complex to watch over the girl, yet he couldn't let his brother take the blame. The kidnapping of Tanaka's granddaughter was Ryuki's responsibility.

Now, late in the evening in downtown Tokyo, he waited alone in a conference room on the top floor of the Tanaka Building. He'd hoped that this day would never come, yet he felt unusually calm as he sat at the conference-room table waiting for the chairman to arrive.

He shook his head as he panned his gaze around the room. He preferred the traditional decorations of his Japanese ancestry: low-profile tables around which people would sit *seiza*-style, hanging scrolls with Japanese calligraphy, and silk-embroidered art. But Tanaka favored a Western style. The room smelled of the twenty black leather high-back chairs, and the long table they encircled was made of black wood that gleamed with a heavy polish. Ebony, perhaps.

The far door opened, and Shinzo Tanaka strode through the

doorway. The man was in his mid-sixties. Bloodshot eyes betrayed a depth of emotion beneath his otherwise stone-like expression. Two bodyguards followed one step behind him, closed the door, and effectively blocked the exit.

Ryuki felt a surge of anxiety as he waited for his long-time boss to speak. As Tanaka's second-in-command, Ryuki had known the man for nearly a quarter century, yet he'd never seen him look as haggard as he did this evening.

"Ryuki." The elder's gravelly voice was heavy with emotion. "How ... how did this happen?"

"I'm sorry." Ryuki bowed his head as he nervously traced the outline of the knife in his front right pocket. "It all happened very quickly. The man broke into the apartment, the child's mother was knocked unconscious, and the child was taken, all in less than a minute. The American police are involved, and I have our people looking into it as well."

Tanaka's face darkened as he pressed his lips into a thin line. "You promised me that my granddaughter would be safe in America."

"I did." A cool sense of resignation washed over Ryuki as he bowed before his boss. "I'm prepared to give a most sincere apology."

He drew from his pocket a knife, a packet of gauze, and a pristine white silken cloth, then laid them all on the table. He placed his left fist on the middle of the cloth with his pinkie extended, and bowed his head with a deep sense of regret. This was his first time ever disappointing the man. He prayed it would be his last.

Gritting his teeth, he picked up the knife, flipped open the razor-sharp blade, and sliced heavily across the last knuckle of his pinkie.

The knife sliced through the fibrous tendons, and he felt them snap like rubber bands. He tightened his core and barely suppressed a grunt of pain.

When the deed was done, he used his right hand to bundle the severed tip of his finger in the white silk. His head still bowed, he gave the grotesque offering to Tanaka, who grimly accepted the apology.

The wound flared with heat, and Ryuki wrapped the injured finger with a gauze impregnated with a clotting agent. With a fresh cloth, he cleaned the blood from the table.

Tanaka pulled out a chair and sat across from him. "Ryuki, we must find my granddaughter. She's my son's only child."

Ryuki felt the man's pain even through his own. Tanaka had already lost his son—killed in the US in a drive-by shooting—despite having kept him from their life, just like Ryuki had sheltered his brother. And now the man feared he would lose his granddaughter too.

"I will get more of our people on this," Ryuki said.

Tanaka leaned forward and slid a note across the table. Ryuki retrieved it with his right hand.

"I'm giving you permission to reach out to the Italians in our American territory," Tanaka said. "There is one there that I'd trust with this."

Ryuki cringed at the slight. The implication was that he himself had fallen out of trust, at least with regard to Tanaka's granddaughter.

"Before approaching him," Tanaka continued, "get permission from his superior. Promise whatever you need to acquire his help. I'll cover the expense." He stood, and the bodyguards opened the conference-room door. "Take the next flight and arrange this with the head of the Bianchi family from New York City."

Ryuki stood as well, and Tanaka placed his hand on his shoulder and squeezed. "Bring my granddaughter safely back to me, Ryuki. She's my only living heir." His tone brooked no argument. "Nothing else is more important."

Ryuki bowed, and Tanaka gave him a light shove toward the exit. "Go!"

As he strode quickly down the hallway, Ryuki unfolded the paper and looked at the English name scrawled on it.

He pressed the button calling for the elevator and wondered who Levi Yoder was.

~

Levi woke to the pre-dawn sounds of New York City rising from several stories below his Park Avenue apartment. With a luxurious stretch, he yawned and stumbled out of bed. It was just before five a.m., earlier than he normally liked to wake up, but as he padded out of the bedroom, he couldn't help but smile at what he saw.

Standing next to the wall-mounted bookshelves, bathed in the warm glow of an antique Italian lamp, was a statuesque woman in her early thirties. She was wearing nothing but one of his button-down shirts as she thumbed through a thick three-ring binder of old medical journals she'd pulled from a shelf. She had straight shoulder-length black hair and mocha-colored skin, both of which contrasted beautifully with the white shirt.

Last night was the first time he'd brought Madison to his apartment—an apartment owned by the Bianchi family, one of the largest of the New York Mafia families. It was a baby step into his secret world.

"You're up early," Levi remarked.

Madison looked up at him in silence for a few long seconds. A smile creased her delicate features.

"What?" He frowned as he looked at himself and then back at her.

"You're just cute. I didn't think anyone still wore pajamas to bed anymore." She tapped a finger on the binder. "You've got a strange collection of books. Is reading medical journals a hobby of yours?"

He shrugged, walked over to Madison, and kissed her on the cheek. "Good morning to you, too. Hopefully, you're good with eggs, because that's the only breakfasty stuff I have in the fridge. I'll go make us some ham and cheese omelets."

Madison huffed loudly. "Levi, don't ignore me. What's with all this medical stuff? It seems like odd reading material for someone to have unless, well, you know—you're a doctor."

Levi grabbed a carton of eggs from the refrigerator and spoke over his shoulder as he prepared breakfast. "Well, I'm obviously not a doctor. You know about how I had cancer a dozen years ago? At the time, the docs all said it was a terminal case, yet obviously I managed to cheat death. But I eventually realized that I didn't come out of that time in my life totally unscathed."

"What do you mean?" Madison now stood at the entrance to the kitchen, and she sounded concerned. "Are you saying the cancer has come back? You haven't relapsed, have you?"

"No, nothing like that. It's hard to explain. Back then, so many things had happened at once: my wife died in a car accident, I had terminal cancer, and I was struck with a debilitating fever that really knocked me out. And then, suddenly, all on its own, the fever broke and my cancer went into remission. And other things were different too.

"The world seemed to be filled with more colors than I'd ever noticed before. The sounds that had always been there, in the background, were more obvious to my ear. Hell, even the smells of the city were stronger and more distinct. At first I wrote it all off as a strange side effect of the cancer. But after a while, some ... other things ... became hard to ignore."

"Like?" Madison rested her chin on Levi's shoulder, watching as he deftly cracked eggs into a mixing bowl. He felt the warmth of her pressed against him and wondered how much he could say without her thinking he was nuts.

"Well, it was little things. Like I could remember random facts without even trying. For example, I could tell you that the restaurant two blocks north of here had chicken piccata on its Daily Specials menu ten days ago, and it was $10.99. The only reason I know that is because I was walking past the place and saw the sign. I can tell you the license plate number of the Uber driver who brought us here. Hell, I know the ticket stub number for the opera that I attended with a friend of mine two weeks ago."

Madison took a step back. "Are you serious?"

Levi poured the beaten eggs into a pair of hot skillets. "Yup. That's one of the reasons I started combing through those books, trying to figure out—"

"Why didn't you just go see a doctor?" Her voice took on an excited tone. "Are you seriously saying you can remember *everything* you've ever seen?"

Levi nodded as he sprinkled chopped ham and cheddar cheese onto the half-cooked eggs, and carefully flipped each of the omelets onto themselves. "Pretty much. Go ahead. I know you're dying to test me."

Madison reopened the three-ring binder, which was an assembled collection of old issues of the *American Journal of Medicine*, and flipped through the pages. "Okay, this one's from October, 2015. It's an article about fevers of unknown origin—looks like you bookmarked it. What's it say just above table one?"

With a flick of his wrist, Levi flipped both omelets over and sprinkled a bit more shredded cheddar cheese on top. In his mind's eye, he recalled the image of the green-hued medical journal and mentally turned the pages to the appropriate article. It had been one that had particularly intrigued him. He recited the text word for word:

"Petersdorf also classified fevers of unknown origin by category, that is, infectious, malignant/neoplastic, rheumatic/inflammatory, and miscellaneous disorders. Fevers of unknown origin also may be considered in the context of host subsets, for example, organ transplants, human immunodeficiency virus, returning travelers."

He looked over his shoulder as he turned off the stovetop's flame, and Madison stared open-mouthed at him.

"Holy shit, that's amazing. Why haven't you become a doctor or something?"

Levi laughed as he grabbed two large dishes from the cabinet and slid a perfectly cooked omelet onto each of them. "It doesn't exactly work like that. Just because I can remember things doesn't mean I understand everything I'm reading. I've got other books on those shelves about electronics, physics, and other subjects. So yeah, I can tell you what a resistor or a capacitor is, but I don't know beans about what to do with them. Well, maybe I sort of do, but not really."

"So basically you have a photographic memory."

Levi shrugged. "I guess. In those journals I learned that photographic memory—they call it eidetic memory—it's not really something adults have. Sometimes a real small percentage of young kids might have it, but it goes away before adulthood. The only instances of eidetic-like memory in adults were associated with people with some form of traumatic brain injury. And I didn't have anything like that—at least not that I know of.

"I don't know, maybe the fever, or the cancer, or both, did a number on me. Anyway, the memory thing does come in handy sometimes, but it's not exactly a key to being a genius. I'm far from it."

He sprinkled a few finely chopped scallions across the omelets and motioned toward the dining area. "Let's get you fed. You've got a long day ahead of you."

Madison's gaze followed Levi into the dining room. "Levi, you're really full of surprises. I'm sorry, I should be helping—"

"Nonsense, you're my guest. Grab a seat. I'll go get some orange juice."

Levi hustled back to the kitchen and smiled to himself as he thought of the beautiful half-naked woman in his living room. It was strange for him to share private aspects of his life with someone. His biological family knew nothing of what he'd just shared, and his mob family only knew small pieces.

He couldn't help but wonder what the future might hold for the two of them.

Levi stood at the back of the common room in Harlem's YMCA with Carmine and Paulie, watching Madison leading her class. She wore a white gi with a black belt cinched around her narrow waist, and she was putting a group of nearly two dozen neighborhood kids through several basic martial arts forms. Her students ranged from around five years old to late teens, and represented the rainbow of races and cultures that made up the neighborhood and New York City itself.

To Levi, Madison was the personification of grace and beauty in a slim five-foot-ten-inch package.

He had to admit, their relationship was complicated. To say they were friends was to make too little of it, but to say they were a couple ... well, it wasn't quite that either. They didn't even live in the same state—she lived in DC, he lived in New York City.

But it was their jobs that truly made their relationship complicated. After all, she was a covert operations officer for the CIA ... and he was one of the leading members of a prominent Mafia family. She didn't know that part, but she did know he was involved with some less-than-savory characters. And that was enough to make things awkward from time to time.

They'd met nearly a year earlier while Levi was overseas, taking care of some private business. He found himself in a situation that ended up forcing him to cooperate with people who turned out to be agents of the CIA—including Madison. He'd been smitten from the moment he first saw her.

It was hard to imagine a more unlikely pair. He wasn't sure where their relationship was going, but she had his undivided attention. That was undeniable.

"You know," said Carmine next to him, "if she really wants to teach kids, I could probably find her a nicer place uptown."

Carmine and Paulie were the mobsters who'd accompanied Levi here.

"Nah," said Levi. "She knows the guy who runs this place and wanted to do him a favor. The way I understand it, this guy saved Madison from an orphanage in Okinawa back when she was a kid. He got her together with her grandma who lives out in LA."

"Okinawa? She doesn't look Japanese ... no, you know, I take that back. I guess I kind of see it now. I figured she was Hawaiian or something. You know, like one of those hula dancer types."

Levi smiled. "Not even close."

His friends had certainly been surprised when he showed up yesterday at the mob-run apartment building with a girlfriend on his arm. They were naturally curious about her, especially since Levi tended to keep that side of his life fairly quiet, but he hadn't really talked to any of them about her yet.

"I think her mom was Japanese and her dad was a black GI," Levi explained.

"Nice," Carmine said, though following his gaze, Levi wasn't sure if he was talking about Madison or about the group of Latina moms who were across the room watching their kids practice karate.

"Is this what she does, teach karate?" Paulie asked.

Levi craned his neck to look up at Paulie, who stood nearly six foot ten. "This is just a hobby, something she's been doing since she was a kid. She works out of DC doing political analysis and stuff." Political analyst was Madison's official cover, since her real job title was strictly confidential. "We don't talk too much about work. It saves some awkward questions, if you know what I mean."

Paulie nodded. "Yup, it can be tough. My Rita and I have been married for almost ten years, and she still thinks I'm an accountant. It's just easier that way."

A door opened and a tiny Asian girl walked in. She couldn't have been more than five years old, and she wore a yellow dress with a wide black belt and puffy sleeves. Her black hair was pulled back into two ponytails, each of which was tied with a matching yellow ribbon. In her hands, she carried a small box tied with red ribbon. She scanned the room, and when her gaze landed on Levi, she walked directly to him.

Curious, he knelt so that he was eye level with her. "Hi there. Is there something I can I help you with?"

With a serious expression, she bowed and began speaking in rapid Japanese.

Levi blinked with surprise and wondered how she knew he'd understand her. After all, with his dark-brown hair, blue eyes, and a rather pale complexion, nobody would have confused him for Asian. But he had lived in Japan for a handful of years and was fluent in the language.

Levi smiled as the tiny doll of a girl related her memorized message.

"Yoder-san," the girl said, "my name is Kimiko and my father wishes you good health and prosperity. He hopes to invite you to visit so that you and he can talk in private." With both hands, she presented the box to him.

Levi took the box, returned her bow, and said in Japanese, "Thank you, Kimiko."

He untied the ribbon and opened the box. Inside was a stack of one-hundred-dollar bills and a rolled-up parchment. Levi thumbed through the stack of money and whistled with appreciation. Then he unrolled the parchment. It was a formal, handwritten letter, its Japanese calligraphy gorgeously done with a brush, in a traditional style.

Yoder-san,

I have contacted Don Vincenzo Bianchi, and he has given me permission to reach out to you.

I am Mr. Shinzo Tanaka's US representative and would very much like to have a meeting with you. I would not ask this unless I felt the cause was justified. There is an innocent life at stake, and I humbly request your assistance on behalf of my superior.

I've enclosed something to compensate you for your time. I hope to hear from you tonight.

Sincerely,
Ryuki Watanabe.

The rest of the note was repeated in English, and gave an address and a time later that evening. It was signed with a reddish-brown thumbprint whose hue resembled the color of dried blood.

Levi looked at Kimiko with curiosity as she tapped at Paulie's leg. "Sir?" she said, staring wide-eyed at the large man.

With an amused expression, Paulie leaned down. "Yes?" He spoke very softly, with a warm and friendly tone.

"You're very tall," she said matter-of-factly, in perfect English. "Can I sit on your shoulder so I can touch the ceiling?"

Levi watched with wonder as the giant man engaged with the

guileless little girl. For a man who could tear a person apart limb from limb, Paulie was very gentle with Kimiko as he lifted her onto his right shoulder and stood.

Kimiko reached up, touched one of the ceiling tiles, and let out a peal of high-pitched laughter. "I did it!"

Laughing, Paulie carefully set her back on the ground.

She held out her hand with a serious expression and shook his hand. "Thank you, Mister. I'm going to tell everyone at school about you, but I don't think they'll ever believe I saw a giant." Then she shifted her gaze to Levi and again spoke in Japanese. "I have to go. My dad's driver is waiting for me. Maybe I'll see you later?"

"It's possible," Levi replied in Japanese.

The girl ran out of the common room just as the class began to disperse.

Levi felt a tap on his shoulder and turned to see Madison smiling at him. "You made a new friend?" She nodded toward the exit.

"I suppose so." He shrugged and gave her a peck on the lips. "We all done here?"

"Pretty much." Madison snaked her arm under his suit coat and around his waist, giving him a squeeze. "Though I think next time, you should teach the class with me."

"I don't know, I kind of like watching you do it. So—what time do you need to be at Penn Station?"

"I've got an early day tomorrow, so my train's scheduled to leave at three."

They walked toward the exit, and the YMCA staff began moving the furniture back into place.

Levi glanced at his watch and sighed wistfully. "Maddie, these weekends go by too quickly."

She tightened her grip around his waist and leaned her head against his. "I feel the same way. But hey, unless something happens, I should be off for two weeks right around Christmas. If you think you can deal with me for that long, we should plan something. It's only a little over a month away."

Carmine had already gone ahead to get the car, but Paulie had hung back and now chimed in. "You know, the wife and I had a really nice time at the Poconos for our fifth anniversary. The resorts are all probably booked, but I know a few people. I can probably get you guys into one of those two-story champagne tub suites and stuff. It's nice and romantic."

Madison bumped her hip against Levi's. "Hmm, romantic sounds nice." She gave Levi a quick kiss on the cheek. "Let me go change and I'll be right back."

Levi's gaze followed her as she darted past a few people talking in the hallway. He imagined what it would be like to be with Madison in a hot tub filled with bubbles.

He looked up at Paulie. "Okay big guy, if you have some strings you can pull, I'd appreciate it."

Paulie grinned. "Not that it's any of my business, but you two look good together. I think you guys should make a more permanent arrangement."

Levi laughed and shook his head. "It's complicated." He pictured the giant mobster playing the role of Yenta, the matchmaker from the Broadway play *Fiddler on the Roof*.

He glanced again at his watch. "Hey Paulie, can you go out there and make sure Carmine knows we'll need to head straight to Penn Station before going to the Helmsley? I've got to talk business with the don, and Madison can't be around for that."

Driving along Park Avenue, the sedan rolled just past East 86th Street and pulled up to a stately old building with two marble columns on each side of the entrance. The words "The Helmsley Arms" were emblazoned in gold leaf above the ten-foot doors.

As Levi hopped out of the car, the cool damp of the late fall in New York City hit him. The earthy smell of fallen leaves and exhaust filled the air, an unmistakable signature of when and where he was.

The doors opened as he approached the building's entrance, and Frank Minnelli, the head of security, appeared in the doorway. He was in his early forties, the same age as Levi, and was dressed in an almost identical tailored suit.

He motioned to Levi. "Come on. We're waiting on you."

Together they walked past the two burly mobsters who were guarding the entrance, across the building's marble-floored foyer, and into the elevator to the top floor.

"So," Levi said, "I'm guessing someone reached out to Vinnie?"

The elevator doors slid open, and they started down a short wood-paneled hallway.

"You better believe it," Frankie said with a snort. "But I'll leave that for Vinnie to tell."

Two more mobsters hopped up from their chairs and opened a set of double doors. Frankie and Levi walked through into Don Bianchi's parlor.

Levi couldn't help but be amazed at how far up his friends had come since they all started out together in Little Italy over twenty years ago. The huge room had two fireplaces, was finished with ornately carved wood paneling, and was well-appointed with beautiful paintings and a museum-quality marble statue of the Venus de Milo.

At the far end of the room, Don Vincenzo Bianchi, the head of the Bianchi crime family, sat at his large mahogany desk, wearing reading glasses and poring over a sheaf of papers. As the two men walked in, he motioned for them to approach.

"Come in, guys. Frankie, you and I need to talk about a few things, but first let's all get this Tanaka syndicate business out of the way."

Levi took a seat in one of the two reddish-brown leather armchairs in front of the desk, and Frankie sat in the other.

"Vinnie," said Levi, "what's this about someone getting your permission to reach out to me? Who are these people? Are they some new Asian outfit?"

"They're hardly new." Vinnie removed his reading glasses, tossed them on the desk and rubbed his eyes. "Frankie, how many made men and connected guys do we have right now?"

Frankie frowned. "I think with Carlo Moretti last month, we're at a hundred twenty-seven made men, and I'm not sure on the complete number, but we've got right around one thousand earners in total."

The don drummed his fingers on the desk and turned back to Levi. "I got a call this morning from the number two guy in the Tanaka syndicate. They're a pretty serious group out of Japan. In the last handful of years they've expanded beyond the island and have been muscling in on some of the Tong businesses on the West Coast. Heck, they even have a presence here in the city.

"Levi, you and I have both agreed that it's best you not be part of the day-to-day business dealings of the family, especially with some of the stuff you've been doing with the feds. But you know what we're dealing with when it comes to these other groups. Let's just say this Tanaka syndicate has ten times our manpower, and they've got resources everywhere."

Vinnie leaned forward and poked his finger in the air for emphasis. "They've made us an offer contingent on your helping them out with something. And it's a really serious offer."

"The message I got said something about an innocent life," Levi said. "Do you know what they want from me?"

Vinnie shrugged. "I have no idea. What I do know is these Yakuza types are vicious when angered, and I'm not interested in sending you into a meat grinder. This Ryuki guy, the syndicate's number two, he said that he'd guarantee your safety—that he just wants an opportunity to have a sit-down with you. He was extremely polite, like a lot of those Asian types are. But frankly, I don't like it.

"Levi, you and I go back to the beginning. I love you like a brother, and I'll tell you, I don't know what to make of this. This guy was really vague—he wouldn't even tell me why he was looking for *you* specifically. So what I'm saying is, if you don't want to go, you've got my complete backing on that. It's your call."

Frankie cleared his throat and frowned. "Levi, I did a little checking on this Tanaka syndicate—or tried to. Their main guy is a man named Shinzo Tanaka, but there's almost no record of him. I can see that he was denied entry into the US a handful of years ago, but that's about it. The man's a ghost. This Ryuki guy, his number two, is the same. No record. No beef with the local or Japanese law.

"But that's official records. Word on the street is different. There, everyone knows these two. And the word is, stay away from these Yakuza nuts. These guys make us look like choirboys." He jabbed his finger in Levi's direction. "So be careful. I can't read this one, and that makes me a little crazy."

Levi heard their warnings, but his curiosity was gnawing at

him. Why did they want to talk to him specifically? How did that little girl manage to pick him out of a crowd of people at the YMCA? And how did she know he understood Japanese?

He looked at Vinnie and smiled. "Is the offer they gave for my help worthwhile?"

Vinnie returned the smile. "I wouldn't have told him how to reach you if it wasn't a sweet deal."

Levi hopped up from his chair and rapped his knuckles on the desk. "In that case, I guess I shouldn't keep the man waiting."

CHAPTER TWO

With a sense of trepidation, Levi stepped out of the elevator on the eighty-sixth floor of the Freedom Tower, now known as One World Trade Center. He strode past a large sitting area with Western-style decorations—plush leather chairs and a coffee table with business magazines and a neatly folded issue of the *Wall Street Journal*—and stepped up to the receptionist's desk.

He wasn't sure what he'd expected, but when he'd mentally prepared to meet one of the top men in a notorious Japanese crime syndicate, he hadn't expected to meet them in a place that looked like a banker's office. Yet this was clearly the right place: "Tanaka Industries" was emblazoned in large silver letters on the wall behind the receptionist.

She gave him a brilliant smile, and bowed ever-so-slightly. "Mister Yoder, you're a bit early. Mister Watanabe hasn't arrived yet."

She had only the slightest accent—likely she had been born in Japan but came to the States as a young teen. She was in her mid-twenties, tall, had a willowy build, and her pale skin resembled fine ivory. And she was beautiful.

Levi glanced at his watch. He was fifteen minutes early. "I suppose I'll just—"

The elevator doors opened again, and two Asian men stepped out.

The receptionist's eyes widened, and she motioned to the two men with an open hand. "Here comes Mister Watanabe."

The men looked a lot alike—they were clearly related—but the one on the left looked a bit older, a bit richer. His suit was custom-tailored, while the other's looked like it had been purchased off the rack. An expensive rack, but still.

"Mister Yoder?" The man on the left extended his hand, and Levi shook it. "I'm Ryuki Watanabe." He spoke in heavily accented English.

Levi responded in Japanese. "Please, call me Levi. Was it your daughter that delivered the package?"

The man's eyebrows raised, and he smiled. A beaming sort of smile that betrayed an inner pride. "It was." He motioned toward the man standing to his left. "This is my younger brother, Yoshi."

Yoshi shook hands with Levi and said in unaccented English, "It's nice to meet you."

Ryuki turned to the receptionist and he spoke in rapid-fire Japanese. "Hiromi, is my conference room prepared?"

"*Hai.*" Hiromi nodded curtly. "Everything is ready."

Ryuki extended his arm toward a corridor leading past the receptionist's desk. "Please, Mister Yoder, let's talk in private."

Levi followed Ryuki. The man's brother didn't join them.

They passed several closed doors before entering a room that made Levi feel as if he'd walked out of New York City and into a traditional Japanese tea house. On the walls hung scrolls of

Japanese calligraphy, and across the room was a silk-embroidered dragon mounted in a polished rosewood frame. It had to be nearly fifteen feet wide and nearly six feet tall. The floor was covered with a large tatami mat, and at its center was a tea kettle, several closed jars, and service items that Levi recognized as being for a traditional tea ceremony.

Without even thinking, he automatically removed his shoes at the entrance to the room, as did Ryuki.

Ryuki motioned toward one of the cushions arrayed on the floor. "Please, make yourself comfortable. If you don't mind, I'd like to prepare tea before we talk."

Levi kneeled on a cushion, folded his legs underneath his thighs, and sat back on his heels. He'd learned all about tea when he'd lived in Japan, and he'd grown an appreciation for it. He felt a familiarity as he watched Ryuki prepare their beverage. He was clearly not committing himself to a formal tea ceremony, but the moves he made in preparing the tea were all deliberate and almost had a religious overtone to them. He uncapped a canister of bright green matcha, a form of powdered tea, scooped it into a bowl, tapped the spoon twice on its rim, and gently lifted the kettle of boiling water.

As the man stretched forward to whisk the tea, Levi caught glimpses of colorful tattoos underneath his long sleeves. More noticeable was the bandage wrapped tightly around his left pinkie. Judging by the finger's length, Levi had to assume that the mobster had recently committed *yubitsume*, a ritual act that literally meant "finger shortening." As a member of the Yakuza, he'd have done that to atone for some great transgression. And as he was the number-two man in the Tanaka syndicate, such a transgression would involve disappointing Shinzo Tanaka himself.

Was that why Levi had been called in?

Ryuki leaned forward and placed a bowl of tea in front of Levi. "I hope it's to your liking."

Levi lifted the bowl with both hands and bowed slightly to his host. "Thank you for this." He closed his eyes and breathed deeply of the steam coming up from the tea. It had a fresh plant-like aroma that immediately brought him back to the tea he'd had when he lived in Japan. He sipped at it and sighed with satisfaction.

It had the same pleasant bitterness that he associated with high-quality green tea.

Ryuki tilted his own bowl back and drank deeply. He looked at Levi, and his lip curled in a half-smile. "I'm rather impressed that you seem comfortable sitting in a traditional style. That's quite unusual for an American."

"That's easily explained. I lived in a *kyokushin* dojo in Tokyo for several years."

The mobster raised an eyebrow and nodded. "You're a man of some surprises. That also explains your excellent Japanese. Anyway, let's get to business. My superior asked me to solicit your assistance with someone who is quite dear to him. His granddaughter. She's been kidnapped."

Levi sat up straighter and canted his head. "I don't mean to be insulting, but why tell me? How can I help?"

Ryuki shrugged. "I'm not sure why Mister Tanaka specifically named you. However, he was quite insistent."

Levi was about to say something when the mobster held up his hand.

"Please, let me explain a bit about the missing child. Her name is June Wilson. As I said, she is Mister Tanaka's granddaughter. She's five years old, and Mister Tanaka is willing to do just about anything to get her back." Ryuki's face clouded and his voice grew deep with obvious emotion. "My youngest, Kumiko, the one you met—she's the same age as Mister Tanaka's granddaughter. I have trouble imagining how I'd be if such a thing happened to her."

Levi's stomach tightened at the thought of a child being hurt or missing. "When did the kidnapping happen?"

"Three days ago, in Maryland. My brother will show you the location."

That didn't bode well for the child. Levi had read that three quarters of kidnapping victims that were murdered were killed within the first three hours after abduction.

He sighed. "I didn't yet say that I would help."

Ryuki leaned forward and spoke with an urgent tone. "What can I do to convince you to help?"

Levi shook his head. "I don't know anything about what happened. Have the police gotten involved? Have they brought in the FBI or anyone else? Has the kidnapper reached out with any demands?"

"My brother witnessed the incident and can answer many of your questions. But there's been no contact from the kidnapper. We have the security videotapes of the kidnapping, and you can interview the mother as well. She was attacked, but left unharmed."

Levi huffed with impatience. "Well, let's bring your brother in here. I need to know everything about what happened if I'm to have any chance of helping."

Ryuki nodded, but his brow wrinkled with obvious worry. "I must explain one thing before bringing Yoshi in. I've kept him from the type of life that you and I share. I'm sure you know what I mean."

Levi nodded. Yoshi was not a member of the Yakuza. He was a normal.

"Please, keep that in mind when talking with him. I want him to be kept out of the business. There are some things he cannot know about."

"I understand."

"When you find the missing girl, I need to know who it is that took her." Ryuki's eyes narrowed and his demeanor turned cold. Levi caught a glimpse of the predator hidden within his polite host. "I would like to have this kidnapper turned over to my men instead of the authorities. I will pay your expenses. Anything you need, whether it is information, weapons, men, I will do everything I can to provide it, as long as it's in pursuit of finding Mister Tanaka's granddaughter. If you manage to find her and bring her back alive, I will honor the deal I made with your superior."

Levi had no idea what that deal was about. Was it about drugs? Prostitution? Territory? An alliance? He preferred not to know. He'd refused to get personally involved in that side of the business.

Picturing the mobster's little girl as a prisoner, Levi felt indignation building within him. How could anyone ever harm a child? He sighed. "Bring your brother in."

"So, you will help?" Ryuki's tone was hopeful.

Levi nodded. "I'll do whatever I can."

June sat against the gray cinderblock wall of her new room, holding the Raggedy Ann doll. The room was lit by a single bare bulb hanging from the ceiling, and was almost completely empty—just a rubber mattress, three smelly blankets, a few old picture books, and a toilet. Next to the toilet was a giant package of toilet paper—the same kind Mommy would get from Costco.

Tears welled up in her eyes, but June admonished herself—*crying doesn't help*—and angrily wiped them away.

She had no idea how she'd gotten here. She remembered Mommy going to the front door to get the pizza, opening the door, and then falling backward. A man in a ski mask caught her and broke her fall. When June ran to her, the man sprayed something in June's face. It smelled weird, kind of sweet.

And then she woke up in this place.

"How long do you think it's been?" she asked the doll.

Suddenly, the light turned off and the room was cloaked in darkness.

"It's coming." June's voice quavered and she tightened her grip on the doll.

Chains rattled on the metal door at the top of the stairs. The hinges creaked, and she heard the familiar sound of heavy footsteps approaching.

Then, from somewhere in the darkness, came the robot's voice.

"Do you like the darkness?"

"No," June responded, as calmly as she could muster. She didn't want to sound scared.

"If you don't do exactly what I say, I will leave you here in the darkness. Do you understand me?"

"Yes," she responded, her voice shaking against her will. She *really* didn't like the dark.

"I want you to say in a loud, clear voice, 'Mommy, it's Tuesday and I'm okay.'"

June heard a spring-like sound, like when Mommy pressed down on the toaster to heat up some frozen blueberry waffles.

"Mommy, it's Tuesday and I'm okay."

She heard the spring-like sound again—nearby, just ahead of her.

"Very good," the robot voice declared. *"Now I need you to stick your pointer finger up in the air. You'll feel an ouch. It will be okay."*

June cringed as she slowly raised her hand.

Something grabbed tightly onto her finger, clicked in the darkness, and bit into the tip. After squeezing hard, it let go.

June shoved her finger in her mouth and shuddered as she tasted something salty. Was it blood? What did that thing do to her?

The robot's footsteps moved back up the stairs. The door opened and closed, and chains rattled.

The light turned back on.

Near her bed, the robot had again left food for her.

June crawled forward and surveyed what he'd left behind. A packet of blueberry Pop-Tarts, two peanut butter and grape jelly Uncrustables—still cold from the freezer—two juice boxes, and two whole-milk containers, each with a straw attached.

She wondered what Mommy would think. Mommy would never have let her have this kind of junk food.

June hugged Raggedy Ann and whispered in her ear, "Do you think Mommy's okay?" Her vision blurred as tears fell onto the doll. She was trying to be brave, but she didn't know how long she could do it.

She was so scared.

She pressed her face against the doll and closed her eyes. "Mommy, where are you?"

THE INSIDE MAN

∼

Helen Wilson sat across from Levi at her dining room table. She was an attractive redhead in her late twenties, but there were dark circles under her eyes, almost certainly from lack of sleep. Still, she was composed, much more so than he'd have expected for someone whose child was forcibly taken from her apartment only days earlier.

"I'm sorry," she said, "but I'm not sure if it's smart for me to be talking to you. I work at the FBI, and they've taken over this case. And besides, June's grandfather isn't someone I can trust. I'm sure you know, but he's not exactly an upstanding individual. The only reason I even let you in was because I trust Yoshi. He and I used to work together a long time ago."

"Listen, I understand completely." Levi felt the pain emanating from the woman. "I'm here only because I'm personally committed to finding your daughter. I've promised to do everything I can. Mister Tanaka has made no demands on me other than to get her back home to you, and to bring her kidnapper to justice. Could you please just humor me? I've already seen the security tapes, and we know it wasn't the pizza delivery guy. He was found dead only fifty feet from this apartment—"

Helen gasped and her hand flew to her mouth. "Nobody told me that. Oh, the poor guy."

"Miss Wilson, can you tell me what you remember?"

Her shoulders slumped and she shook her head. She seemed to struggle with her thoughts. "I don't know. I remember ordering the pizza. June and I were having a late Friday night playing Uno together. The front gate rang and I buzzed the driver through. I remember opening the door, but I don't remember a thing after that. The next thing I knew, Yoshi was hovering over me using smelling salts to try and wake me."

Levi had spent the last twelve hours with Yoshi, and had heard everything he had to say, but it hadn't helped much. The videotapes didn't do much to clear things up either. They showed only an average-sized man in a dark-gray ski mask, escaping with June Wilson slung over his shoulder. Hell, it could even have been a woman.

"Miss Wilson—"

With a trembling hand, Helen pushed a lock of hair from her face. "Please, just call me Helen."

"Helen, did you suffer any injuries?"

"No. I mean, I was knocked out, but I don't have a mark on me, if that's what you're asking."

Levi frowned. "Not even a bump on your head or bruising from when you passed out?"

Her lower lip trembling, she shook her head. "It all seems like a nightmare I can't wake up from."

"Helen, how much do you know about kidnapping?"

"Nothing. It's not what I do." Helen's voice quavered. "I'm just a budget analyst."

"Well, kidnapping falls into three categories. Nearly half of all kidnappings are known as family kidnappings. Perpetrated by someone related to the child. The others are pretty evenly split between acquaintances and strangers. So, the obvious question is—and I'm sorry if this is awkward or you've already told the FBI—where is June's father?"

Tears welled up in Helen's eyes and she took in a deep, shuddering breath. Levi felt for the woman.

"June's father died before she was born. He was a graduate

student at Georgetown, and as he was walking to his car, he was killed in a drive-by shooting."

"I'm sorry." Levi scribbled some notes on his legal pad. "What was his name?"

"Jun Tanaka. And yes, I now know he's Shinzo Tanaka's only son. But he was never involved in any of his father's business. In fact, he'd been living in the States since he was old enough to go to boarding school. I never knew about what his father did until after Jun had been killed."

"Are there any other relatives that you know of on his side? What about your family?"

"I don't think Jun had any other family in the States." Helen frowned. "But I've got a sister—she's married with four kids. They live in Arizona. My parents live in Arizona, too. They're usually on a golf course, I think. We don't talk much."

"Have you told them about what happened?"

She shook her head. "I know I should have called them, but I haven't. I'm really not sure why, but I feel kind of paralyzed inside. It's not—"

"Listen." Levi reached across the table and patted her hand. "I'm not judging you. I think it's completely understandable that you're not in a normal state right now. I don't know what I'd be like in your situation. When's the last time you saw your family?"

"Almost a year ago. June and I went to Arizona for Christmas."

Levi sat back in his chair and mentally scratched off the Wilson family—for the moment anyway. No reason to pursue that angle yet. He still needed to do more research on the Tanaka family, but he doubted they'd done it, because if they did, why hire him to get her back? No, this didn't feel like a family-motivated act.

He spent the next twenty minutes asking Helen about her friends, co-workers, the preschool that June had attended. Then a knock sounded on the front door.

"One second," Helen announced across the apartment. She got up from the table, looked through the peephole, and opened the door. Two men in FBI windbreakers stood outside. "Hey guys, what's up?"

"Just here to check and see how you're doing."

Levi closed his notebook, walked over, and tapped on Helen's shoulder. "I've got a few things I want to look into based on our talk. Are you going to be around tonight if I have more questions?"

"Of course."

Levi excused himself and squeezed past the two men at the door. As he turned toward his rental, he heard one of the men ask, "Who was that?"

Levi got in his car, pulled his cell phone from his suit pocket, punched up the address of the preschool, and started in that direction. As he turned on Wisconsin Avenue, he dialed Denny.

The phone rang twice before a groggy voice in New York City answered, *"Yeah?"*

"Denny, wake up. I need some of your skills kicked into gear."

For the next ten seconds, all Levi heard was the muffled sound of Denny rolling out of bed. *"Man, you do realize I also run a bar, right? I didn't get home until seven a.m., and it's not even noon."*

"Sorry, but this is important."

"Okay, I'm up. What do you need?"

"There was a child kidnapped Friday night around 10:15 p.m. in the 8000 block of Wisconsin Avenue in Bethesda, Maryland."

Levi turned left on Montgomery Avenue.

"Damn son, you're away from home base. Hold on, I'm logging into the computer. What do you need?"

"There was a Domino's delivery car. It was a Honda, that's all I've got right now, but it was leaving the Flats8000 apartment complex. It was dumped behind a restaurant five miles east of here. I need background video from anywhere along the vicinity of that route. I'm figuring a security camera from one of the buildings along the way might have caught something as the car was leaving."

"Got it. All right, I'll see what I can get through the online security systems. Do you care if I pull in some of my Maryland resources to help? There might be some tapes that aren't hackable or online. I assume you need this right away?"

"The sooner, the better. We don't have time to waste. I'll cover whatever hours and expenses are needed for this."

Levi pulled into the preschool's parking lot and turned off the ignition.

"How old's the kid that's missing?"

"She's five."

"Damn. Okay, I'm calling the cavalry. I'll let you know what we find."

The phone clicked off.

Levi put his phone back into his inside jacket pocket, tilted his rearview mirror down, and peered at himself. He smiled and combed his fingers through his dark-brown hair.

"Time to sweet-talk the principal."

Whether it was Levi's story about the missing child, his blatant flirtation with the divorced fifty-something principal, or that he was dressed like a respectable person in a thousand-dollar suit, he didn't particularly care. He only cared that it had worked, and that the head of the school had given him the go-ahead to talk to June's teacher, and had called ahead to let her know he was on his way.

Levi heard the kids talking loudly as he knocked on the door to Ms. Ledbetter's pre-K classroom. There was a shushing sound, and the teacher announced, *"One two three, eyes on me."*

The class immediately quieted.

The door was opened by a short middle-aged woman with round Harry Potter–like glasses. "Oh, that was quick. Mister Yoder?"

He nodded, leaned down and whispered, "This will just take a second, okay?"

"Of course. Please, come in."

The teacher led him in front of a group of three and four-year olds, all sitting cross-legged in a half-circle. She snapped her fingers three times, and in a surprisingly commanding voice for someone her size, she said, "Okay, students, we have a visitor who needs to ask a very important question. I want you to show him how responsible you are and give him all of your attention. This is Mister Yoder. Class, what do we say to visitors?"

The kids all yelled, "Good morning, Mister Yoder."

"Hello, class." Levi smiled and pulled a pencil from his suit pocket. There was a trick he'd learned when training dogs on his parents' farm, and he figured it might work with these kids. "Can everybody see this pencil?"

"Yes," they all responded enthusiastically.

"Okay, I want you to keep your eyes on this pencil and when

it stops moving, I'm going to ask an important question. Here goes…"

He slowly moved the pencil back and forth until every kids' eyes were following it. When it floated in front of Levi's nose, he stopped and asked, "Has anyone seen June Wilson since you left school on Friday?"

Levi focused on each kid's expression, looking for any unusual reaction: their eyes darting away, the child's body tensing suddenly. Anything to suggest they were keeping a secret. But the only reaction he got was confusion. Heads shook and a few kids said "no."

One of the kids asked, "Is she sick?"

Levi smiled at the blonde girl who'd asked the question. "No, she just had to go somewhere for a little bit. I'm sure she'll be back soon." He addressed the class, "Thank you for letting me visit."

The teacher snapped her fingers twice. "What do we say to Mister Yoder?"

The kids all responded in unison, "Thank you for visiting, Mister Yoder."

Levi waved at the kids, gave the teacher a nod, and walked out of the classroom.

"I hope Denny gets somewhere with those video records," he grumbled to himself.

As he left the building and walked across the parking lot to his car, three unmarked sedans with flashing lights on their dashboards came flying up over the curb and nearly ran him over.

Their doors flew open and multiple voices yelled, "Hands up!"

Before he knew it, he had a half-dozen men with guns trained on him.

Levi lifted his arms above his head.

Three men with FBI windbreakers approached and slammed him to the ground. The side of Levi's face connected with the pavement, and it took every ounce of self-control he had not to fight back. One man trained his nine-millimeter Glock at his head, and another had his knee in the small of his back. Within seconds, they'd clamped cuffs around his wrists and ankles.

"What the hell is going on?" he asked.

"Shut up," was the only reply he got.

One of the men frisked Levi, then they lifted him up and dumped him into the back seat one of the dark-gray Crown Victoria sedans. Two men sat on either side of him, sandwiching him in, and the car pulled away from the school.

Levi's cheek burned from the scrape he'd received on the pavement. He rubbed it against his shoulder and growled, "Can someone tell me why the hell you've picked me up? I haven't done anything."

The agent sitting in the front passenger seat turned and gave him a venomous glare. "You have no idea?"

"None. If you're arresting me, I expect there's some kind of charge. Why'd you guys pick me up?"

Over the last year, Levi had dealt a lot with federal law enforcement. They'd used him to help nab some crooked feds who were dabbling in underage sex trafficking. They were usually pretty level-headed, but this crew was pissed.

He shrugged his right shoulder to work out a cramp and the agent on his right gave him a sharp elbow to the ribs for his trouble.

"Oh, sorry about that," the agent grumbled insincerely.

"Well? Am I going to hear any reason why you guys have picked me up?"

The agent in the front scowled. "Sure, why not. We got a call about a man half the Bureau's been looking for, and lo and behold, you were exactly where they said you'd be."

Levi frowned. "I don't understand. Why would anyone be looking for me? This has to be some kind of mistake. What have I supposedly done?"

The agent on Levi's left looked like he was going to spit in Levi's face. "Special Agent Bruce Wei. Special Agent Tony Mendoza. Special Agent Tran Nguyen."

Levi shrugged. "Is that supposed to mean something to me?"

The agent's jaw muscles clenched, and he glared daggers at Levi. "They were all murdered while off-duty, one of them in front of their kids." A cold smile creased his stone-like expression. "We have reports of someone matching your description at the scenes. Buddy, you're up against three first-degree murder raps."

CHAPTER THREE

Levi's arms were cuffed behind his back, and his shoulders throbbed. He was seated on a metal chair, bolted to the floor, in front of a table with a brown Formica top. His holding cell, a six-by-ten-foot room with drab gray walls, was otherwise empty. And it was cold—very cold. Not quite cold enough to see his own breath, but it was probably in the fifties.

This certainly wasn't the J. Edgar Hoover Building in DC. This place was some dump out on the outskirts of nowhere, and from the various turns and the time it had taken to get here, he figured they were somewhere near Quantico, Virginia.

He wondered when they'd come for him. It had been twenty minutes since he'd been shackled to the chair, and he figured they were trying to soften him up. Wear him down for an interrogation. It's what he would do. But he'd dealt with much worse conditions before. So he just closed his eyes and focused on his breathing. The dull ache of his scraped cheek and sore muscles faded.

Seconds turned into minutes, and his senses absorbed the tiny details of his surroundings. Through the metal chair, he felt the dull vibrations of the world outside.

Somewhere in the distance, he sensed a car's engine idling, and then the opening and closing of a car door.

He heard the murmurs of voices, then footsteps echoing through an unseen hallway. Both grew louder.

Levi opened his eyes just as the door to his room opened. A tall man he'd not seen before entered, and the door swung shut behind him with a metallic clank.

The man was an agent straight out of central casting. Late forties, generic dark-gray suit, dark glasses, humorless expression. He took a seat on the other side of the bare table and stared at Levi for a few long seconds, making a sucking sound through his teeth.

"Mister Yoder, I'm Special Agent O'Connor with the FBI, and I'm afraid you're in serious trouble."

Levi tilted his head to the side and cracked his neck. "Whatever the charges are, it's a load of crap. I didn't do anything."

"The agents who picked you up already told you what you're charged with, Mister Yoder." O'Connor frowned. "And I got your records. I know everything there is to know about you and your association with the Bianchi crime family out of New York. You're also a paid informant, which I'm sure your mob cronies wouldn't take too kindly to—"

"That's bullshit. I don't know anything about any crime families, and even if I did, I'd never talk to the feds about them. Why did you guys really pick me up?"

O'Connor stared at Levi for a full ten seconds before responding. "We have evidence placing you at the scene of the murder of three federal agents. Couple that with your known involvement in the sex-trafficking—"

"You're not pinning that shit on me!" Levi snorted, and shook his head. "Your records are bullshit. I helped you assholes find some crooked feds who were taking bribes. *They* were the ones importing and playing with underage prostitutes. Is that it? You're trying to set me up as some kind of revenge tactic for your pedophile buddies? I want my phone call. Get me my lawyer."

The tight control Levi maintained on his temper was starting to fray. He'd spent two months on contract to the FBI's child sex trafficking division, looking for and finally finding two of their agents who'd been taking kickbacks from one of the other East Coast mob families. It was an ugly business, and the more Levi had looked into it, the more disgusted he'd gotten with some of what the other families had gotten themselves into. But he never dropped the dime on anyone but the dirty feds.

It was the FBI agents who were violating their oaths, not him, and not even the Mafia associates he'd dealt with.

But now it looked like the FBI wanted payback. Levi had prepared himself for just such an event. He had both videotapes and audiotapes of almost everything. These federal bastards weren't going to take him down.

O'Connor glared at Levi and shook his head. "You're not getting *anything* until I say so. Those three agents you killed were my friends, and I intend to—"

"You intend to what?" Levi strained against his shackles and puffed out his chest. "You have rules you need to follow, Agent O'Connor. I know my rights. I know I didn't do what you're claiming I've done. Get me my lawyer."

The agent sat back and blew out a loud breath. "Listen to me,

Yoder. I can make your life miserable if you fight me. Sure, you'll eventually get your phone call. But I'll make sure you don't get bail. I'll make sure you're in the hole for months, maybe even years before your case comes to trial. I'll bury you."

Levi glared at the agent. He wasn't wrong. No matter how confident he was in being able to convince others of his innocence, this asshole could make things difficult for him.

"I know I didn't murder anyone," Levi said. "You've looked me up. I'm clean and you know it. I've done nothing but help you assholes clean up your—"

"You never gave up your mob contacts—"

"That wasn't the deal I made. It was your guys that were dirty. I gave you the evidence you needed to take two dirty feds off the streets. You should be kissing my ass, but instead you're hassling me over something you know I didn't do."

O'Connor leaned forward and growled. "I don't know any such thing. What I do know is that we have mob-connected murders of three federal agents, and you've been implicated in those murders. I should just put you into the system. I heard about what happened the last time you were put in. It got a bit bloody, didn't it?"

Levi glared. The last time he had been put in lockup, on trumped-up charges, he'd been attacked by Russian mobsters.

O'Connor chuckled. "Oh, you didn't think I knew about that? I've got your number—"

"You don't have crap. Need I remind you that all the charges against me were dropped?"

"You murdered two people in that jail."

Levi laughed. "What, are you some long-lost cousin of the dead Russian mobsters who tried to kill me? Give me a fucking break. Self-defense, and you know it. Reliving history is making me all teary-eyed and nostalgic, but what is it that you really want from me?"

"I want answers. Did you have anything to do with murdering agents Wei, Mendoza, or Nguyen?"

"No."

"Do you know who did?"

"I have no idea. All bullshit aside, you're barking up the wrong tree on this."

"You willing to take a polygraph on that?"

Levi smiled. Whatever so-called evidence this agent had, the guy probably knew it was crap. He was on a fishing expedition.

"I have no problem with a polygraph, Agent O'Connor." Levi frowned. The longer he sat around wasting his time with these people, the harder it would be to find Tanaka's granddaughter. "So what's it going to take for you to get out of my hair? Believe it or not, I actually have things to do."

O'Connor shifted in his chair and drummed his fingers on the table. "You might be under the impression that you're calling the shots here, but you're not. Your ass is mine until I say otherwise. However, I might be able to work a deal." He rapped his knuckles on the tabletop and nodded. "Assuming you can pass a polygraph exam, we might be able to work something out. Your access to some of your mob buddies could prove useful in this investigation. I might be able to convince the higher-ups to treat you as a cooperating witness."

What O'Connor didn't realize was that Levi would never give up a family member to the feds. Things in the family were handled by the family. *Always.* He pictured a five-year-old girl in the hands of a kidnapper and swallowed the bile rising in his throat. "And that will get me out of these cuffs and my freedom?"

"Out of the cuffs, yes. Freedom ... well, that all depends on the details of whatever deal is made. No matter what, you're still a suspect until we resolve the case to the Bureau's satisfaction."

"Fine." Levi shrugged, not seeing that he had much choice in the matter. Not without major legal hassle and lots of time that he couldn't afford. There was an innocent girl on the line. And who knew, maybe they weren't lying just to get his help—maybe they really did have some informant falsely pointing the finger at him. But who?

"You're smarter than you look." O'Connor stood and put a phone to his ear. "It's me. He's ready to submit himself to a polygraph. Bring in the equipment."

That settled it. Whoever was on the other end of that phone call had been expecting this outcome. They wanted Levi to voluntarily submit to a lie detector test.

But why?

∽

After filling out a long questionnaire and being hooked up to the polygraph equipment, Levi sat back against the metal chair and focused on his breathing.

He'd practiced with a polygraph machine a dozen times, but this one was a bit different. There were more leads attached to his fingers, which Levi knew was intended to measure his skin's galvanic response—the electrical changes triggered by various emotional states. Two pneumography tubes were wrapped around his chest and stomach to measure his breathing. And finally, a blood pressure cuff was wrapped around his right upper arm.

The polygraph examiner, a heavyset man in an ill-fitting suit, tapped a few keys on a laptop attached to the polygraph equipment. "Mister Yoder, we'll be going over the answers to your questions you filled out earlier. I need to let you know that..."

Levi's mind drifted away from the words of the corpulent examiner and he began meditating. Preparing himself for the questions he knew were coming.

Years ago, he'd learned from an Indian guru the art of transcendental meditation, and it had proven useful for clearing his mind. It was especially useful back then, because the death of his wife had been eating at his soul. And since then, he'd learned several variations of the same skill, mindful techniques that allowed him to relax while at the same time enhancing his senses.

He heard the examiner's labored breathing, felt his own heart beating at a slow rhythmic pace, and even sensed the hum of electricity powering the fluorescent lights in the hallway outside the room. He imagined his mind as floating separate from his body. He heard and saw everything, but in an emotionally detached sort of way.

He wasn't looking directly at the examiner, but he knew when the man picked up the previously-filled-out questionnaire. Levi felt absolutely nothing when the man spoke.

"Mister Yoder, I'm going to ask you a series of control questions that are intended to create your baseline physiological responses. These will help me calibrate the equipment. After I ask each question, please say 'no' as your response. Do you understand?"

Levi nodded.

The examiner shifted uncomfortably in his chair. "Mister Yoder, you are forty-one years old, is that correct?"

"No." In fact, Levi was forty-one.

"Are you the current President of the United States?"

"No."

"Have you ever told a lie?"

"No." The pace of Levi's breathing remained steady as the questions continued.

The examiner soon finished with the control questions, and he went on to ask Levi about his mob ties. Levi lied about nearly everything on that topic. When the questions touched on his whereabouts on certain days in the last two weeks, and his knowledge of certain agents, Levi told the truth. He had nothing to hide on those counts.

After about thirty minutes, the questioning stopped and the examiner tapped repeatedly on the laptop's keyboard. The man's face was red, and despite the coolness of the room, his forehead was damp with sweat. Finally, he closed the lid of the laptop, detached it from the wires that were still connected to Levi, and walked with it out of the room.

Levi was left alone in the room for a full ten minutes. His arms, which were still bound to the chair, ached from lack of movement.

The door suddenly flew open and O'Connor walked in, his stone-like expression giving way to displeasure. "Yoder, what the hell kind of Mickey Mouse bullshit did you pull? What's the trick?"

Levi looked up as the agent roughly removed the leads from his fingers, the blood pressure cuff, and the tubes around his chest. "Agent O'Connor, I have no idea what you're talking about."

The agent harrumphed and shook his head. "It doesn't matter. I got a call from my SAC. I'm bringing you in."

Levi shrugged his still-sore shoulders as he followed Agent O'Connor through the halls of the FBI's field office in Washington, DC. They'd travelled nearly thirty minutes in the agent's sedan, and aside from the agent's instructions to "buckle up," the trip was made in complete silence.

Several passing FBI staffers glanced curiously at Levi's visitor's badge. That, plus the time it had taken for the security folks to get a ledger from another room for him to sign, gave him the distinct impression that visitors weren't often seen in this field office.

O'Connor stopped at a closed door and knocked.

A voice sounded from within the room, *"Come in."*

The agent opened the door and motioned for Levi to enter.

Levi walked into a cramped office furnished with a single Formica-topped desk and several government-issued drab gray metal cabinets. Stacks of paperwork were piled on every flat surface.

A gray-haired man in his late fifties stood behind the desk and motioned to a chair. "Please, Mr. Yoder, take a seat."

O'Connor closed the door, and sat within arm's reach of Levi. "Mister Yoder, this is Special Agent in Charge Gary Michaels."

Levi was familiar enough with how the FBI was organized to know an SAC was high up the food chain. There'd be no reason for the three of them to be in the same office. This Michaels guy was likely in charge of many if not most of the employees in this building. Levi wondered what the big to-do was.

"Mister Yoder, before we get into the details of what you're here for, I want to make perfectly clear how serious your situation is. You've been accused of the first-degree murder of three federal agents. We have testimony placing you at the scene of these incidents. I have more than enough to hold you for three days in detention, and due to the severity of the crimes, I can make sure that when your arraignment comes up, you won't be given bail. I need you to understand the gravity of your situation."

Levi gritted his teeth and studied the SAC. The tone of his voice and the way he held himself clearly indicated he was used to being in charge and wasn't playing. He seemed cold and intelligent, and he wasn't up for any BS from someone like him.

"I understand, sir."

Michaels nodded curtly. "Good." He grabbed a sheet of paper from one of the stacks on his desk and looked at it. "Are you agreeing to be a cooperating witness and to assist us in identifying the suspects involved in the deaths of Special Agents Bruce Wei, Tony Mendoza, and Tran Nguyen?"

"Yes."

"You will not, and I repeat, will *not* engage or attempt to apprehend any suspects associated with this investigation. That is not your job. Any evidence you find, you'll bring back for us to act on. Is that clear?"

"Crystal, sir."

"Good." Michaels turned to O'Connor. "Agent O'Connor, I happen to know that Nick Anspach just came in from the Quantico lab. Take Mister Yoder to visit with our forensics expert—"

"But—" O'Connor protested.

"No buts, just do it, Frank. You hear me?"

"Yes, sir."

Michaels jabbed his pointer finger at Levi. "Mister Yoder, we aren't going to ask you to wear a tracking device as long as you're checking in daily with Agent O'Connor. He'll be your bureau liaison for the duration, and you'll take your cues from him."

Levi glanced at O'Connor and frowned. "I don't understand. If you want me to look under every rock for whoever did this, I can't exactly be playing 'Mother May I' all the time with Agent O'Connor."

Michaels's eyes narrowed and he shook his head ever so slightly. "I think you'll find Agent O'Connor isn't a micromanager."

O'Connor twisted in his seat to face Levi. "Mister Yoder, can I ask you to wait outside in the hallway for a second? I need a word in private with Mister Michaels."

"Sure."

Levi exited the room, and closed the door quietly behind him—then pressed his ear against the wall outside of Michaels's office. He heard the gruff tones of O'Connor's whisper.

"How can we just let him go ... with that polygraph..."

Levi pressed harder against the wall. What was it about his polygraph?

"Frank, it's not my call."

"If it's not you, then—"

"Just shut up and do this thing. There's some ... I barely understand it, myself."

The voices got even quieter and then ... silence.

Levi stood up straight just as Michaels's door opened.

Agent O'Connor stepped into the hallway, barely glanced at him, and said, "Follow me."

∽

As they walked down the stairs to the second floor, Levi asked, "Agent O'Connor, when your guys picked me up, I was in the middle of following up on a lead regarding a kidnapping. The mom works for the FBI and—"

"What's her name?" O'Connor glanced at him with a wide-eyed expression.

"The girl's name?"

"No, the mom's name."

"Helen Wilson."

The agent paused at the door leading from the stairwell to the second floor and focused on Levi. "I'm familiar with that case. We've got people on it." O'Connor frowned. "I appreciate your concern for the kid, but that's not your issue. I don't want to hear about you spending time on anything other than finding out who took out three federal agents. Are we clear on this?"

Levi *so* wanted to smack this guy into tomorrow, but he pulled in a deep breath, let it out slowly, and nodded. "Understood, Agent O'Connor."

"Good."

But as O'Connor led Levi from the stairwell and down a wood-paneled hallway, Levi gritted his teeth. There was no way he was leaving the Tanaka kid's kidnapping to the feds.

Nick Anspach, the forensic examiner, looked to be in his forties. He had platinum-blond hair and scars from what looked to be a nasty burn on the right side of his face. And as Levi shook the man's hand, he noticed that the man was missing half of both his pinkie and ring finger.

"It's good to meet you, Mister Yoder."

Agent O'Connor stood in the doorway to the forensic examiner's office. "Nick Anspach is one of the FBI's best forensic examiners." He turned to the examiner and hitched his thumb at Levi. "Mister Yoder is a cooperating witness on the Mendoza, Wei, and Nguyen case."

Levi noted the neatly arranged desk, nothing out of place, everything oriented just so. The only detail of the office that had any level of disorder was the pictures tacked to the wall behind the desk. Nearly thirty pictures of Anspach at various social gatherings. A drink in his undamaged hand was a common theme, and in many of the shots, FBI employee badges were present. A popular guy.

"Nick, a few ground rules on our CW here. He doesn't have credentials, so I'm handing him off to you. He obviously needs an escort. He's cleared to look at the evidence we've gathered on the three homicides, but he can't remove or get copies of anything that's in evidence."

Anspach nodded. "Anything else?"

O'Connor shook his head. "No, that's it. I've got to catch up on other things."

Just as the agent turned to walk out, Levi asked, "Hey, what about my car? I was parked at that preschool when you guys picked me up."

O'Connor looked over his shoulder at Levi. "I've already gotten it taken care of. By the time you and Nick are done, it'll be parked outside the building." He left the office, closing the door behind him.

Anspach motioned toward a chair. "Mister Yoder, why don't you grab a seat and we can go over what we've gathered on these cases."

"Mendoza was killed in New York City eight days ago." Anspach's voice was soft, almost as if he were whispering.

Levi flipped through the Mendoza case file as the forensic examiner sat on the opposite side of the desk. There were nearly fifty pages of notes, interviews, and other forensic reports. The agent's autopsy stated that the man's carotid artery had been severed by a deep laceration across the front and side of the neck.

With a lopsided grin that pulled slightly at the scar tissue on his cheek, Anspach slid a pad of yellow sticky notes toward Levi. "You can't have any of the records, but O'Connor didn't say you couldn't jot down a few notes."

Levi returned the examiner's smile and tapped the side of his head. "Thanks, but I'll see if I can keep it all up in here." He tapped on the file. "This happened in the middle of the day in Central Park. How is it that this guy hasn't been caught?"

Anspach shrugged. "I can't say. Frankly, I didn't do the initial investigation, but I talked to the guy who did, out of the New York field office. Initially it looked like a random mugging, but nothing was stolen."

Levi flipped to the next page in the file and was greeted by an artist's sketch of an Asian man. "Is this the suspect?"

Anspach held a grim expression. "Yup. It happened right in front of Mendoza's wife and two kids. The sketch is based on the wife's description." He reached across the desk and tapped on the Asian man's cheek. "She also stated that she scratched him something good across the left cheek. We got a DNA sample from underneath her fingernails and it matched that of a Chinese male."

Levi wondered why the hell he was even involved in this. *I'm a six-foot Anglo with blue eyes and one hundred and eighty pounds. There's no way I'd be confused for a five-foot-seven Asian guy weighing one hundred and forty pounds.*

Levi huffed with frustration and focused on the artist's drawing. One of the earlier pages in the file had listed Mendoza's kids as being five and seven, both boys. What kind of animal would attack someone in front of his two kids?

The examiner slid a thicker file toward Levi. "This is what we have on the Nguyen and Wei incident. It happened only about an hour from here. It was a car bomb that took them both out, and—"

"I don't get it." Levi began flipping through the new case folder. "One New York murder and two near here. Why are these three murders being lumped together? I'd think they'd be handled by two different field offices, wouldn't they?"

Anspach tilted his head and stared silently at Levi for a moment before answering. "O'Connor didn't tell you?"

"O'Connor hasn't told me dick about any of this. What am I missing?"

"Well—I guess it doesn't do any harm telling you. They're all part of a sex tourism taskforce."

"You mean child sex trafficking?" Levi's lip curled up with revulsion, and his mind drifted to the image of the missing Tanaka kid.

"Not *only* children, but yes. Import of foreign nationals for … less than honorable reasons. Even though slavery has been abolished in this country for over one hundred and fifty years, it still exists." Anspach's face took on a haunted expression that implied the forensics specialist had seen some things he'd rather not have seen.

Levi looked over the reports on the bomb used to kill the two agents. One of the printouts showed a picture of an Asian man. "You found a fingerprint on a bomb fragment?"

"Lucky as hell, really. In the FBI lab over in Quantico, we have some really good processes to help bring out latent prints. I managed to find a print amid all that junk from the scene, and as you can tell in the report, it led to a hit in IAFIS."

"Aye-fiss?"

Anspach chuckled. "Oh, sorry. FBI acronym, we've got boatloads of them. That's our fingerprint database."

Levi scanned the IAFIS report on a Kiyoshi Ishikawa—thirty-two years old, a Japanese foreign national on an expired student visa. Current whereabouts were unknown. The section of the report titled, "Criminal Record and Associations" included a list of relatively minor beefs with the local law in DC. But Levi's heartbeat echoed loudly in his head and a chill raced up his spine as he read the next line aloud. "A known member of the Tanaka syndicate."

Anspach grumbled something unintelligible then said, "From what I know, they're a really bad set of folks out of Japan, trying to make inroads in the US. But to be honest, that's not my area of expertise, so I can't really give you much insight on them."

As Levi skimmed the rest of the report, his mind raced. After another five minutes in silence, he pushed the file back to Anspach. "Are these files everything you have?"

The man's right eye twitched in what looked like a painful tic, and the scar tissue next to the corner of his eye creased. "I'm afraid that's it." He motioned to the sticky notes and pencil. "You sure you don't need to take any notes?"

Levi stood and shook his head. "I've got what I need."

CHAPTER FOUR

Back in his rental car, Levi had just called Madison when a capitol police car flew past the FBI's DC field office, its siren blaring. "Maddie, are you okay?"

"I'm fine." Her voice came over the car's speakers. She sounded stressed. *"What's up? You don't normally call during the weekday."*

"Well, believe it or not, I'm in DC and I have a few hours before I need to catch the train back. Are you able to grab a bite?"

"Oh ... I wish I could. To be honest, I've been feeling kind of blah, so I'm heading to the doctor to get checked over. Maybe I'm getting the flu or something."

Levi frowned. Something didn't sound right. She seemed to be upset about something. "Well, I can go with you—I've got time. Just let me know where to meet you."

"No, that's perfectly all right. You go take your train, Seriously, I mean it."

"But—"

"*Levi!*" Madison raised her voice, then laughed. "*Do you really need me to tell you that I'm going to my gynecologist and I would prefer you not be there? I'm fine, just not feeling one hundred percent. I'll call you on Friday and we'll figure something out, okay?*"

Embarrassed, Levi shifted the car into gear. "Okay, I suppose I understand. Have fun."

"*Not exactly the kind of thing you tell a girl going to her lady parts doctor, but okay.*" Levi heard a smile in her voice. "*I'll talk to you later.*"

He tapped his destination into the car's navigation system and pulled away.

~

Standing in the middle of Union Station, Levi pressed his cell phone tightly against his ear, trying to hear Denny's voice over the noisy crowd of evening commuters.

"*Levi, that Domino's delivery car was abandoned in the back of a run-down taqueria near the corner of Arliss Street and the Garland turnaround. Across the street is a beauty school with a security system that snapped some wide-angle shots from around that time. The photos aren't good enough to identify anything useful like a plate, but there was a dark-colored Suburban parked in the back of the taqueria after the restaurant was closed. I had a local check with the owner, and nobody there owns anything like that and the owner didn't see a thing.*"

"That's great, Denny. Did you by any chance catch what direction the Suburban was going when it left the parking lot?"

"*As a matter of fact, yes. A library next to the beauty school had a video camera pointing at Walden Road. Right around the time the Domino's car got dumped, the library camera shows a black Suburban going north on Walden Road."*

"That's great."

"Don't get too excited. I wasn't able to track it any further. That's mostly a residential area, and there's not much in the way of security cameras around there. I spread my net pretty far, pulled in lots of local favors, but I couldn't find the car again. It could have parked in someone's garage, but more likely it's gone. Walden is one of those through streets that runs straight across residential areas. That Suburban could be anywhere."

"Shit, okay." Levi began walking toward the gates where his train was set to depart from. "I'm still in DC, but I'm taking the Acela to Penn Station, so I'll be back in the city in a few hours." Levi spotted a familiar profile fifty feet ahead, and steered toward the man. "Listen, Denny. I have to go. Gather up whatever you have for me, and I'll see you sometime after midnight."

"Gotcha. I'll be at the bar, as always."

Levi ended the call and stepped up behind the Asian man staring up at Amtrak's schedule board.

He placed his hand on the man's shoulder and said, "Yoshi, funny seeing you here."

∼

Levi and Yoshi sat next to each other in the coach section as the train sped north to Penn Station. The conversations of late-evening commuters buzzed all around them. Yoshi had wanted to go into the quiet car, but Levi wanted their conversation to be drowned out by the surrounding noise. In Levi's mind, everyone was a suspect, and there was a lot about this mobster's brother and the whole Tanaka thing that bugged the hell out of him.

It was hard to imagine that it was only twelve hours ago that he had been interviewing Helen Wilson in her dining room. He replayed that conversation and found himself focusing on a just a couple sentences she'd said.

"The only reason I even let you in was because I trust Yoshi. He and I used to work together a long time ago."

"So," Levi said. "Why'd you quit working for the FBI?"

Yoshi had leaned his head back against the headrest and closed his eyes, but now he sat up straight and twisted in his seat to face Levi. "How the heck did you know I worked there? Did Helen say something?"

"Not in so many words, but yes." Levi studied the man. His posture was stiff, and he looked Levi directly in the eyes, somewhat defiantly.

But then Yoshi sighed wistfully, and his posture softened. "It's hard to explain."

"Listen, no bullshit." Levi leaned. "I'll figure it out, but for everyone involved, it's a lot better that I know what's going on. Everything. There's no way you'd leave the security of a government job with the Bureau to be some two-bit security lackey unless there's a good reason." He noticed a rather expensive Tag Hauer chronograph on Yoshi's left wrist. An image from this morning's interview with Helen flashed into his mind's eye, and he smiled. "Let me guess, your brother was supplementing your pay, and the Bureau got wind of it."

Yoshi cast his eyes downward. "You're close. Ryuki asked me to start looking after Helen a few years back. I didn't ask for any compensation, but he started depositing money into my account, and someone at work must have noticed. I passed the lie detector tests, because I honestly didn't even know about the deposits yet, but still, after that I was sort of set aside by my bosses, and I can't blame them. I always knew that if my brother came to the States, it might pose a problem for my career.

"So I talked with Ryuki and he arranged for my security guard position. That made it easier to keep watch on Helen, and especially to keep watch over June. It's why I had the night shift. During the day, I volunteered at June's preschool. At night, I was keeping things normal for the two of them as much as I could."

Levi gave just the slightest hint of a smile. "Does your brother know you and Helen are a thing?"

Yoshi's complexion turned white. "How … no… Did Helen say—"

"No, she didn't. Your watch did." Levi flicked his finger at the steel wristband of Yoshi's watch. "Helen has a matching woman's version of your watch. I'm thinking she couldn't afford that kind of bauble on an FBI analyst's salary."

Yoshi leaned forward and put his head in hands. "I'm such an idiot." Then he sat up straight and looked at Levi with a worried expression. "It's not like … I mean, one day I was checking in on her, and it just sort of happened. We both knew at the same time, but we also knew we had to keep it a secret."

Levi understood—Yoshi was worried what Tanaka would do if and when he found out. Yoshi had gotten involved with, in effect, the widow of the mob boss's only son.

He chuckled and patted Yoshi on the shoulder. "You have some balls on you, I'll give you that. Is there anything else you haven't told me? Anything about June or the mother? Anything. It may not seem important, but it could be."

Yoshi shook his head and spoke with a quavering voice. "No.

I love that little girl as if she were my own. I'd give my life for either of them. I've told you everything I know."

"Good." Feeling a small sense of relief, Levi leaned his head back against the headrest. He hadn't been sure about Yoshi, but now, he mentally crossed him off the list of issues he had to resolve.

Still, his mind raced with the next steps. He needed to juggle two completely separate cases at the same time. The sketch artist's rendition of the Asian man loomed large in his mind.

A visit to Chinatown was definitely in order.

∼

At midday Levi walked along the streets of Flushing, right around Fortieth Road in Chinatown. It was a mild late-autumn day, and the streets were crowded with people, but the only non-Asians among them were a couple of ConEd folks working on an electrical panel on the side of a building.

Normally, Levi wore the family uniform, which for a made guy like himself consisted of a tailored suit and Italian loafers. But, today wasn't a normal day. He was on the prowl, and he needed to blend in, so he'd dressed like a tourist: sneakers, jeans, a button-down shirt, and a Yankees windbreaker.

For Levi, every part of the city had its own unique signature—a sound, a smell, and even a feel that was unmistakably its own. Here, that signature included the scents of ginger, soy, and star anise, and amid all that, the smell of a hot dog stand hidden behind a panel truck with Chinese characters on its side.

But today these streets felt … different. Gloomy, even during a bright and sunny day. It was as if some invisible cloud of oppression hung over the area. As if everyone in the neighborhood was having their energy sapped from them.

As he walked slowly along the narrow street, Levi's eyes darted back and forth, looking for his target. Plenty of people stared right back at him from the shade of the awnings that hung over the entrances to the local shops. None of these people caught his attention.

And then he spied the girl—just a wisp of a thing.

She was probably no more than eight or nine years old. Certainly prepubescent. Yet, she wore gaudy eye makeup, garish lipstick, and a barely-there miniskirt with her right shoulder exposed to the fifty-degree weather.

Levi gritted his teeth. This was one of the girls he'd heard of in this part of town. A sex slave. Maybe a refugee from Cambodia, Vietnam, or China. This kind of stuff shouldn't be happening. Not here. Not in his town. His stomach churned with a mixture of disgust, fury, and sadness.

He pulled out his cell phone and pretended to look something up, but really he was focusing the camera on the girl. He zoomed in.

He saw the goosebumps on her skin as she stared longingly at the nearby hot dog stand.

He snapped a picture and put the phone away.

Then he walked across the narrow street, handed the man working the hot dog stand two bucks, and said, "I'll take a dog."

The vendor fished the hot dog from the steaming water, put it into a warm bun, wrapped it, and handed it to Levi. "Thank you, sir."

The girl was now staring right at him.

He walked over to her and handed her the hot dog. "Here you go, dear. Have a snack."

The girl stared wide-eyed at the gift lying in her hand—but she seemed frozen, uncertain what to do.

"Go ahead, eat it," Levi said in his best Mandarin. He had no idea what language the girl spoke.

A man materialized out of the shadowy recesses between two buildings, and yelled something in a dialect of Chinese that Levi wasn't familiar with, and stalked menacingly over.

The girl looked up at the intimidating man, fear enveloping her face.

The man slapped the food to the ground and growled at Levi with a thick Chinese accent. "Fifty dollars, not hot dogs. You want a fuck, it is fifty dollars. Girl top notch. First class."

Levi's body stiffened as the man walked closer, raising his voice. "Fifty dollars, white boy. You owe fifty dollars. Pay me."

Clenching his fist, Levi spat out, "I don't fucking owe you jack shit."

He felt a hand touch his shoulder, and he turned to see an attractive Asian woman standing inches away. Her floral perfume enveloped him. "I was wondering when you'd get here," she said with a smile. Then she leaned into him, snaked her arm around his neck, and gave him a firm kiss on the lips.

Before Levi could even react, she grabbed his upper arm and began pulling him across the street. "You shouldn't be here," she whispered.

The man who'd been acting as the little girl's pimp screamed after them, again in an unfamiliar dialect. The woman yelled back at him over her shoulder as she led Levi away.

Levi noticed that many of the merchants had fallen back into the recesses of their stores, only to be replaced by a new set of people. A rougher crowd seemed to be gathering. Likely members of a local street gang. Certainly members of the local Chinese tong.

As the woman, whose grip was surprisingly strong, pulled him toward a storefront, Levi began to smile. Across the street, between a Chinese laundry and a fruit and vegetable stand, stood the man from the artist's sketch. The sketch had been remarkably accurate, including the angry red scratches on his left cheek.

Levi lost count of how many gang members the pimp's ranting had brought out onto the street.

The woman opened a door—an attached bell rang brightly—and pulled Levi through. "I'll keep you safe." She said.

Levi couldn't help but feel amused at the thought. He had two guns on him, both with fully-loaded magazines, and several knives, and he was quite capable of trading blows with most anyone he came across. Yet this woman was doing her damnedest to rescue *him*.

The woman yelled a few words at an old man who was standing in the back of the store. He pulled aside a rack of clothing, revealing a metal door. Without releasing her grip on his arm, the woman entered a code on a number pad beside the door, and a *snick* came from the locking mechanism. She opened the door, pull him roughly forward into a spacious living area—far more luxurious than anything he'd have expected to find in this neighborhood—and slammed the door shut behind them.

Levi stared at his "rescuer" with both amusement and astonishment. "Um, Miss—"

She gestured toward a leather sofa. "Just sit down. You'll be okay." The woman pointed at a plush leather sofa in the twenty by thirty-foot room.

His gaze followed the statuesque figure of the Asian dragon

lady as she left the room. He shook his head and studied his surroundings.

The room was much more luxurious than any place he'd have guessed existed in this neighborhood. He sat on the sofa, and appreciated the firm yet giving nature of its cushions. It was very comfortable. The smell of tanned leather coming off the furniture along with the leather's supple and fine-grained texture confirmed it to be a high-quality item. The decor was a mix of Asian and Western sensibilities. A few silk tapestries hung from the walls, very Chinese, yet the sofa and burnished walnut coffee table were quite Western. In fact, Levi wouldn't be surprised if the sofa has been made in Italy.

When the sound of a shower running came from somewhere on the far end of the apartment, he felt a sudden sense of amusement. A strange man was sitting in this woman's living room, under unusual circumstances, and she was off to take a shower? He admired her moxie.

After a few minutes, the woman returned. To Levi's surprise, she was completely naked.

As she padded nonchalantly across the room, Levi had to consciously remind himself to not let his mouth hang open. She had a dancer's body—well-proportioned, muscular, and slender all at the same time. And accentuating her pale skin was one of the most complex and beautiful tattoos Levi had ever seen. It was an undulating Asian dragon that curved along the slopes and valleys of the woman's fantastic figure.

The woman removed a silk robe from an old-style wooden coat stand, wrapped it around herself, and asked, "Would you like some tea?"

She spoke English very clearly, with what sounded like a slight Russian accent.

"I suppose … sure, if it's not too much trouble." Levi stood.

The woman immediately snapped her fingers and pointed to the couch. He sat right back down, puzzled yet desperately curious about this woman.

Before long she was bringing over a tray with a tea kettle and two small Chinese teacups. She poured for the both of them and sat across the coffee table from him.

He grabbed the hot cup of tea—and had a flashback of a time not that long ago when a beautiful woman had tried to poison him. But when he sniffed at the tea, and couldn't detect anything odd, he sipped it. It was a very good black tea.

"I saw what you did."

Levi tilted his head at the woman. "What do you mean? You mean argue with that man?"

"No." The woman waved dismissively. "You gave the girl some food. Why did you do that?"

Levi sat back, surprised by the question. "I don't know. I guess she looked hungry and I felt bad for her."

"Why?"

"Why did I feel bad for her?"

The woman nodded.

He paused as he wondered who this woman was. She clearly wasn't afraid to be alone with him. Far from it. And the way she had initially approached him, with the kiss … maybe she was a hooker? No, probably not. But maybe? Levi needed to be careful how he answered. He had no idea what this woman's reaction would be to him saying that he simply hated the idea of a girl that young being on the streets.

"It was cool outside, and she looked like she could use something warm to help her fight the cold." It wasn't a lie.

The woman stared unblinkingly at him for a few long

seconds. Then she nodded. "You're a good man. That's why I helped you." She motioned toward the door they'd entered through. "You must wait here another twenty or thirty minutes. By then the boys will have gone on to more interesting things." She drank the rest of her tea, stood, and without another word walked out of the room.

Levi pulled out his cell phone to text Paulie to meet him at Denny's, but found he had no signal in this building.

It was about twenty-five minutes later when the mysterious woman reappeared. She was now dressed in regular street clothes.

"The streets are clear," she said. "Come with me."

Levi followed her to a door in the back corner of the room. She threw a few latches, then opened it to reveal a dark alley behind the building just off Fortieth Road.

"You'll be fine," she said. "Just don't come back."

Levi stepped through the doorway and turned to shake hands with the woman, but she backed into her apartment and closed the reinforced door with a finality that matched her words.

Levi looked at his phone. He had full signal again. As he walked to the nearest subway station, he hit a number on speed-dial.

"Ya?" The man's voice responded.

"Paulie, I'm about to send you a picture."

"Another kid?"

"Yup. Same as before. This time in Flushing, Chinatown, next to a Chinese laundry."

"Got it. Hey, the guy I'd trust is out on the don's business today. It'll have to wait at least until tomorrow. Is that cool?"

"Yup, just tell him to be careful. This is a tong lair, and

they've got muscle on call. Let me know what it costs, I'll cover it."

"Consider it done."

Levi hung up and glanced over his shoulder as he took the stairs down to the Main Street Station.

Tonight he'd be meeting up with Mendoza's killer.

CHAPTER FIVE

It was late in the evening, prime time for the seedier side of the city to come out. Levi unsealed a plastic bag that held the clothes he'd use for this kind of foray into the city. Tonight, Levi wasn't one of the sophisticated elites of New York, strutting around in a fancy suit. As he removed the thread-bare pants and shirt from the sealed bag, the whiff of stale beer and urine hit him. This was always the tough part: getting used to the stink.

He slipped the clothes on and looked at himself in the mirror. He hadn't shaved that morning, but one day's stubble wasn't quite good enough to pass for a drunken homeless person. So he added a bit of face grease and a touch of makeup to add dirt in strategic places—like in the creases of his ears, the edges of his nose, and on the backs of his fingers and hands. He knew how to make himself into a passable bum.

The phone rang and he put it to his ear. "Frankie?"

"Ya, the place is ready. I've got a few boys waiting in there, so you shouldn't have any trouble once the package arrives."

"Thanks. I appreciate the favor."

Levi hung up and double-checked himself in the mirror. His hair was now greasy and disheveled, and he looked like he hadn't showered in months. It wasn't a perfect disguise, but he was counting on the smell, which had the uncomfortably strong scent of ammonia coming from the urine, to keep most people from looking at him too closely.

He slipped on the shoes, which were the part of the disguise he felt most proud of. They were so scuffed and torn that they looked like they were about to fly apart at the seams. In fact, the outer layer of the shoe was almost completely sewn together from fragments of a larger shoe. But underneath, Levi wore a sturdy and comfortable pair of walking shoes.

Soon he would be strolling the streets, heading for the nearest subway entrance.

～

Levi staggered into his position near the Chinese laundry he'd spotted earlier. The outside vents coming from the laundry's dryers kept him warm, but also blew his stench toward the others in the street, who kept their distance.

The type of people on the street at night were of a quite different sort than what he'd seen during the day: more hookers —none of whom, thankfully, paid him any attention—more customers for the hookers, and more gang members. Some of the gang members had set up games of checkers; others were drinking shots, and yelling at each other. Still others were brazenly selling drugs. He'd seen much worse in parts of China, but it bothered him to see this was happening in his own back yard.

He'd done some research during the day, and had figured out that the dialect being spoken around here, both earlier and now, was Cantonese. He still didn't understand any of it, but it at least gave him an idea of what part of the world some of these people were from. Likely the coast of China, or Hong Kong. Maybe these gangs were offshoots of the Triad. He knew what type of people they were, not that this surprised him. Anyone willing to exploit kids was already beneath contempt.

Levi had spent nearly two hours lying in the alley, obscured by a large piece of cardboard acting as a blanket, before he spied his target.

The man with the scratched face was laughing about something with a handful of others who'd been selling small packets of what he assumed was heroin or methamphetamine.

Levi now covered his nose and mouth with a painter's mask and pulled a ski mask over his head. He was ready for what was coming.

When his target happened to glance his way, Levi purposefully sneezed, letting the cardboard slip slightly down, showing him lying in the shadows, and more importantly, revealing a wallet lying next to his body.

Through half-closed eyes, Levi saw the man start walking toward him.

When the man reached Levi, he looked side to side, smiled, and leaned down to pick up the wallet.

Levi squeezed a bottle that almost instantly filled the alley with a cloud of mist.

The man gasped with surprise, breathing in the mist, and lurched upward. Then with a gurgling sound he fell heavily to the ground.

The mist was a potent anesthetic known as Sevoflurane—a

chemical Levi had learned of during his brief interaction with some CIA operatives.

Holding his breath, Levi grabbed the man by one arm, and lifted him into a fireman's carry. He took him deeper into the alley, racing through the darkened corridor between buildings, and passed across several poorly lit streets. He was no more than a shadow flitting from one darkened corner of the city to another until he stopped at a doorway, knocked twice, paused, knocked once, and then three times.

The door opened, and Paulie's six-foot-ten silhouette filled the entrance. He relieved Levi of his burden and whispered, "The safe room's ready."

∼

Levi squeezed the capsule of smelling salts under the mobster's nose. The unconscious man lurched away from the sharp smell of ammonia, straining against the leather bindings that held him to the metal chair bolted to the floor.

Following the man's movements, Levi kept the capsule directly under his nose until the man's eyes opened wide.

"Rise and shine," Levi said calmly as the man squinted against the bright lights aimed directly at him. In the room were three of Levi's mob associates, including Paulie and Sonny. Men he trusted implicitly. "I have a few questions for you. You answer them, and you're free to go."

The man strained against the loops of leather once more and spit at Levi. "Fuck you and your questions."

He spoke English like a native. Maybe he was one. Levi knew practically nothing about this guy.

"Listen, this doesn't have to go down hard. I have a few

questions that I need answers to. The cops are looking for you. Worse yet, the feds want you real bad. Bad enough that they reached out to me."

"Who the fuck are you?" The man moved his head back and forth, trying to see past the glare of the lights. "I haven't done shit." The mobster began yelling at the top of his lungs for help.

The men in Levi's crew just stood back and smiled.

Levi let the man continue for a full minute before he said, "This room is completely soundproof. Nobody will hear anything."

Paulie took a step closer to the captive, bringing his huge arms came into view, and clenched his fist. His knuckles popped loudly.

The captive's lip curled with disdain. "Go ahead, beat the shit out of me. I'll remember you fuckers and I'll get you back in spades."

Levi chuckled as he studied the scratches on the man's face. "It looks like you got into a catfight. Tell me about it. How'd you get those scratches?"

"Fuck you."

With a lightning fast movement, Levi smashed the heel of his hand against the man's nose, resulting in a sickening crunch.

Blood spurted down the man's face, and for a moment, Levi thought he'd need another one of the smelling salt capsules. But the man shook his head, blood splattering everywhere, and he smiled with blood-streaked teeth.

"Is that the best you've got?"

Levi held his open hand out toward Paulie and he felt the handle of a ball-peen hammer being placed in his palm. He waved the hammer around, as if testing its heft. "Listen to me, my friend. It's completely up to you how far this goes. Let me go ahead and explain—"

"Or what, you're going to brain me?" The mobster sneered, blood dripping from his chin. "You're boring me."

Levi grinned at the captive and shook his head. "Oh, I wouldn't do that. It would end the fun. Believe me, you'll talk to me. Even if I have to give you a transfusion to keep you alive, you'll be talking." He waved the rounded head of the hammer in front of the man's face. "You know, I've never actually hit anyone on the head with a hammer. It's not really my thing. I'm not a violent person. In fact, I'd rather not have anything to do with violence. But here I am, looking at someone who has a story to tell, and he's not talking to me." He looked over his shoulder at Paulie. "Doesn't that hurt your feelings when someone doesn't want to tell you his story?"

Paulie nodded and shared Levi's smile.

Hitching his thumb toward Paulie, Levi leaned closer to the mobster. "You're hurting my friend's feelings, and that's rude." He slammed the hammer down on the man's pinkie, smashing the bones into tiny shards.

The mobster screamed with pain and lurched against his bindings.

Levi made a *tsk-tsk* sound. "You see that? That's not good when the bed of your fingernail turns blue like that. That means I crushed all the blood vessels in the finger. If it isn't treated soon it'll turn black and you'll probably lose it. A pity, really. All I wanted was your story."

The man's breathing was ragged from the pain, but he was alert.

Levi had seen a variety of reactions to torture. Some people caved before it ever got physical. Others needed shots of adrenaline to keep their heart pumping. Some even needed the help of so-called truth serums to relax them, to weaken their resolve. Levi didn't know how far, this guy would go, and he didn't care. This mobster had killed a father and husband, and he'd done it right in front of the man's family. There were few things Levi could imagine that were worse. The Bianchi family, the particular branch of La Cosa Nostra that Levi was affiliated with, they frowned on such things.

Levi stared into the man's face and growled, "Where did you get those scratches from?"

The mobster closed his eyes and gritted his teeth for a second before answering. "Will you let me go if I tell you?"

"It depends on if I believe you. Make me *believe* your story."

The man took a deep breath and let it out slowly. "Fine. My brother's funeral was a closed casket one. We never really knew why he'd gotten so messed up in the accident. And then there was a guy. Someone gave me some photos of him and proof that he'd tortured and killed my brother." The mobster's voice grew thick with emotion. "I was just getting revenge on the bastard who killed my brother. He was a sick fuck too. Tortured him and practically shredded his body."

Levi motioned for the man to stop. "One thing at a time. Who gave you these photos?"

Bubbles of blood dripped from the man's nose as he screwed up his face in thought. "I don't know. Some envelope just showed up at my place. Slid under my door."

"Do you still have the photos?"

He nodded. "At my apartment."

Sonny had the mobster's wallet. He read the address from the man's driver's license.

"Ya, that's my place."

"Is it near here?" Levi asked.

"Ya, real close."

"Where do you keep the photos?" Levi asked.

"In my sock drawer in my bedroom."

"You live alone?"

The man nodded.

Levi placed his thumb onto the man's broken finger and spoke with a tone full of warning. "If we find out you're not being honest with us, I'll make sure you live, but you won't have the use of your arms, legs, or anything else"—he glanced meaningfully at the man's crotch—"that you hold dear. So, I'll ask again." He pressed on the broken remains of the man's pinkie. "Are you telling us the truth?"

"I am." The man nodded vigorously and squirmed with discomfort.

Levi turned to Sonny. He was one of the family's best second-story men. "Sonny, go check out the man's sock drawer and bring back whatever you find."

Sonny, who was a tiny guy, built like a jockey, soundlessly slipped away.

Levi turned back to his prisoner and smiled. "Now, tell me about those scratches. Tell me about the day you got them. Don't leave out any details."

Levi studied the photos Sonny had brought back from the Asian mobster's apartment. They were taken in what looked like the remnants of a bombed-out building, and they were pretty bad.

Two people were featured. Mendoza, whom Levi recognized from the FBI case file, and a naked Asian man with burnt skin and bloody gashes across his body. His forehead was particularly messed up, and there was a misshapen dent where his right cheekbone should have been, as if he'd been hit with something heavy.

In one of the pictures, Mendoza was smiling for the camera as he relieved himself on the other man's naked body.

This must have been the Asian mobster's brother.

Levi held his cell phone in one hand and the pictures in the other. He was torn about what he was about to do.

They'd already moved the unconscious mobster to another location. The pickup spot. He had no way to explain or excuse what he saw in these photographs, and a part of him felt that Mendoza probably deserved what he got.

He sighed as he shoved the pictures in his pocket and dialed a number.

"O'Connor."

"Hey, it's Yoder. I've got eyes on Mendoza's killer."

~

The tinny sound of a bell greeted Levi as he walked into Gerard's, a hangout of his in his old neighborhood of Little Italy. In the old days, the bar seated no more than a dozen customers and there was room for only six tables, but now the place was under expansion. The aroma of basil and garlic hit Levi as he entered, and a deep voice greeted him from the newly expanded room that would eventually be the bar's kitchen.

"Hey, Levi! How can you know this *mameluke* for so long and never teach the guy to make a proper marinara?"

Levi smiled at Gino "Three chin" Romano, a three-hundred-pound mobster stirring a large pot on the newly-installed stovetop. Denny, the owner of the bar, was paying close attention to the ingredients Gino tossed in, but he glanced up at Levi with a look that said he needed rescuing.

Levi nodded toward the fat man. "Hey, Gino, you going to make some pasta to go with that?"

"What do you think?" The round-faced mobster looked as if he'd been insulted. "I've already showed my guy Denny how to roll out noodles and use a *chitarra* for my classic *spaghetti alla chitarra*."

It was midday, the day after Levi had given up Mendoza's killer, and his stomach rumbled, reminding him that he hadn't eaten since yesterday. Gino's specialty was that damned spaghetti he handmade and cut on a traditional Italian pasta cutter that looked like a bunch of guitar strings in a wooden frame.

"All right, but you'll need to get on it without Denny's help. I need him."

Gino wiped his hands on the towel he'd tucked into his expansive waistband and motioned Denny away. "Go on, I'll finish this up."

Denny walked over to Levi and gave him a wink. "Maybe I shouldn't have told Gino that I didn't know much about cooking and Rosie would be doing all the cooking for the bar."

Gino overheard. He yelled across the bar, "The best cooks are all men, you just remember that!"

Levi laughed, put his arm over Denny's shoulder, and led him toward the back of the bar. "Listen, if he's getting pushy, I'll take care of it—"

"No, nothing like that." Denny waved Levi's words away. "I actually like learning new stuff, and he's certainly enthusiastic. It's no problem." He jabbed Levi playfully in the ribs. "I've been around you people long enough. I'm no church mouse. I've got a voice."

"Good." Levi nodded approvingly. He'd felt a bit weird about some of his mob associates starting to hang out at Denny's place. After all, it had been *his* hangout for years. But once Levi had gotten back into the business, and recruited Denny to help with some security items the family had needed, some of the guys had taken a liking to Denny.

It was an association that amused Levi, because he couldn't have imagined someone less Italian than Denny. Denny was a black guy, born in Queens, with an IQ that rivaled that of the smartest folks in the world. Yet he got on great with his mob associates, and in turn, Denny's legit business was booming.

In the back, out of sight of the front room, Denny pressed his finger against a spot on the tiled wall. Something in the wall clicked, and Denny pushed open the hidden door to his secret back room.

~

Denny scanned photos from the Mendoza case into his computer, and frowned as they started to pop up, one by one, on his monitor. "Damn, Levi. This stuff's nasty. It reminds of those Abu Ghraib pictures—you know the ones, that prison in Iraq that hit all the papers."

"It's bad stuff, no arguing that," Levi said. "I just need to know what I'm dealing with. After what you've told me about how photos can be messed with, I wanted you to give me your opinion on these. That guy in the photos, the living one, is supposed to be a fed."

A new image of Mendoza flashed on the screen, and Levi

winced. Mendoza was smiling for the camera, one foot planted directly on the head of the battered, naked body on the dirt floor.

"A fed? Why the hell would he pose like ... I guess it takes all types."

Denny picked up a photo, flipped it over in his hands, sniffed at the paper, and shook his head. "This didn't come from any photo lab. Someone printed this on photo paper, probably from a good quality inkjet printer." His fingers were a blur as he typed. "Let me mask off parts of the picture and see if I can do a fragmented reverse-image lookup."

"Denny, try speaking non-techno-geek for a moment. What did you just say?"

The screen became a blur of images popping in and out of view. "If I had an electronic copy of the original photo, I'd be able to tear it apart and figure out if it's a fake pretty darn quick, and maybe even where it was taken. But since I don't, and the quality of these pictures kind of sucks, it's hard to tell if they were digitally manipulated. Which, if I wanted to send someone a doctored-up photo, this is how I'd do it. Anyway, I've snipped out a piece of the background image and I'm scanning all of the images that I can find on the internet to see if there's anything out there that looks like a partial match."

Levi was somewhat proud of himself for having followed all of that. He watched photos of broken buildings near war zones flip in and out of view. "Got it. And what if you—"

"Bingo!" Denny pointed to an image. "A perfect match."

Levi leaned in, grabbed the original photo, and compared it to what was on the screen. "Holy shit, that's the same scene, but the fed isn't there. And look, where the body is, they blurred it out for the paper, but whoever printed this photo had access to the original. What the hell?"

With a few keystrokes, the picture zoomed out and a newspaper article showed the headline, "Meth Lab Explodes in Elmira Heights."

"Levi, the photo with that fed posing on the dead body is starting to look sketchy."

Shock registered as Levi processed this new information.

Denny's fingers became a blur again as he typed. "I just grabbed a mask of the fed with that pose. Let's see if that shows up somewhere."

Almost immediately after he submitted the query, an image of Mendoza popped up on the screen. It was him with the same pose, but instead of one foot perched on a dead man's head, it was perched on a soccer ball. The caption under the photo stated that Anthony Mendoza was the new soccer coach for the YMCA in Queens.

"Son of a bitch." Levi realized that the mobster he'd just handed off to the FBI had been set up. But why the hell would someone try to get some street gang hoodlum to go after an FBI agent?

"You want me to check the rest of these?"

Levi closed his eyes and leaned back in the metal folding chair he'd been sitting in. "Yes. I want to know if *any* of them are real."

As Denny typed away at the PC, he glanced at Levi and said, "Oh, by the way, I'm expecting something to arrive tomorrow that I want to show you. One of my other customers prepaid for a custom piece and then his situation changed, so he didn't need it anymore.. It's just weird enough that you might find a use for it."

Levi waved dismissively. "I have enough guns for now."

"It's not that kind of piece. Trust me, you've never seen one of these."

Levi opened his eyes and stared at the back of Denny's head. "Oh?"

Leaving an image of Mendoza on the screen, Denny hopped out of his chair and said, "Hold on, now that I'm thinking about it, I need to grab something to measure your eyes."

"My eyes?" Levi watched as Denny jogged past him and disappeared into a maze of shelves loaded with all sorts of gadgetry. He came back lugging what looked almost like a misshapen microscope with a chin rest.

Denny motioned for Levi to come closer. "This is a keratometer. It'll measure the curvature of your cornea so that I can fit another custom job to your eyes." He adjusted the chin rest. "Okay, just put your chin here and press against the forehead rest."

"And you have to measure my cornea for this?" Levi frowned, but then shrugged and placed his chin on the device. "Okay, whatever."

"I think you'll get a kick out of it." Denny sat on the opposite side of the optical instrument and adjusted some knobs. "Just stare at the reflection of your eye and keep the other eye closed." He examined the machine, adjusted more knobs, then scribbled something on a piece of paper. "Okay, all done. I'll get something fitted for you as soon as I can, but come by tomorrow. I'll have finished the upgrade of your hat, and I think you'll like those changes too."

Levi mumbled a positive response and focused once again on the screen where Mendoza's face stared blankly at him. Who would have set up Mendoza to be assassinated? And who would have had access to the unblurred images from a meth lab explosion?

"Okay, picture number two is fabricated as well," Denny said. "Moving on to the next."

"Figures," Levi growled.

His mind drifted from Mendoza to the Tanaka mob boss's granddaughter. He really needed to get back down to the DC area to continue his investigation. Were there any other clues, any communications to the mother? He needed to interview her again. Maybe he missed something.

And then there was O'Connor. He'd be expecting something on the Wei and Nguyen cases, and the only lead he had was a member of the Tanaka syndicate who was missing. Maybe Yoshi's brother would be some help with that.

Denny's computer beeped, and he exclaimed, "Oh shit, Levi. Helen Wilson's Gmail account just received an e-mail with a wave attachment."

"A wave attachment?"

"You know, a .WAV file. A sound file." Denny clicked on the mouse, and a little girl's voice came over the speakers.

"Mommy. It's Tuesday and I'm okay."

The girl's voice was followed by the sound of something being pressed against the microphone. Then a synthesized, almost robotic voice.

"You have two weeks to collect ten million US dollars and wire it to the bank account specified in the e-mail. If funds are not received by then, you will never see your child again."

CHAPTER SIX

As Levi stepped off the elevator at Tanaka Industries, he was greeted by Ryuki Watanabe. The number two man of the Tanaka syndicate held a grim expression and said nothing as he led Levi through the near-empty offices of what was officially an import and export business.

Ryuki stopped at a door that had the mobster's name printed on it in both Japanese and English, and the two men stepped into a spacious office. The mob leader sat behind a large mahogany desk and slid his desk phone between them.

Ryuki spoke in Japanese, his voice was tense and he clipped his words. "I woke my superior as soon as you called. He's waiting for our call. You have the data?"

Levi nodded.

The mobster pressed a button on the phone and a dial-tone filled the room with a long string of different tones as the international number was dialed.

The phone rang once, before an older man answered in Japanese.

"It's about time, Ryuki. I've been waiting over an hour!"

Levi cut in. "Tanaka-sama, I'm very sorry. This is Levi Yoder, and it is my fault for the delay. I struggled with midday traffic to get here—"

"Ryuki told me about the news. I want to hear it myself."

"Understood. It is in English. Do you want me to—"

"No, I can understand well enough, thank you."

Levi raised the volume on his cell phone and played the recording he'd taken at Denny's.

"You have two weeks to collect ten million US dollars and wire it to the bank account specified in the e-mail. If funds are not received by then, you will never see your child again."

Ryuki's face showed no emotion as the message played.

For a long moment, the mob boss's heavy breathing was all that came over the speakerphone. The he said a single word that Levi didn't understand. Some type of Japanese slang? Mob code word?

Ryuki responded with a *"Hai"* and bowed his head in acknowledgment at the phone.

"Yoder-san, was there anything else in the message?"

"Yes, it was the little girl. She left a message to her mother."

"Ah, do you have it? I have never heard my granddaughter's voice."

"Yes." Without even thinking about it, Levi bowed his head to the phone. He rewound the recording to the beginning and put it close to the phone.

"Mommy. It's Tuesday and I'm okay."

There was an eerie silence on the line for a few long seconds. *"So, that is my only heir."* The tense emotion coming in the mob boss's voice sent a chill up Levi's spine. "Yoder-san, I'm too closely involved in this to be of good judgment. I require your counsel on this. What would you do if this was your child?"

"I'd destroy the people responsible," Levi responded without hesitation.

Ryuki's stone-like expression cracked, and he gave Levi an approving nod.

"But, I would not react immediately." Levi continued. "We need more information."

"And, how would you intend to get this information?"

"Tanaka-sama, I had planned on asking Ryuki about this, but I have some resources ... information from the US FBI. They are looking for a Kiyoshi Ishikawa, who they believe is a member of your business. I don't know the truth, but—"

"Ryuki," Tanaka's voice was loud through the speaker, giving off a gruff authoritative tone. *"Do you know this name?"*

"Yes." Ryuki nodded and began flipping through a small box of index cards. "He asked permission to go back to Japan to visit his ailing father, and I gave it. I have an address for him in Ryogoku." He pulled out an index card out and slid it across the desk to Levi. It showed the father's address, written in Japanese.

Levi nodded. "Tanaka-sama, I have people who I trust helping me, but the FBI believes that Ishikawa-san has killed two of their agents. I've been warned by them to not investigate your granddaughter's kidnapping. They claim it's being taken care of, but... Well, I don't like to believe that the FBI could be behind this, but it seems interesting to me that some of those involved know about both your daughter's heritage and Ishikawa's relationship to it. Maybe—"

"You think they are using my granddaughter as leverage to get Ishikawa?"

"I don't know. But I'd like to question Ishikawa. It might be best if I go to Japan to do it, because Ishikawa would likely be unsafe coming back."

"*Ryuki, give Yoder-san use of the plane. I will try to be back in Tokyo for this, but in case I am not, arrange for Yoder-san's reception.*"

"*Hai,*" Ryuki nodded at the phone and looked over at Levi. "I will call to get the plane fueled. How long will it take for you to be ready?"

Levi glanced at his watch. It was three in the afternoon—people were still at work. "I have to make a few phone calls. As long as I don't have any problems with my contacts, I can be ready in an hour or so. But I don't have a change of clothes or—"

"*Ryuki will arrange for anything you need to be waiting for you when you land. We must not waste time.*"

Levi stood. "Okay, I'll go outside and make some calls."

"*Yoder-san, I very much look forward to meeting you in person.*"

"As do I, Tanaka-sama. As do I."

∼

Standing outside the entrance to One World Trade Center, Levi had to hold his phone a few inches from his ear as O'Connor yelled, "*There's no fucking way you're leaving the country.*"

Levi shook his head and paced. He needed the FBI to not interfere; even if he took a private jet, he'd have to check in through customs on arrival, and he was pretty sure the FBI would lose their minds if his passport suddenly triggered an alert showing that he'd landed in Japan.

"Listen to me," he said. "I don't give two shits who took out your agents. You guys are the ones who asked me to look into these incidents. I delivered Mendoza's killer, and now you're telling me that I'm not supposed to follow where the leads go?"

"You're just lucky that the DNA we got off that mobster matched Mendoza's killer. My SAC's happy about that, but you fucked that guy up royally. He's still being treated at the hospital."

"I don't know what you're talking about. That guy was like that when I spotted him."

"Ya, whatever. Tell me again, why Japan?"

"Did you even look at the evidence on the Nguyen and Wei case?" Levi leaned against the wall near the skyscraper's entrance. Men and women in business suits walked past. "One of the bomb fragments had a latent print that got an IAFIS hit. I've got the inside track to where our guy is, and that's somewhere just outside of Tokyo. He's being protected by his mob connections. So, if you think you can go there and get him, then do it. Otherwise, it seems like I've got to do your dirty work."

"We don't have clearance to pursue any suspect on foreign soil."

"Then stop jerking my chain. I may not have this opportunity later. Maybe I can give him a reason to come back to the States—"

"How the hell would you manage that?"

"Leave that up to me. I just don't want my passport flagged if I land in Japan. Do I have clearance to pursue the lead, or not?"

"I can't authorize a cooperating witness to leave the country."

Levi gritted his teeth and slowly breathed in and out, trying to keep his cool. "Then who can?"

"I'll call you back in fifteen minutes."

The line went dead.

Levi would have liked to check in with Denny next, but doubted he'd be able to reach him. The electronics whiz had detected signs of someone trying to hack into one of his firewalls and had immediately shut all of his systems down. He was now probably in one of his quiet rooms, a place he'd shielded against all electronic signals. It was where the man did his most risky work, none of which Levi understood.

Levi scrolled through a series of contact numbers that Denny had given him, found the one he was looking for, and hit the call button. The phone rang once ... twice ... and a woman's voice answered. *"Office of Public Affairs, Federal Bureau of Investigation."*

"Hi, I'm trying to reach Nick Anspach, A-n-s-p-a-c-h. This is somewhat important, and he's either at the DC field office or somewhere in the main lab in Quantico. Can you help me out?"

"Sir, who may I say is calling?"

"Tell him it's Levi Yoder."

"One second, sir." After putting him on hold for half a minute, the operator came back on the line. *"Sir, I'm connecting your call."*

The phone rang once, and Nick's soft-spoken voice answered. *"Mister Yoder? I'm a bit surprised to hear from you."*

"Please, just call me, Levi. And frankly, I didn't think I'd call you either, but circumstances are what they are. I'm going to ask you something that might be out of line, but there's a little girl at stake. I need your help."

"Um ... okay. I can't promise anything. What did you want to know?"

"A five-year-old girl was kidnapped a few days ago out of her mother's apartment in Maryland. I was hired by a family member of the victim to try and find her. And to be honest, the Nguyen and Wei case is eating up all my time, and the longer she's out there somewhere, the less chance I'll find her alive. I figured since you're a forensics specialist, maybe you could help me track something down."

There was silence on the line for a few seconds before Anspach responded. *"I don't think I can help you in any official capacity."* His tone gave Levi the impression there might be a "but" coming. *"Any formal analysis of a scene would have to come through the normal channels. Although ... if it's a kidnapping and the victim might have been taken across state lines, the FBI might already be involved. If so, maybe there's something I can do."*

"They are involved, but for obvious reasons, they aren't sharing what they've learned with me. I just want the girl found alive, whether it's me who finds her or someone else. And I might have some information that could help."

"Oh? Like what?"

Levi explained that the girl was the daughter of an FBI employee, that he'd tracked down the Domino's car to a parking lot, and that there was video footage of a black SUV speeding off from the scene, heading north.

"Levi, I'm not at all familiar with the case, but if you have those security tapes, we have people here who specialize in

enhancing video images. You never know, we might be able to get a license plate."

"I don't have the tapes right now, but I can probably get them—"

Levi's phone beeped. It was O'Connor.

"Listen, I've got Agent O'Connor on the line. I'll work on getting you those tapes, but I have to go."

Levi switched lines, and O'Connor's gruff voice erupted from the phone. *"Mister Yoder, you've got some angel looking over you. My SAC approved your trip. Call me the moment you're wheels down on foreign soil. I don't care what time it is."*

"Roger that. I'll keep you posted." Levi hung up.

At that moment Ryuki exited the building. He looked around, spotted Levi, and walked over. "Yoder-san, the jet is being fueled and a flight plan has been filed. Do you have everything you need?"

Levi patted at his suit jacket's breast pocket and felt his passport and the gun in his shoulder holster. "I have my passport, and I'm also carrying two guns and a few knives."

Ryuki patted Levi on the shoulder. "I expected as much. You need not worry. Your safety is guaranteed." He led Levi toward Fulton Street, where a long black limousine pulled up to the curb. A tall muscular man, whose neck was easily as thick as Levi's thigh, stepped out of the front passenger seat and opened the rear door.

Ryuki shook hands with Levi and said in a hushed tone. "You may leave your weapons with our pilot for safekeeping. He is a trusted member of the organization. Do you have any questions?"

"So, just get on the plane, and someone will be there to meet me and take me to Ishikawa-san?"

"Yes. My superior wants to meet you as well. Whether that happens before or after your meeting with Ishikawa-san, I'm not certain." Ryuki placed his hand once again on Levi's shoulder and leaned closer. "You will be treated as an honored guest. No need to worry."

Levi nodded and stepped into the cavernous rear compartment of a brand-new Mercedes Maybach. The smell of warm leather engulfed him as the large man gently closed the door behind him.

Levi leaned back into the comfortable seat and worried about what kind of link there might be between Ishikawa and the kidnapping of June Wilson.

∽

The speaker in the plane's cabin crackled to life, and the pilot spoke in lightly-accented English.

"Mister Yoder, we're on final approach to Narita airport, and should be landing on runway A in approximately fifteen minutes. That will be 6:35 p.m. local time. The temperature is forty-three degrees Fahrenheit, or approximately six degrees Celsius.

"I've been told by our contact at the terminal that Mister Tanaka will not be able to meet with you until tomorrow morning. But he has arranged for some of his men to escort you into the city."

The speaker clicked off, and the Gulfstream G650ER banked slightly. The sound of the landing gear being lowered murmured through the cabin.

The last time Levi had been in a private jet, he was flying over Russian territory as he and two CIA operatives left a military installation hidden in Siberia. That seemed like almost a lifetime ago.

This jet was much more luxurious than that one—the equivalent of an executive's office in the sky. It gave Levi pause to think of how much money this syndicate must generate to be able to afford not only a jet like this, but to fly it nonstop to Tokyo with only a single passenger.

As the plane flew ever lower, the pressure adjusted in the cabin and Levi closed his eyes. He hated to admit it, even to himself, but landings always made him nervous.

∼

As he stepped onto the stairs that had been rolled up to the jet, Levi was hit by a cool breeze carrying the scent of gasoline. It was cold enough for his breath to form clouds of mist.

At the base of the stairs he was greeted by four Japanese men dressed in identical suits, ranging in age from late thirties to early fifties.

Given the buzz of activity on the tarmac, it was easy to believe that the Narita airport was one of the busiest travel hubs in the world. Levi had once read that well over a hundred thousand travelers flew into and out of the airport every day. Even in this part of the airport where the private aircraft were serviced, the sounds of aircraft taxiing, landing and taking off were all around them. It was no wonder the men who normally worked on the tarmac wore hearing protection.

The eldest of Levi's welcoming group stepped forward and gave a deep bow, which Levi returned. Levi noticed the man's left hand was missing two knuckles. He was always aware that he was dealing with the Yakuza, and from what he'd been told, the Tanaka syndicate held a particularly ruthless reputation.

"Mister Yoder," the man said in accented English. "I'm Hirofumi Hidetada, but please, call me Harry."

"Only if you call me, Levi." Levi gave the man a smile, and Harry's face brightened.

Harry motioned to his three companions. "Accompanying us tonight are Daishi, who goes by the name of David, Chujiro, who prefers Charlie, and Akinori, who goes by the name of Alan."

Levi bowed respectfully to each and began speaking in Japanese, which got an unexpected reaction from the group.

"Please," Harry said, looking apologetic. "May we all speak English tonight? We are slated to start working for Mister Watanabe in the US early next year, so we would like more practice with someone—"

"I understand perfectly," Levi gave the men a thumbs up. He glanced at his watch. "It's almost seven. What's the plan?"

Harry motioned toward a waiting limo, "We heard that you had lived in Japan before, so the boss suggested we show you something unique. Across the street from your hotel is the perfect place. We're going to attend a Burns Supper."

"Burns Supper? What's that?"

All four men smiled, and Harry said, "You'll see. I think you'll find it entertaining."

○○○

Just as June was about to take Raggedy Ann to bed with her, the room was cloaked in darkness and she let out a squeal of surprise. The chains on the metal door at the top of the stairs rattled.

She cringed, because this meant only one thing.

The robot man was coming.

She didn't know how long it had been since he'd last been here, she just knew she was hungry and hadn't had anything to eat in a long time. Hopefully, he had some food.

The stairs creaked, and footsteps drew closer.

"I brought you something to eat and something new to wear."

The voice sounded like it was directly in front of her, but June couldn't see a thing.

"Thank you, Mister Robot. When can I see my Mommy?"

"Soon. Maybe very soon."

June felt a cold hand grip her ankle, and gasped.

"Just stand still and I will put this on you."

"Okay, I won't move." June said, her voice quavering.

The man tightened his grip on her ankle and slipped her foot through something. He did the same with her other foot, then put her arms through the arm holes of what felt like a sleeveless shirt or jacket. And it was very heavy.

The robot pressed something on the back of the jacket, and a tiny light on the front of the jacket, no bigger than a pinhead, turned red.

"Don't try to take this off. It's how I know you're behaving. Also, don't go near the ladder or try to take this off. If you do, your mommy will never see you again. Do you understand?"

June nodded vigorously. "I swear, I'll never ever ever take it off."

The robot man placed his cold hand on her cheek.

And then he was gone.

The lights flickered back to life, and she saw a cardboard box filled with food and drinks. More peanut butter and grape jelly Uncrustables, along with juice and whole-milk boxes.

She looked down at herself and saw that what she was wearing wasn't a shirt—it was more like the life jacket she wore when she and Mommy went on a boat, except this one had loops around each of her legs. Even if she wanted to take it off, she had no idea if she could. She ran her fingers over the olive-green canvas and felt wires just underneath the cloth.

How long would she have to wear it?

She heard the robot's voice in her head. *"If you take it off, your mommy will never see you again."*

June vowed, "I won't ever take it off. No matter what."

She grabbed a partly frozen Uncrustable, unwrapped it, and took a bite.

She blinked tears from her eyes. She had sworn to herself she wasn't going to cry again. Not anymore.

Yet the tears began to fall as she thought of Mommy all alone at home without her.

CHAPTER SEVEN

When Levi had last been in Japan, it was during a completely different phase of his life. He'd been mourning the death of his wife and had tossed himself into martial arts. He'd spent his days training in the karate dojo, and his night sleeping on the floor in the back room of that same dojo. He'd struggled to learn the language, and didn't socialize much, and that had set him apart from the others.

In Japan, there's a ritual called *nomikai*—a way that employees or teammates strengthen their bonds with each other after hours. Often it involves going out to a bar or restaurant that served drinks and allowing people to loosen up. Back then, Levi was anything but loose; he had too much going on in his head. There was only one person he'd spent time with—he was young, probably in his late teens, but he too was a bit sullen and a loner—and he'd helped Levi pick up Japanese. But even then, on the rare occasion when they would go out socially, it was usually to a sumo match, never to drink.

So, when Levi found himself sitting with four Japanese mobsters in the banquet hall of O'Shaughnessy's, a Scottish ale house located in the middle of downtown Tokyo, he couldn't help but smile.

The four men took long pulls at their mugs of BrewDog, a Scottish beer that seemed to be well received by his companions, while Levi sipped at his seltzer.

Harry pointed at Levi with his mug. "Are you sure you don't want a drink? The boss is paying for dinner."

Levi clinked his glass with Harry's mug and shook his head. "I'm allergic to alcohol. It makes me sick."

"I'm sorry to hear that. That must be difficult."

"I've learned to get used to it."

The truth was that although Levi could drink alcohol just fine, his body processed it differently. It tended to hit him almost immediately, making him dizzy for a few minutes, and then left him with a headache. Not a pleasant experience.

Levi looked around the place. It was large, easily fifty feet square, with about twenty other tables, all with people talking and drinking beer. It was obvious they were all waiting for some event to begin. He tore a piece of bread from the loaf that had been placed on the table and popped it into his mouth. It was still warm and had a strong rye flavor to it. He grabbed another piece of the crusty rye bread and motioned to the others with it. "So, do you guys know Kiyoshi Ishikawa?"

Two of the gangsters shook their heads, but Charlie, who looked like he was the youngest, nodded. "*Hai*. He and I grew up next door to each other."

"What he's like?"

Harry asked, "Why do you want to know?"

Levi shrugged. "I'm supposed to visit him and ask some

questions. It's a private matter, but I just want to understand—"

The sound of bagpipes erupted from the far end of the dining hall, and everyone at the tables stood and cheered as a bagpiper walked into view, followed by two more men in kilts.

One of the men was carrying a large silver tray with the biggest sausage Levi had ever seen. Attendants quickly refilled glasses and mugs, the people in the banquet hall clapped enthusiastically, and Levi found himself getting wrapped up in the festivities.

The largely Japanese crowd was very enthusiastic about the whole thing as the tray was set on a reserved table at the center of the dining hall.

A large, presumably Scottish man, with a big red beard stepped up to the table. The crowd of nearly two hundred diners immediately hushed and sat back down.

With a dramatic flourish, the man pulled a large knife from a sheath at his waist and pointed it at the large sausage-like roast in front of him. He slowly turned to address the crowd and said with a booming voice, "It is now time to address the haggis."

Levi suddenly understood what he was seeing. He'd heard of haggis—a Scottish specialty made of sheep, oatmeal, and other spices, all stuffed into a sheep's stomach or something like it—but he'd never had it before. Heck, he'd never even seen a haggis until now. And he certainly hadn't expected to be having it in Japan of all places.

The Scottish man's voice echoed loudly through the room.

"Fair fa' your honest, sonsie face,
"Great chieftain o' the pudding-race!
"Aboon them a' ye tak your place,
"Painch, tripe, or thairm:

*"Weel are ye wordy o'a grace
"As lang's my arm.*

*"The groaning trencher there ye fill,
"Your hurdies like a distant hill,
"Your pin wad help to mend a mill
"In time o'need,
"While thro' your pores the dews distil
"Like amber bead.*

*"His knife see rustic Labour dight,
"An cut you up wi ready slight,
"Trenching your gushing entrails bright,
"Like onie ditch;
"And then, O what a glorious sight,
"Warm-reekin, rich!"*

Levi could hardly understand a word the man was saying, but he watched in fascination as the man enthusiastically stabbed the haggis and squeezed it until the contents gushed out of its casing. He acted as through he'd just disemboweled a victim.

As the man continued "addressing the haggis," Levi's phone buzzed with a message.

It was from Denny.

*Figured you might want to know.
A BOLO went out last night from the Maryland State Police for a stolen black Suburban.
About twenty minutes ago, police scanners reported an explosion just outside of White Oak, Maryland. Police on the scene confirmed the remnants to be from the stolen Suburban.*

Levi's mind raced. If the police were there, then hopefully a forensics team was looking into it. He couldn't possibly be that lucky that it was the same car from the video, but...

He quickly texted a reply.

"Ye Pow'rs, wha mak mankind your care,
"And dish them out their bill o' fare,
"Auld Scotland wants nae skinking ware
"That jaups in luggies;
"But, if ye wish her gratefu' prayer"

The man raised the tray as if in triumph and bellowed out the final line.

"Gie her a haggis!"

Everyone in the dining hall broke out with loud applause, and the serving people began streaming in with trays of the night's dinner.

Harry nudged Levi and smiled. "So, what did you think?"

Levi returned the smile. "I didn't understand a word, but it was fantastic."

Harry lifted his mug and all four men clinked glasses repeating what many of the people at the other tables were saying. "The haggis!"

Levi laughed throughout the dinner and enjoyed the men's company. But all the while, his mind was elsewhere, thinking about a five-year-old girl who was probably scared to death—or worse.

The elevator in the Tanaka building dinged as it reached the top floor, the doors slid open and Levi was met by two serious-looking men in suits.

"Mister Yoder." The man on the right addressed him in Japanese and made an upward motion with his hands. "Please, no disrespect is intended, but—"

"I understand."

Levi raised his arms to his sides, and the man to his left frisked him while his companion watched. When the first man was done, they switched roles, and the second man frisked Levi as well.

The men then led Levi down a well-lit hall. Unlike Ryuki's offices in the US, the interior of the Tanaka building was decorated with a Western sensibility. Dark wood paneling, with art pieces that looked to be copies of masters like Rembrandt and Picasso.

Or maybe they weren't copies?

They stopped at a double-door, and one of the men knocked firmly.

A voice responded from within. *"Enter."*

The men escorted Levi into a penthouse office with a three-hundred-and-sixty-degree view of Tokyo. Pillars of shelves held photographs, books, and other bric-a-brac that made the spacious office feel homey.

From behind a massive wooden desk—mostly black with just a few streaks of very dark brown, all of which shone with a heavy polish—a man stood. "Yoder-san, it is very good to see you in person after hearing so much about you."

Levi bowed politely. "It's good to meet you as well. I've been wondering something. If you don't mind telling me, how did you know to look for me? I don't think we've ever met, and I have a good memory for such things."

The mob boss smiled, and his stiffness softened. He turned to the two mobsters standing at the doorway. "Go, I'll call when we are done."

The men bowed and left, closing the doors behind them.

Shinzo Tanaka stepped away from his desk and motioned for Levi to follow him to one of the shelves. "Come here. Tell me if you see anything familiar."

Levi walked over to the shelving, which was also made of the same wood as the desk. It held dozens of leather-bound classics written in Japanese. Levi spotted *1984*, *The Color Purple*, *Fahrenheit 451*, *To Kill a Mockingbird*, and *The Hobbit*.

Tanaka was clearly a fan of Western literature.

On other shelves were photos of Tanaka with other people—probably politicians or power-brokers.

Levi's gaze was drawn to one photo in particular. It was sitting in the center of the shelf, in a place of prominence. It featured a younger Tanaka with his arm around a kid. A familiar kid.

Levi's mind raced back to the dojo where he'd studied over a dozen years ago. He thought of his one friend in the dojo, the loner who'd never used his family name, just his given name.

Jun.

And then all the pieces fell together.

The kid in the picture was the Jun from the dojo.

Helen Wilson's daughter was named June, same pronunciation.

Shinzo Tanaka had his arm around Jun…

Jun Tanaka?

And then it all made sense.

Jun had never talked about his family, and Levi had assumed he was an orphan, so he'd never asked for details.

Levi turned to Mister Tanaka, who held an inscrutable expression. "You're Jun's father. I didn't know."

Shinzo nodded, and a storm of emotions flashed across the man's face. Sadness, pride, anger. And through them all, determination. "My son, I told him to not use his real name. I didn't want him endangered due to my reputation. I'm sure you understand."

"*Hai.*" Levi bowed slightly without thinking. Old habits returned quickly. "I understand perfectly. So, it was Jun who mentioned me?"

A smile bloomed on the older man's face. He placed a hand on Levi's shoulder. "Yes, he told me all about the American. He also told me you were a man of uncommon honor, and believed you were sent away from a mob family, much as he had been. For protection."

"Well, that's not exactly what happened."

"I know." Shinzo patted Levi on the back. "I reached out even then to learn who it was my son was associating with. I have for years meant to meet you and say 'thank you' for helping my son during his toughest years. I'm saddened that we are not meeting under better circumstances."

Levi nodded. "I will do everything I can to find your granddaughter. And speaking of that, may I ask you something? It may be inappropriate for me to ask this, but it has to do with Ishikawa-san."

Shinzo walked to his desk and motioned for Levi to take a seat. "Go ahead."

"The FBI claims that Ishikawa-san left fingerprints on a bomb that killed two of their agents. These agents were assigned to investigate child sex trafficking. Is this something Ishikawa-san may have been involved in?"

Levi's question hung dangerously in the air. He had just suggested that Tanaka's business was profiting from the child sex trade.

The mob boss's face reddened, and his lip curled with revulsion. "I am many things ... many things, but what I am not is a trader in children. I hear many of the Italians frown on involving women in their business, whether it is running business or being witness to such business. Well, it is my code to not involve children in any of my dealings. Are we clear?"

"I'm sorry if I have offended you—"

"No!" Tanaka slammed his fist on the desk, his eyes narrowing. "It isn't you who has offended. If Ishikawa has done anything such as this to disgrace my business, you will leave him to me to take care of."

Feeling a bit relieved that this powerful man's anger wasn't aimed at him, Levi let out a deep breath he hadn't realized he was holding. "With your permission, I would like to interview him, and as soon as possible."

"Done." Shinzo pressed a button on his phone, and the two men who'd escorted Levi into the room reappeared. "Ichiro, Kenzo, take Yoder-san to the address I gave you earlier. He's to extract information from Ishikawa Kiyoshi. Support Yoder-san in whatever he needs. Understood?"

"*Hai.*" Both men acknowledged their superior's request with a deep bow.

Levi stood and bowed to the mob boss as well. Tanaka returned his bow with a nod.

It was time.

Tanaka's men escorted Levi into an apartment building in Ryogoku. The last time Levi had been in this town was when he and Jun went to see a sumo match.

It was nearing midday as they entered one of the nearby apartment buildings. The smell of mildew was strong as they walked through a poorly lit hallway and was led down an even worse-lit stairwell. The building itself seemed to be reasonably well maintained, but it smelled as if it hadn't had air circulating in it for a long time. The musty smell grew even stronger as they entered the basement.

"Does anyone live here?" Levi asked.

"No," one of the men responded. He pulled a set of keys from his pocket and unlocked a metal door at the base of the stairs. "The boss keeps this building for special uses. Such as today."

The hinges squealed loudly as the men forced open the door and waited for Levi to enter.

He stepped through the doorway and took in the details of his new surroundings. It was a large open room with barely anything in it but two men standing at the far end of the basement. They were standing six feet apart, their sleeves rolled up to reveal ornate tattoos. Flecks of fresh blood marred their white button-down shirts.

There was a man between them that was slumped over in his chair, arms tied behind his back, his body strapped to the chair, which was bolted to the floor.

He'd obviously been beaten.

A nearby table held instruments of torture: pliers, hammers, chisels, something that looked like a modified cattle prod, and one particularly vicious-looking chrome-plated corkscrew. Boxes of sterile gauze, alcohol, a set of syringes, and smelling salts rounded out the collection.

These Yakuza weren't playing.

The two men bowed as Levi approached and took several steps back.

"Ishikawa-san?" Levi asked them as he gestured toward the unconscious man.

"*Hai*," they responded.

For a brief moment, Levi felt bad for Ishikawa. He'd been beaten by two of his own gang members, and he probably didn't even know why. The men doing the beating likely didn't know either; Shinzo Tanaka had simply demanded that Ishikawa be softened up for Levi's arrival. To make things easier. Quicker.

And then Levi reminded himself that this guy was likely involved with child prostitution. His pity vanished.

He picked up a smelling salt capsule from the table, grabbed Ishikawa by his hair, and lifted his head up. Blood was oozing from a cut on the bridge of his nose. Levi shoved the capsule underneath the man's nose and popped it open. The strong smell of ammonia wafted up, and the mobster tried wrenching his face away, but Levi held him in place.

Ishikawa's eyes opened, and Levi smacked him with an open hand across the cheek.

"Wake up. I have questions for you."

The man blinked rapidly, not completely conscious. When Levi pushed the chemical cocktail under the mobster's nose again, Ishikawa grunted in Japanese, "I'm awake … I'm awake."

Levi tossed the used capsule on the floor and sat back on his heels in front of Ishikawa. The man's face had scarring that reminded him of Anspach, but more recent. Part of his ear looked like it had been chewed on, and his cheek and temple had the pink scarring that came from severe burns.

"Kiyoshi," Levi said, "Mister Shinzo Tanaka sent me to talk with you. I'm expecting some answers."

Despite the beating he'd already received, Ishikawa paled at the mention of the head of the Tanaka syndicate. He nodded rapidly and said, in an almost begging tone, "I'll do whatever is needed."

"I just need the truth. Tell me about the bomb that you set."

The man looked panicked, and he glanced from side to side. Levi was contemplating what he'd need to do to get the man talking, when Ishikawa's eyes opened wide with recognition.

"I was just trying to break into the building," he said. "I didn't know it had a gas leak. They shouldn't have died—that wasn't my intent. The kids were—"

"Hold on. What kids?"

Ishikawa tilted his head. "The school. It was late when I tried to break in, and there must have been a spark and the whole place blew. I didn't know there was anyone still in the building."

Levi frowned and studied the man's expression. "Where was the school?"

"You don't know?"

"Where was the school?" Levi barked loudly.

"In West Virginia. A small town called Chelsea."

Levi stood and began pacing back and forth in front of Ishikawa. "Tell me more."

"I received a lead that there was cash being stored in the office of the elementary school. Over ten thousand dollars from some school fundraiser. I smelled something as I approached the building—it had to be the gas. I should have known better. But—"

"Was this the only explosion you were involved in?"

A look of genuine surprise was plain on Ishikawa's face. "Y-yes."

"What time was it when you broke into the school?"

Ishikawa furrowed his brows. "It was definitely night time. I think after ten, but before midnight. And when I broke through the door, it must have set off a spark…"

Levi walked away from Ishikawa, hit a number on his speed dial, and put his phone to his ear.

Denny picked up after one ring. *"Hey, Levi, what's up?"*

"I need you to follow up on something. Can you do it right now?"

"Sure, just give me a second—I'm behind the bar. Hey, Rosie, I'm going in the back. One second, Levi."

Levi muted the call and yelled across the room at Ishikawa. "How long ago was this explosion?"

"A few months ago. Early September, I think."

Levi walked back to the stairwell, where his two escorts had been waiting. "Does Ishikawa have any children?" he asked.

One man nodded. "Two. One boy, one girl. Both are young, one is five, the other is seven years old."

"Bring them here."

The man paused for only a second before responding with a nod. "They are close by, visiting their grandfather. I will be back in a few minutes."

As the man departed up the stairs, Denny came back on the line. *"Okay, I'm at my terminal. What do you want to know?"*

"Check on a school explosion. Natural gas is likely. It was in Chelsea, West Virginia, sometime around September. I need to know everything you can find out about it, ASAP."

"One second."

Levi put the call on mute, stepped back into the basement, and pointed at the two men who'd softened Ishikawa up. "Clean him up and untie him." He narrowed his gaze at Ishikawa. "I'm sure he'll behave."

By the time Levi got off the phone with Denny, having gotten the information he needed, the guard had returned with Ishikawa's kids. The kids ran to hug their father, who'd been cleaned up as much as possible. His nose was bandaged, and a towel was draped around his shoulders. He maintained a brave face for their sake, but Levi saw the terror in his eyes. And he had reason to be worried. His kids weren't part of any equation he'd have prepared for.

"Father, what happened to your nose?" the little boy asked.

Ishikawa smiled and cupped both of his kids' faces in his hands. "I accidentally fell. This American man is a doctor, and he's helping fix it."

The little girl broke away from her father and hugged Levi around the waist. "Thank you, Mister. Thank you so much."

Levi patted the girl on her head and motioned for the guard to escort the child out once more.

Ishikawa's eyes followed his kids out the door. He waited until they were gone before speaking, his voice trembling. "Please, please don't do anything to them. Anything you do to me, I accept. I don't know what I did wrong, but—"

"Enough!" Levi yelled, his voice a slap across the face. He squatted so that he was eye level with Ishikawa, who was still sitting, though unbound, on the chair. "You cannot even imagine what I'll do to your kids if you lie to me again. I just talked to someone who said there have been no explosions at any school in Chelsea, West Virginia. So, what explosions *have* you been involved in? What bombs have you set?"

"Bombs?" Ishikawa blinked, a plain expression of surprise etched on his face. "I've never... I don't know anything about bombs. I've never even been close to one, I don't think. Nobody in our station is a bomb-maker, I'm sure of it. I swear to you, I have no idea about any other explosions or anything about bombs."

Levi studied the man's face. The pale clamminess of his skin was obvious, but the reaction he'd had. He'd seen it hundreds of times. It was the reaction of a man who was confused and surprised. Levi didn't need a polygraph to know that Ishikawa was telling the truth.

He hadn't set the bomb that had killed Nguyen and Wei.

"Ishikawa-san, the explosion wasn't in Chelsea. It was just over the city line in the town of Ghent." Levi patted the man on the knee and stood. He turned to the two men watching over Ishikawa. "Let's bring Ishikawa-san back to the boss. It is up to him what's to be done, but I believe Ishikawa has done nothing wrong."

Upon hearing this, whatever had kept Ishikawa upright in his chair gave way, because the man pitched forward and would have smashed face-first onto the floor if Levi hadn't caught him.

The two men grabbed Ishikawa by the arms and half carried half escorted him toward the exit.

Levi patted Ishikawa on the shoulder and whispered, "Don't go back to the US yet. You are being looked for."

As Ishikawa began to thank him, Levi's mind was already thousands of miles away.

The only lead he had to the two agents' deaths had just fallen apart.

O'Connor still wanted his pound of flesh, but this time, Levi was going to disappoint him.

CHAPTER EIGHT

Levi was met in the lobby of the Helmsley Arms by the head of security for the Bianchi family.

"Hey, Frankie. What's up?"

Frankie motioned toward the apartment building's entrance. "Let's go take a walk. You and I need to talk."

Levi studied Frankie's grim expression, and with a sigh of frustration, he followed Frankie back onto the streets of New York City.

As the two men walked along East 86th Street, Levi's breath came out in warm jets of mist. Frankie was bundled up in a winter jacket, while Levi was wearing the same suit he'd just spent the last two days in.

"Come on, Frankie, I'm freezing my ass off out here. What's going on?"

"One of our guys was rubbed out." Frankie said it bluntly, giving Levi a sideways glance. He continued walking at a brisk pace.

"Shit."

Levi hated the risks of their business. More and more, the Bianchis had been involving themselves in legal ventures, but even then, nothing was without risk among people who stretched the laws. Sometimes personalities between the different families clashed, and other times it was just a case of being in the wrong place at the wrong time. The city could be a dangerous place, even for a connected guy.

But this wasn't the kind of thing Levi usually dealt with; this was the kind of thing Frankie was usually all over.

"Who was it, Frankie? And why are you telling me about it?"

"You probably never met him—a working stiff named Jimmy Costanza. He was one of our connected guys. We got a note delivered, along with two pieces of him: his finger and his manhood."

"What?" Levi stared at Frankie in disbelief. It was one thing to have someone shot. It was very old school to have souvenirs delivered to a man's family. Levi didn't think that happened anymore.

Frankie dug a folded piece of paper from his pocket. "Here, take a look."

Levi opened it and scanned the text.

Stay out of Flushing and our business.

There was a reddish-brown smear on the paper. Dried blood.

Flushing? The family didn't have any business in that area that Levi was aware of. But—

"Oh, shit."

"Ya, oh shit. Vinnie asked me to ask you to stop whatever it is you're doing there. I don't want to know any more than I have to, but Paulie told me about those kids you've been lifting. He said Jimmy was doing favors for him and probably got spotted by one of those Chinese bastards. Well, whatever it was you had them doing, he died because of it."

A chill ran up Levi's back. If Paulie had used Costanza to take care of that girl he'd spotted, that meant the Chinese may have been following him. And if so, they might know where she'd been taken. His blood turned to ice.

He stopped and faced Frankie. "I'll take care of this with Vinnie, but right now I have to go!"

He raced back to the apartment building, dialing a number on the way. As soon as the call was answered, he yelled into the phone, "At the Helmsley, I need a car, no questions. Get there ASAP."

Levi broke all sorts of speed limits to get to Lancaster, Pennsylvania, in two and a half hours. He called Paulie repeatedly on the way, but didn't even get voicemail—either the man's cell phone was off or it had no signal.

As he drove up the path to his family's farm, he spied another car—a black Toyota Camry with New York plates. His heart thudded heavily. Cars were a rare thing in this out-of-the-way Amish community.

He hopped out of his borrowed vehicle and began trudging up the icy path. It had snowed recently in the countryside.

Levi's mom walked out of the barn up ahead, looking to see who had arrived. Her face lit up when she saw Levi. "Lazarus!" she called, using his given name. Though she was in her late sixties, she hustled over quickly and wrapped him in a tremendous hug. "It's been so long! You should visit more often." She admonished him in Pennsylvania Dutch, the language he'd grown up with.

He kissed her on both cheeks and nodded toward the other car parked nearby. "Whose is that?"

She tucked a stray lock of her fading blonde hair back under her white prayer cap. "You don't know? It's the translator you sent for the new girl. She seems very nice."

Levi felt the blood draining from his face. "Where is this translator?"

Mom pointed off into the distance, toward the one-room school building that Levi had attended in his youth. "They're in school, of course. The kids are doing really well. They'll be thrilled to see you."

Levi kissed his mom on the forehead and said, "I'll be right back. I just want to check on things."

As he jogged the quarter mile to the school, he patted his suit, checking to make sure his weapons were where they should be.

He hadn't sent any translator.

He hopped up the steps to the school and opened the door, ready for anything.

He was greeted with a scene that could have come from a Normal Rockwell painting. A dozen kids ranging from five to ten years old, were at their desks, writing in their notebooks. A woman, her back to him, was talking to a girl at the far end of the classroom.

"Daddy Levi!" shouted one of the kids in delight. Heads turned, and several kids hopped out of their chairs and rushed over. As they encircled him, hugging him from all directions, they tugged at his heartstrings. He remembered where he'd found each and every one of them. Images etched forever in his mind.

These kids were victims of the streets, abused in unspeakable ways. Brought from foreign lands—Vietnam, Cambodia, China, and others—most had lacked any English, leaving them at the mercy of the pimps and slave lords that hid in the shadows of nearly every major city.

The best he could do was give them a chance. Levi had paid heavily for the documents that would give them American names, a US citizenship, and a healthy start to a new life. And now, as he looked into their smiling, healthy faces, he knew it had all been worth it. For all the sins he'd committed, and would continue to commit, he hoped this would be a balm to his restless soul.

"So, you're the one."

Levi looked up at the woman who'd spoken, and he gasped in recognition. This was the woman who'd "rescued" him in Flushing. The same woman, who under her clothes, had an undulating dragon tattoo across her taut, athletic body. Her arms were draped over the girl he'd tried to help that day—the girl who'd only wanted a hot dog.

He spoke to the kids in Pennsylvania Dutch. "Go now to Grandma Yoder and tell her I said you all deserve a treat. I want to talk to this woman."

The kids cheered, and poured out of the school, however one of the kids, Alicia, she turned to the girl standing in front of the woman and spoke in what Levi assumed was Cantonese.

The woman nodded and both girls raced from the schoolhouse, leaving Levi alone with her.

"What are you doing here?" he asked, trying to keep the anger he was feeling from his voice.

The woman approached him with a relaxed self-confidence.

"I should ask you what these children are doing here. Why did you have Mei stolen from her manager?"

"Manager?" Levi felt the heat rise up into his neck. "You mean *pimp*. How the hell did you find this place?"

The woman stepped closer, within arm's reach. She wasn't at all intimidated by him. "Why did you have her taken?" She motioned toward all the other desks in the room. "And the other kids, are they like Mei? Did you steal them all?"

Levi's sixth sense tingled, he sensed something was amiss. Was she a cop? Was she trying to entrap him into admitting something?

"Raise your hands," he said. "I need to frisk you."

"You're not touching me," the woman growled, giving him a look of revulsion. She took a step back. "Lock the door and I'll show you that I'm not hiding anything."

Levi took a step toward the door, closed the latch, and watched as the woman unzipped her dress, letting it fall to the ground. She kicked it over to him, followed by her shoes and undergarments. She then raked her fingers through her long jet-black hair. Levi had never encountered anyone who would so casually get naked in front of a stranger.

The woman brazenly stood naked in the middle of the classroom as Levi inspected her clothes for a listening device. "Why are these kids here? You realize that these people would kill you for taking them."

He tossed her clothes back to her, and she quickly got dressed. "How did you find this place?" he asked.

She stepped closer and glared at him. "Answer my question first. Why are these kids here?"

Levi studied her. She was aggressive—pushing him. Why?

He unclenched his fists and shrugged his shoulders. Her demeanor was setting him on edge.

"I wanted more for them," he said. "They didn't deserve to be victimized."

The woman tilted her head and stared unblinkingly at him. "So, all of these kids are like Mei? And now they're off the streets. But for how long?"

Levi frowned. "What do you mean for how long? Forever, if I have anything to do with it, and I *do*. These kids aren't going back to the streets, *ever*. Do you understand me?"

The woman took a step back, and her expression softened just a bit.

"How did you find us?" Levi asked again.

The woman shook her head. "I can't tell you that. Just know that you're lucky you weren't the one who took her—or you'd be the one cut into pieces."

She growled a warning. "Stay away from where you found Mei. I won't be able to help you next time." She stepped around Levi and moved toward the door.

Levi placed a hand on her shoulder, but she spun around and back-fisted his hand away. "Don't touch me." she snarled. "Don't worry—they'll never hear about this place from me. Nor will you ever see me again. But don't you dare come looking for me, or all bets are off."

And with that, she threw open the latch and walked out of the schoolhouse.

Levi contemplated going after her. He also worried whether this place was still safe for the kids. But he didn't have any real alternatives. What else could he do? He had nowhere else he could take them.

His muscles ached with pent-up anxiety. He needed to punch

something—hard. He sat on one of the kids' chairs, feeling somewhat paralyzed.

The door creaked open, and a face peeked into the classroom. It was Alicia. She was one of the first kids he'd taken from the street. She'd run away from whoever had smuggled her into the States, and Levi had found her rummaging through a dumpster no more than ten blocks away from his Park Avenue apartment.

"Hello, baby girl." He said in Mandarin. "You can come in."

Alicia walked in with the new girl in tow. "Mei wanted to thank you," she said in English that was much better than he last remembered her speaking.

Mei looked nothing like the kid Levi had met in Flushing. Gone were the gaudy makeup and improper clothing. Now she wore a modest, dark dress with a white prayer cap. She looked just like everyone else in the community—apart from being Asian. Levi smiled at how young and innocent she looked. He knew she was damaged and scarred on the inside, but hopefully, in time, she'd put her past aside and find a new life.

She walked up to Levi, her eyes tearing. She started to say something in Cantonese, but after only a couple of words, she began to cry.

Levi knelt in front of her and wrapped her in his arms. She hugged him back tightly, as if she'd never let go. He closed his eyes and choked down the lump in his throat. "Tell her that she'll be safe here."

Alicia smiled. "She knows that already. Miss Lucy told her that none of the bad men would find her here."

With Mei hugging him tightly and not letting go, Levi glanced at Alicia. "Miss Lucy?"

"The lady that was just here." Alicia patted at Mei's back.

"Mei said Miss Lucy snuck her candies when her … well, when the bad man wasn't looking."

Mei's sobs began to subside, and Levi felt her shuddering breath on his neck.

There were times when Levi felt like coming here and never leaving. He could almost imagine himself with the kids, almost like a real father … but that wasn't going to happen. He could do more good out there, in the real world. To him, this place was like a cheat—an escape from reality. He could never bury his head in the sand again. He was done running from his problems.

Mei finally pushed back from Levi, and with her eyes downcast, she said something in Cantonese.

Alicia covered her mouth and giggled. "Mei wants to know if she's allowed to have a second cookie."

Levi burst out laughing, hugged both kids to him, and led them to the door. "Let's all visit Grandma Yoder for another cookie."

∽

When he'd first asked Mom if she'd be willing to look after a child he'd rescued from the streets, she didn't hesitate. His mom was a deeply religious woman, and she felt strongly that it was a commandment from God to do things for others, especially those less fortunate than ourselves. The Jews had a name for this—they called such an act a *mitzvah*. But upon seeing Mom with the kids, Levi could tell she wasn't just doing it because it was the right thing: she loved those kids. And more importantly, those kids knew it and returned her affection.

It was a bit gut-wrenching for Levi to leave the kids behind, but they were where they belonged. And he had other demands on his time. He had only ten days until the kidnapper's deadline. Ten days for him to unravel the mystery of the kidnapping while somehow managing to keep O'Connor off his ass and stay out of jail.

As he walked into Gerard's, Denny called from behind the bar. "Hey, Levi."

It was midday, and there weren't any customers in the bar, but the place was full of activity. Woodworkers had begun hanging cabinets, and stonemasons were busy marking off a new countertop for the expanded eating area. Rosie, the brown-haired Puerto Rican woman who worked for Denny, was wiping the bar clean of the dust coming from the work area. She gave Levi that frustrated look she always did when he showed up. Probably because more often than not, it left her with one less set of hands to deal with customers.

"We won't be long," Levi promised.

She shook her head, and rolled her eyes. Rosie was a realist, and knew better.

Levi and Denny went to the secret room in the back, and as the door sealed shut behind them, the noise from the front room vanished.

Denny wiped his hands on his pants. "I've got some stuff you'll really want to see."

At the back of the workshop, past the rows of the metal shelves, sat a plain table with several packages on it. Beside it stood a mannequin wearing what looked like a wet suit.

"What the hell is that?" Levi asked, looking at the mannequin.

Denny ripped open a Fedex package and glanced at the wet suit. "Oh, you mean Henry? I'll introduce you to him in a second. But first, let me show you this." He pulled from the package what looked like a plastic contact lens container.

He picked it up, shook it lightly, and heard water sloshing inside. Yup, contact solution. "Why the heck do you think I need this?" Levi had never worn glasses—in fact his vision was a notch or two better than normal.

Denny smiled. "Humor me. Open it and put that contact in your right eye. If you've never done it before, I can do it for you."

Levi felt a tingle of excited anticipation … almost like unwrapping a present. Denny fancied himself a real-life version of Q, the gadget-master for James Bond. And though Levi was certainly no James Bond, the electronics whiz *was* pretty remarkable when he set his mind on doing something new and creative.

Levi unscrewed the cap and examined the contact submerged in what looked like standard contact solution. "Why does this thing look like it has little silver stripes running through it?"

"Those are fiber-optic channels. Actually, it's a bit more than that, they're bundled arrays of carbon nanotubes, but let's just keep things simple. Trust me, you won't even see them when you put it on."

Levi looked at his hands. "Shouldn't I wash my hands or something?"

"Really?" Denny gave him an amused look and pulled out a bottle of contact solution. "Show me your right hand."

Levi extended his hand, and Denny squeezed the solution on Levi's hand and all over the floor.

Levi rubbed his fingers together, not sure that they were any cleaner now than before. "What's this thing do?"

"Stop being a baby, I've never steered you wrong. Just put it in your right eye. That's the one I measured it for."

With a sigh, Levi scooped the contact onto the top of his index finger. As he moved it toward his eyeball, he wondered why anyone would wear contacts. The idea of putting something directly on your eye seemed nuts. Yet here he was doing exactly that.

"Just press it on gently and it should just suction cup right onto your eye. It'll automatically orient itself once you blink a few times."

Levi did as he was told, and the world turned blurry as he blinked the excess contact solution away. But as he was about to rub his eye, Denny stopped him.

"No—don't rub your eyes. Here." He handed Levi some tissues. "Just dab the wet away."

Levi dabbed away the wetness, then looked around. "Okay, now what? I don't see anything different. Am I supposed to?"

Denny took a pen from his shirt and handed it to Levi. "Take a look at that."

Levi felt that kid-like excitement building within him. He knew this had to be more than just a pen. He gave Denny a hint of a smile.

He turned the "pen" over in his hands and twisted the cap, revealing a ball-point nib. This was one of those fancy non-disposable pens with black lacquer and gold fittings. Thicker than he'd have expected for a normal pen, but otherwise ... just a pen. Levi felt a wave of disappointment.

"Press the metal clip," Denny suggested.

Levi pressed down on one side of the gold clip. It clicked, and the top of the pen flipped open, revealing a clear glass lens. An image flickered into view in Levi's right eye, almost as if by magic.

"Oh, shit."

Denny laughed.

The image was confused and blurred. "What am I seeing?" Levi asked. "Oh, wait..." He aimed the pen, and the image hovering in front of his right eye followed the pen's movement.

A little to the right, the pen aimed at Denny, focusing on his mischievous smile contrasted with his dark complexion.

Aiming the pen, up, the image displayed in front of his eye shifted to the ceiling tiles. They needed a fair bit of dusting.

Denny chuckled as Levi aimed the pen at different targets. "As you can tell, holding the clip down is what activates the video transmitter. While it's active, if you push or pull the cap, you'll be able to—"

"Hah!" Levi laughed as he zoomed in on the far end of the workshop. The image was now clear as day. It was almost like he was looking into a transparent viewfinder. "This is awesome."

"That's not all of it. Give me five minutes, and I'll link the pen via Bluetooth to your phone and you can stream a video directly to it."

Levi let go of the clip, and the image vanished. He shook his head and chuckled. "Denny, you're always good for a surprise. I can think of all sorts of uses for this. Was this the custom thing you'd talked about?"

"No, that's just one of the things I've been working on." Denny motioned for the pen and handed Levi a bottle of contact solution. "Give me your phone and I'll link it to the pen. You put the contact back into its case."

Levi stepped over to a mirror and tried to figure out how to remove the contact without blinding himself.

"Just swipe the front of the contact with the tip of your finger," Denny said. "Once you dislodge the seal, it'll come right out."

Levi pried open his eyelids with one hand and awkwardly removed the contact with the other. He put the contact back into its case and turned toward the mannequin. "Okay, so I can't help but notice this goofy-looking mannequin…"

"Hey! That's Henry."

"I'm guessing Henry comes with the custom item you were talking about—the wet suit?"

"It's actually a dry suit."

"Wet suit, dry suit, whatever. What's the story with that?"

"Pretty simple, actually. I had some two-bit second story guy dump a pretty good deposit for something custom, and he ended up not showing up to collect. I figured out he's doing five to ten years in Sing Sing, so I'm stuck with Henry." Denny slid Levi's phone back across the table. "Well, this guy asked me for something that'll defeat a thermal imaging system. Henry's wearing the result of that request."

Levi pocketed his phone and examined the suit. On the back was a slight bulge, almost like a thin backpack. "What the thing on the back? And wouldn't the rubber eventually get warmed up by body heat?"

Denny hopped out of his chair, flicked a switch on the side of the backpack, and a barely noticeable hum began to emanate from the suit. "This is a three-ply suit with a fine mesh circulator running across every square inch. It's made of a specially-treated waterproof Cordura that's tear-resistant, tough as nails, and provides the perfect foil for the recirculation when layered properly."

"Ah." Levi studied the suit with a new appreciation. "I get it. So, is the thing on the back the water reservoir with a heating or cooling element?"

"Yup. Well, it's not water, exactly, but you got the idea. And it's good for both cold and warm. There's two separate thermostats connected to the two different layers of mesh. So the layer closest to your skin can keep you at a comfortable temperature while the outer one can be set to whatever environment you need. Anywhere from twenty degrees to a hundred and twenty degrees."

"Whoa, below freezing? Really?"

"I told you it's not water. Anyway, since the guy who requested it isn't coming back, and you're about the right size, and you're always into weird situations … I figured I might pawn this off on you."

Levi gave his friend a sidelong glance. "Word of advice, 'pawning off' aren't the words you should use when trying to make a sale."

Denny shrugged. "Well, are you interested?"

"I'm afraid I don't have a need for it. It's cool as hell, though."

Denny sighed. "Oh well. It was worth a try. C'mon." He motioned for Levi to follow him. "I've got your new baseball cap all fixed up like you asked."

Levi's cap was sitting next to Denny's computer. Of all the devices Denny had come up with, this was one of Levi's favorites. By sending out narrow beams of light deep in the infrared spectrum, and monitoring for reflections coming back, it allowed him to detect whenever someone or something was looking at him. It had already saved his life once.

Denny picked it up. "No more need for a separate battery. The tech is evolving pretty rapidly when it comes to molded lithium-ion batteries. The power's all hidden within the brim and structural ribs of the cap. Works just the same as before though, and it can charge wirelessly."

He pointed at the tiny, nearly-invisible holes surrounding the edge of the cap. "I've fixed the bigger problem, too. You said some security cameras were showing you light up like a Christmas tree when you wore it? That won't happen anymore. I've adjusted the wavelength of the light it sends out, so it's beyond what any surveillance equipment should be looking for."

He pointed at a darkened smudge under the bill of the cap. "And this is a pressure switch. Press it once and it'll kick off a diagnostic, which will tickle all the posts. Press it again to turn it off."

"Awesome." Levi touched the inside of the cap, feeling the tiny metal posts that just barely protruded from its liner.

"Oh, on a more serious note. You'll want to see this." Denny sat at his computer and pulled up what looked like a photograph of someone's computer screen.

Levi sat on the stool next to him. "What's that?"

"It's a copy of the forensics report from that Suburban that blew up. You remember, the one I texted you about? Anyway, I looked through it and figured you might want to know about—"

"How the hell did you ... never mind." Levi focused his attention on the poor-quality photograph of a computer screen. It must have come from one of Denny's contacts inside the intelligence community. Likely a former classmate of the MIT grad.

Denny zoomed in on the image. "It looks like the car was doused with an accelerant and set on fire. Nothing accidental about it. I'm not exactly sure why, but the FBI got called into this, and they found a few latent fingerprints. Oh, and check this out."

Levi's attention focused on the section of text that Denny highlighted.

IAFIS match to a Giancarlo Fiorucci. Known associate of the Marino crime family out of Virginia. Current residence: unknown.

"Son of a bitch." Levi realized that his search had taken an unexpected turn. He pressed one of the quick dial buttons on his phone and waited. The phone rang once … twice … and then a loud bout of static erupted from the receiver. The signal was terrible in Denny's workshop.

"Hey, Levi." Frankie's voice crackled across the line. *"Vinnie wants to talk to you about this Costanza thing and where you've been."*

"Perfect, I just got back and I need to talk to him too. When is he available?"

"Come by for dinner. I'm sure you remember that it's Michael and Vanessa's birthday tomorrow, and the family is having a big party at the Waldorf, but tonight's just us."

Levi winced as he realized he hadn't gotten anything for Vinnie's kids.

"Hey, Frankie. How's our relations with the Marino family out of Virginia?"

"The Marinos? Those guys are nothing but a bunch of momos with big chips on their shoulders 'cause they own some of the DC politicians and lobbyists. We've got a cousin over there who's one of the boss's capos. Why are you asking?"

"I might need some introductions. Let's talk after dinner."

"All right, man. Five o'clock is when Vinnie's wife gets back with the kids from school. If you're not around for their party tomorrow, you might want to do something nice tonight, if you know what I mean. Dinner's at six."

"Okay, Frankie. See you then."

Levi hung up and glanced at his watch. He needed to get something for the kids.

"Hey, Denny, out of curiosity, does it say on that report who did the on-scene forensics?"

"Hang on." Denny started scanning through the images he'd been sent and just about when Levi was going to tell him it didn't really matter, Denny smiled and zoomed in on the image displayed on the screen. The monitor was suddenly filled by a small section of the report.

Crime Scene Analysis completed by: Nick Anspach

"Well, I guess he ended up following up on that lead for me. I probably owe that guy a beer."

CHAPTER NINE

A bell chimed as Levi opened the door to Rosen's Sporting Goods. A pimply-faced teen was scanning a woman's purchases at the counter, and the woman's toddler was swinging a pair of snow boots into the back of her legs.

The cashier looked up and nodded at Levi. "My grandmother's in the back with someone. I'll let her know you're here."

"Thanks, Ira."

"Ira is the other one. I'm Moishe." The teen rolled his eyes as he scanned the next item.

Levi chuckled. He wasn't sure if he'd ever called one of the Rosen twins by the right name on the first shot.

As he waited, a line formed at the checkout. Everyone seemed to be buying all sorts of snow gear. Snowshoes, parkas, bibs, skis. The weather forecast had warned of a blizzard. Levi fully intended to be down in DC and would be happy to avoid the disaster that the New York City streets would turn into this weekend.

"Moishe!" A woman's voice erupted from somewhere in the back. All Levi could see was a gray-haired bun bobbing up and down as she walked past a tall sales rack.

An Asian man also emerged from the back of the store, heading straight for the exit. He didn't look familiar to Levi, certainly nobody he'd seen in Chinatown before, but judging by his clothes and the way he carried himself, the guy was almost certainly in Levi's line of work.

Not a surprise. Esther was not what she seemed to be. Under that grandmotherly façade was a shrewd businesswoman who had no reluctance about dealing in anything she could profit from—including things that weren't exactly legal to purchase.

"*Bubbaleh*, you should have called your brother in from the back. I don't like such long lines." Esther apologized to the customers for their wait and helped her grandson speed up their checkouts. Soon the line had died down, and Esther came over to Levi.

He held up a small shopping bag and smiled. "I come bearing gifts."

Esther gave him a suspicious look and peeked inside the grocery bag. "Oy, you wicked man. Entenmann's, and this time, it's the black and white cookies you bring me. Now I *know* you want something." She motioned for him to follow as she waddled toward the back.

"Wait," Levi said. "Something I need might be in the front. Or at least, I hope so."

Esther stopped and cocked an eyebrow at him. "Oh, really?" She walked over to him, smoothed out his suit jacket and patted him on the chest. "So, what can I do you for, *boychik*?"

"Well, I've got a set of nine-year-olds that I need a last-minute birthday gift for."

Esther gave him a disapproving stare. "You forgot the birthday for Don Bianchi's twins?"

"I didn't forget, exactly, I just—"

"Pfft, enough with the excuses." She waved dismissively at him. "What's the budget?"

Levi shrugged. "I have no idea. I need something nice, and … do you have any ideas?"

"I just got in two more Segway Drifts I haven't put out on the shelves yet. If you want them, I think they'll be a hit with the kids. And they come with helmets."

"I have no idea what those even are."

"You've heard of a Segway?"

"Aren't those the scooters that automatically balance when the rider steps on them?"

Esther held an amused expression on her round and slightly wrinkled face. "Imagine roller skates with the same technology."

"Really? That sounds kind of cool. And you have two?"

"I do." Esther wagged a stubby finger at him. "But don't think you'll sweet talk me into giving you any deals on those. They're flying off the shelf as it is."

"Fine, I'll take them both."

As Esther turned toward the back of the store, Ira, Moishe's brother, walked in. "Ira, go back in the storeroom and take out the trash, and while you're there, grab the Drifts for Mister Yoder and gift-wrap them. They're still in the new inventory rack." She motioned for Levi to follow. "I've got some of your stuff ready for pickup."

"My stuff?" Levi wracked his brain trying to remember what he might have had on order. Normally, Esther was good for both semi-auto and automatic weapons, body armor, and even explosives that had somehow gotten "lost" from a military depot. All the standard equipment for the trade.

They walked to the rear of the store, past the grandson who had his arms full with two Segway boxes.

She led Levi to a table in the far corner of the supply room in the back. She plopped down in front of it, and pointed at the chair next to her.

Levi took his seat. "Esther, can you remind me what I had on order? I don't remember—"

"*Oy gevalt*, you think I just make these things up? Remember when you said I need to talk to Mister Wu, that tailor of yours? Well he and I worked out a deal, and since he had your measurements, I figured you might be my test subject for this." She leaned over, picked up a long flat box, and laid it on the table. With a flourish, she opened it to reveal what looked like an exact copy of the suit he was wearing.

Confused, Levi pulled the box closer and felt the material. The cloth was a bit thicker, stiffer, heavier. It wouldn't drape the same way his regular suit did.

"*Nu*, try it on."

Levi removed his suit jacket and tried on the new one. "Why is this thing so heavy?"

Esther waved away his question. She stood, ran her hands over the lapels, and took a step back with her face tilting to one side and then the other. "It looks good. How does it feel?"

"Honest?"

"What kind of *meshuggener* question is that? Of course, honest!"

"My other suit is more comfortable. This feels heavier than it needs to be, and it's kind of stiff."

"What, you expecting paper-thin linen to stop a bullet or a knife?"

"Oh." Levi's mouth dropped open.

"That's all I get is an 'oh' from you? That's not as good as the vest I made you, but then again, there's nothing better. But you got me thinking about it, and with some of my sources, I put a few things together. That's three layers you have. Outside is the wool suit you're used to, but woven underneath is something new, a nanofiber that's lighter and stronger than Kevlar. It should stop a forty-five at point-blank range. But so you don't get hurt as much, underneath I had Mister Wu put in an STF liner—"

"STF?"

"Shear-thickening fluid. It's not that new, we've known about non-Newtonian fluids forever, but this stuff is good. The faster something hits it, the more resistance it gives. That's why your suit, my dear *boychik*, is a bit heavier. I'm thinking I could market this even to the normal people out there."

Levi smiled at Esther. She looked exactly like you'd think an old Jewish grandmother with a sweet tooth should, but she was one of the most knowledgeable people he knew when it came to weapons and armor. He shrugged his shoulders and worked his arms back and forth. "You know, now that I realize why this feels like it does, I think I could get used to it."

Esther beamed at him and pointed at the box. "Perfect, I got you two suits, and also an all-black set of fatigues, for when you don't need to look presentable. All I'm asking is for you to use it, and let me know how it works for you."

"You mean be your guinea pig—"

"Oy, let's leave the pigs out of it. You're just one of my favorites who I want to see safe, that's all. Oh, and if you get shot, I definitely want to take a look at the suit and whatever else you were wearing. Research, you know."

Levi chuckled as he folded the suit jacket, placing it back in the box. He glanced at his watch and winced. "I have to get going."

Esther came closer and spoke in a conspiratorial whisper. "You know it's not my business to get involved in your kind of politics…"

What she meant was that she didn't want any mob-related drama since she had customers on all sides.

"Well, I care what happens to you, my *boychik*, and because I care, I'm letting you know something. I'm seeing things that make me nervous. The Japanese, the Yakuza are getting very agitated with the Hong Kong members of the Triad that are here. And the Triad members, who are also my customers, they've been asking about those who you're close to."

In other words, the Italians.

"I don't see your side reacting yet," Esther continued, "but the Chinese, they're loading up. I figured you should know. Be careful."

∼

"Oh my God, the kids are going to kill themselves." Phyllis, declared in her nasal voice.

Vanessa and Michael had their helmets on and were standing on their new Segways with huge smiles on their faces as they drifted around Don Bianchi's parlor. Both Vinnie and his wife, Phyllis, looked on with pained expressions as their kids laughed, wobbled, and seemed to be getting the hang of Levi's gifts.

Frankie had his arms crossed and was cringing each time the kids wheeled their arms trying to get used to their new gifts.

"So, kids, do you like them?" Levi asked.

The nine-year-olds leaned forward on their new skates and zoomed directly at Levi. They smashed right into him, and all three of them fell to the ground, laughing.

"Okay, that's enough of that," Vinnie exclaimed. "Get those things off and thank your Uncle Levi so we can get to dinner. I'm starving."

Levi hopped up onto his feet and held out his arms for a hug. "It's okay. I don't bite. But I might bark sometimes." He let out a small Chihuahua-like yip.

The kids rolled their eyes and gave him hugs, thanking him repeatedly for the presents.

"Come on, let's go." Vinnie declared as the maid appeared in the doorway to the parlor, indicating the food was ready.

Vinnie's apartment occupied the entire top floor of the Park Avenue building, and it still amazed Levi when he thought of how far his friends had come. It wasn't that long ago that they were all tough young kids on the street. Well, at least Vinnie had always been a tough guy. Levi had more often just found himself in situations where he had to decide whether or not to defend his friends.

He'd always defended his friends.

Phyllis nudged Levi as they walked toward the dining area. "So, where's this girlfriend I heard about?"

Levi cocked an eyebrow. Vinnie's wife had made it her personal mission in life to find him someone, and he'd always brushed off her attempts. It wasn't exactly something he wanted someone else to do for him.

"She lives in DC."

"Oh, come on. You know what I mean. I want to meet her—"

"Phyllis," Vinnie said, "leave the poor guy alone. You think you're some kind of matchmaker?"

"I'm just looking out for him," she insisted.

Vinnie looped his arm over Levi's shoulder and pulled him toward the dining room.

The travertine dining room table easily sat fifteen, and Levi silently wondered how in the world Vinnie had even managed to get that monstrosity into the building. It sure wouldn't fit in the stairwell or the elevator. A crane?

Frankie took his seat near the end of the table. Vinnie motioned Levi into the empty seat to his left and said, "Whose turn is it for grace?"

The kids both pointed at each other, and Phyllis shook her head. "Vanessa, it's your turn."

The cute blonde girl stuck out her lower lip, but bowed her head. Everyone else bowed their head as well.

Vanessa spoke in a very clear voice. *"Benedici Signore noi e il cibo che stiamo per mangiare. Benedici la nostra madre e il nostro padre, e tutta la nostra famiglia."*

Vinnie nodded approvingly and shifted his gaze to his son. "And Michael...."

Michael clasped his hands together, bowed his head and cleared his throat. "Bless us Lord and the food we are going to eat, bless our mother and father and our whole family."

Vanessa raised her head, but Michael continued with his own extended version of the pre-meal prayer.

"If it's not too much trouble, can you bless Cassie from school, my teacher Mrs. Rodriguez, my cat Whiskers, oh and please bless Maria, Jennifer, Lou from my art class..."

As the precocious child continued rattling off the names of

people and things in his life, Levi looked at Vinnie and Phyllis. He sensed the pride they had in their kids. It gave him a warm feeling, but deep inside, he felt a sense of regret. He'd always planned on having a family. Had things been different, and his wife hadn't died, his kids might now be just a bit older than Vinnie's.

But then he thought of the farm and the smiling faces he'd left behind, and that put a smile on his face.

"Okay, Michael," Vinnie interrupted. "That was very nice."

Levi turned to Vanessa and Michael. "Both of you, that was beautifully done."

Michael smiled and said proudly, "I can do it in Italian, too. Want to hear?"

Vinnie wagged his finger good-naturedly. "You can show Uncle Levi some other time." He turned to Phyllis and complained, "I'm going to starve if we don't eat soon."

Phyllis stood and took the silver lid off the large silver serving tray. Steam rolled up to the ceiling and the aroma of tomatoes, basil, and something fried filled the room.

Vinnie leaned forward, dramatically sniffing the air and moaned. "Eggplant parmesan, my favorite."

Levi suppressed a smile when he saw young Michael's face. Clearly, the boy wasn't a fan.

"Guests first," Phyllis said. She held out her hand, and Levi passed her his plate. Using a spatula, she laid several large pieces of beautifully fried eggplant on the dish. She glanced at him. "Marinara on top?"

"Sure, thank you."

She ladled on some thick marinara sauce, then placed a nest of buttered linguini on the side of the fried items and handed his plate back to him.

Levi breathed in the wonderful smells. "Phyllis, this looks amazing."

Vinnie leaned closer to Levi and whispered loud enough for everyone at the table to hear. "You didn't think I just married her for her good looks, did you?"

"Vinnie!" Phyllis gave her husband an embarrassed smile and demanded his plate. As she loaded it up, she said to the kids, "Don't you think Uncle Levi would make a great dad?"

Levi stared wide-eyed at Phyllis as the kids nodded their approval. Where the hell had that come from?

As she continued filling the plates, Phyllis held a smile on her face every time she glanced at him.

The don leaned over to Levi and whispered, "You and I need to talk about kids after dessert."

"Kids?"

Vinnie winked and put a finger to his lips.

Levi looked over at Frankie. The security chief was suddenly preoccupied with smoothing out a wrinkle on his button-down shirt.

What was going on?

Once everyone was served, Vanessa, who was seated next to him, held her knife and fork in her hands, raised her eyebrows, and gave Levi a look.

"What?" Levi was starting to feel paranoid.

She leaned closer. "We're being polite and waiting for you to take the first bite." She lowered her voice and hissed, "You're the guest."

"Oh, sorry." Levi smiled and took a bite of fried eggplant. It was delicious. "My compliments to the chef," he nodded to Phyllis, who looked pleased and began cutting up the eggplant for Michael.

Everyone began digging into their meal, and Frankie, with his mouth half-full with pasta, prompted the kids to talk about their day at school.

Levi's mind wandered as the kids competed with each other over who could talk louder and faster.

What in the world were Vinnie and Phyllis hinting at? And was Frankie involved? He ate quicker as Frankie's words repeated in his mind.

"Vinnie wants to talk to you about this Costanza thing and where you've been."

~

Levi sat opposite of Frankie on a leather-upholstered wingback chair in front of the fireplace in the don's parlor. In his mind, there was a countdown clock ticking away. A five-year-old girl's life was at stake, and even though everyone else's life moved on, for him, he couldn't shake the anxiety-inducing tick, tick, tick of that countdown.

Ten days left.

"How's the Japanese mob thing going?" Frankie asked. "You making progress for them?"

The question reminded him that Vinnie and the Yakuza had made some kind of business arrangement, likely contingent on his success. "Progress is slow, but that's part of what I'm going to ask Vinnie about when he gets out of the bathroom."

Vinnie walked into the parlor and sat down on the third chair arrayed in front of the fireplace. "Levi, I'm sorry about Phyllis. She got all weird on me when I told her about you rescuing kids off the street and leaving them with your mom."

A tingle raced through Levi as he stared open-mouthed at his friend.

"What? You didn't know I knew?" Vinnie waved dismissively. "Levi, you should know better. I know everything that's going on around me."

"It's my business to make sure he knows," Frankie said with a wry smile.

Vinnie shook his head at Frankie. "What, you need credit for every little thing?"

The two lifelong friends rolled their eyes at each other.

The don continued. "Anyway … I figured it was your business to do what you want, until it interferes with mine. When it does, we need to talk, and that's what we're doing."

"The Costanza thing," Levi said. He felt a wave of guilt over the thought of another man paying the price for something he'd asked to be done. "I'm sorry that happened. I wouldn't have thought—"

"Enough," Vinnie interrupted. "I'm not looking for an apology. It happened."

"Well, it won't happen again," Levi promised.

"I just need to understand what's the deal. What are you doing with these kids? I did a little looking into it. You've spent a fortune on getting these kids official papers. Making them part of the system. Your mom adopting them. Why?"

Levi sighed as he thought of the kids, not as they were now, but as they had been. On the streets. In danger. Innocent, or at least … they deserved to be.

"I don't know, Vinnie. When I was grieving, after Mary's death, traveling in all those Godforsaken places, I saw these kinds of kids everywhere. Kids no older than Vanessa working the streets for some pimp, parents selling one or more of their kids into slavery because they couldn't afford to feed them. These kids were put into situations that no child should ever face. And I didn't do anything about it. I couldn't. There were just … so many."

He felt his stomach tightening as he thought of the hell on Earth that had been life for those kids.

"So when I saw it in my own city, I just … I just had to do something. All of the kids I'm taking responsibility for, they either didn't have parents or their parents sold them to the scumbags who supposedly managed them." Levi's throat tightened at the thought.

Vinnie leaned over and clapped his hand on the back of Levi's neck, and they pressed foreheads together. "My friend, you're an angel in wolf's clothing. If only the world had more people like you. Is there anything I can do for these kids you have over at your mom's place? Do you need some help, you know, financially?"

Levi cleared his throat, smiled, and patted his friend on the shoulder. "No, I've got it. And I know you think I'm crazy for doing it, it's just…"

"Hey, I understand why you're doing it. But you have to realize, even here, there's just too many."

"You can't save them all," Frankie added.

"I can try," Levi replied with a smile.

CHAPTER TEN

Nine days left.

"Levi," Madison's voice crackled as the train passed through a tunnel. *"When do you think you'll be back in DC?"*

Levi chuckled as he glanced out the window of the train. "As a matter of fact, I'll be pulling into Union Station in a few minutes. What's up?"

"Well, I think we need to talk. You have time for a quick bite tonight?"

"I could do dinner, but it's just about eleven, how about lunch instead?"

"No, I've got work to finish. How about you meet me at my place at six, and we'll plan from there. Sound good?"

"Sounds great, see you then."

As soon as the line cleared, Levi's phone buzzed and he put it back to his ear. "You forget something?"

"Not particularly." It was O'Connor's gravelly voice on the

line. Great. *"You're supposed to check in with me, daily. Where are you?"*

"Just arriving at Union Station, going to follow up a lead that I've got."

"Take a break, I want you to meet me at Arlington Cemetery. Special Agent Tran Nguyen is being buried there today at three, and I think you should get a feel for why what you're doing matters."

Levi had been to Arlington once before. When his cousin, a former Army Ranger, died in Afghanistan, he was buried with full military honors. It was during that ceremony that Levi learned just how much his cousin had kicked ass and taken names over in the Middle East. A Silver star, two Bronze stars, and a long list of other achievements qualified him to be buried in what many in the armed forces considered to be hallowed ground. Nguyen must have been a similar ass-kicker to be getting buried there.

"I'll be there."

"Good. I'll meet you at the Visitors' Center at two thirty."

Levi hung up just as the train came to a stop. Just enough time to check into his hotel, change, and head over to the funeral.

∼

Levi followed Agent O'Connor toward a crowd of nearly a hundred people who were all gathered in front of a flag-draped casket, all of them with heads bowed in respect for the man who'd sacrificed everything for his country.

An orange-robed Buddhist monk spoke to them in what Levi presumed was Vietnamese, and a few dozen soldiers in full dress uniform formed an outer contingent.

O'Connor let out a deep breath and shook his head. "Dead, because he wanted to stop child sexual exploitation." He looked Levi in the eye. "I wanted you to see what the spear tip of this fight looks like."

And with that, he turned and walked away.

Levi stayed back from the crowd, leaning against the trunk of an old magnolia tree. O'Connor hadn't needed to bring him out here for him to take this seriously. Levi already lived his life by the motto of "do the right thing." And what Nguyen had done—not the dying part, but the rescuing of kids—that was most certainly the right thing.

As he scanned the crowd, Levi spotted someone looking directly at him. But almost immediately, the man broke eye contact and shifted his gaze to the coffin.

"So, how did you know Tran?" asked a voice. A brown-haired man had sidled up next to him.

Levi took a step back, startled. Rarely did anyone ever get within arm's reach without him noticing. "I didn't."

"I saw you come in with O'Connor. You working on a case with him?"

"You might say that." Levi replied. He got a soldier vibe from the man, even though he wasn't in uniform. He was built like a linebacker, and wore a cheap but freshly pressed suit. Levi held out his hand. "The name's Levi."

The man shook Levi's hand. "Tim."

"I'm guessing you worked with Tran?"

"Yup. We go back all the way to boot camp."

"Ah, so you were both in the Army?"

"Feels like ages ago, but yes." Tim stared off into the distance, frustration etched into his rugged features.

Levi followed the man's gaze toward the coffin. For a split

second, his eyes connected again with the man who'd been looking at him earlier. This time the man gave him the briefest of nods before walking away from the ceremony.

He shifted his thoughts back to the dead agent and admitted to Tran's coworker, "I'm tasked with trying to track down who did this to him," Levi said. "Do you have any thoughts?"

"No," Tim said with a dejected tone. "I wish I did. Every time we get close to nailing one of these bastards, they slip out of the country. They shift territories. They just shoot their inventory and bury them somewhere. These people Tran and I go after, they care nothing about human life. We're cattle to be exploited. Kids are just easier to control than adults."

Levi couldn't bring himself to even think about killing kids to hide evidence of misdeeds. What kind of twisted thought process would make that seem logical?

"Don't you know where they're coming from?" he asked.

"The pimps? The slavers?" Tim pressed his lips together and gave Levi a sidelong glance. "You're new here, aren't you? Of course, we know. They're coming from everywhere. South of the border. The Middle East. But right now, we're inundated with a flood of Asian kids being exploited."

"Why not stop it at the source? Why wait until they get here?"

Tim snorted derisively. "Oh, we try to get permission to go after them, but we're blocked each and every time."

"The Bureau blocks you?"

"Sure, it's the Bureau sometimes—usually due to lack of jurisdiction. More often it's the foreign country not wanting us operating in their borders."

"And let me guess: when you drop the dime on your suspects

in country, so that their authorities can grab them, they never do."

"They never do." Tim's troubled expression grew darker. He turned to Levi and said, "I hope you nail whoever did this to the wall."

With a shroud of frustration and deep-seated emotion, the ex-soldier turned and walked away.

∽

The sound of the shower running echoed through Madison's apartment as Levi thumbed through one of the many unlabeled workbooks that were lying on her desk. Their relationship had spanned nearly a year, so he'd spent a number of weekends in this small, minimalist apartment. It was a one-bedroom, furnished only with a sofa, an old tube TV on a rickety stand, a desk, a kitchen table with two chairs, and some bedroom furniture. Add in some clothes, disposable kitchenware, and whatever was in her fridge, and that was the extent of her worldly possessions. Levi had poked fun at it in the past, but her rationale was pretty sound.

"It's just me and work. Who am I here trying to impress?"

He respected that.

Levi had met her when she was working the part of an undercover operations officer for the CIA—and as far as he knew, she still was. She never talked about work with him though, not even reminiscing about the time their paths had crossed on the job. Though she was very focused on her work, she kept that part of herself firewalled from him. And ultimately, that was what made Levi a bit uneasy about whatever their relationship was and where it was heading.

He knew more about Madison, with the help of Denny, than she realized. He'd seen her DD-214s, military discharge papers, and he knew she'd been an EOD member of some skill in the Navy. An explosives expert. So, as he flipped through the handwritten pages of one of her notebooks, he wasn't surprised to find that she'd drawn diagrams of IEDs, improvised explosive devices, likely from some type of bomb-tech class. He understood enough to get the gist of her notes—he'd been studying some of the basic electronics books in his library, and could at least read the circuit diagrams she'd drawn.

In the movies, they always showed some poor bomb tech sweating over which color wire needed to be cut to defuse the bomb at the last minute. Almost all of that was crap and nonsense. The truth was, most military and civilian explosives experts didn't try to defuse bombs very often at all. It was usually safer to just isolate the bomb and blow it to smithereens.

But there was definitely a science to bomb-making, and Madison knew it well. She'd written nearly ten full pages solely on the topic of collapsing circuits. As Levi flipped through the pages of her handwritten notes and precisely drawn circuit diagrams, he wondered whether she would give him some lessons on this stuff.

"Nosy, aren't we?"

With a sheepish smile, Levi set aside the notebook, and turned to see the frowning face of Madison. She was fresh out of the shower, one eyebrow arched as if to say, *What the hell do you think you're doing?*

He stepped over to her and gave her a light peck on the lips. "I know, I know, you hate me going through your things. But it was just sitting there on the desk and—"

"And you couldn't resist." She rolled her eyes, turned her naked back to him, and said, "Zip me up."

Levi zipped up the black cocktail dress and whistled appreciatively at the way the outfit hugged her slender curves. "You said you wanted to talk."

"Not now. Let's get to the restaurant."

"Are you driving, or am I?"

"Unfortunately, you'll have to follow me." She gave him a slight frown and waggled her phone. "I'm on call for a case, so I may need to bug out at a moment's notice."

"Okay, let's get going." Levi offered his arm, and she took it as they walked out of the apartment.

The place Madison brought them to was packed with diners, but all Levi could see was Madison's sad, but resolute expression.

"I think it's only fair to you that..." Madison paused as a waiter delivered trays laden with steaks and roasted chicken to the adjoining table. Then she took in a deep breath and tried again. "I think it's only fair to you that we stop seeing each other."

She lowered her gaze to her uneaten plate of chicken-Caesar salad. "Those cramps I was having, it was my body having a really rough time. I'd miscarried before, and I must not have realized it. This time, it was bad. I'm not going to be able to have kids."

Levi's heart dropped to his stomach. He couldn't even imagine what Madison was going through. What she'd *already* gone through—without him. An overwhelming sense of guilt washed over him. "I'm so sorry this happened. I—"

"No, it's for the best. I was never sure about having kids, or even getting married." She gave him a weak smile. "You made me think about all of that and more. But I also know that you need someone who you can share your life with. We have too many secrets between us. It's not fair to you, what I do, what you do… It's not … it's not good for a relationship. I think my miscarriage was a sign—"

"Maddie, that's ridiculous. It's not—"

Madison's phone buzzed and she snatched it off the table and put it to her ear. A few seconds passed, and she nodded. "Understood. I'll be there in fifteen."

She got up from the table. "Sorry, I have to get going." Madison leaned over and kissed his cheek, then walked out of the restaurant, leaving him alone.

Levi stared at the table filled with food. No amount of food could fill the hollow pit he was feeling in his gut.

He waved the waiter over. "Can I get the check?"

The waiter shook his head. "No need, sir. The lady took care of the bill already. Do you want me to wrap this up for you to take home?"

"No." Levi flipped a twenty-dollar tip onto the table. "I'm done here."

Levi got up and walked back to his car. Tomorrow would be a long day.

It was time to meet up with one of the heads of the Marino crime family.

CHAPTER ELEVEN

There were eight days left, and Levi's mental clock ticked ever louder. He adjusted the baseball cap—pressed the hidden switch on its bill to turn it off—as he walked into Ma Kelly's Bistro, a place no self-respecting New York member of the Mafia would find himself in. It was an old Irish pub converted to serve food to folks that didn't care about what kind of animal the meat was coming from. The place was dingy and smelled of stale beer. Not surprisingly, it was nearly empty.

A tall, barrel-chested man got up from one of the tables, and though Levi had never met the man, he could tell that was his guy. Dino Minelli.

"My cousin Frankie says we're all friends," Dino said.

Being friends in La Cosa Nostra had a special meaning. When someone introduced you to another member of the Mafia, they'd say you were either *my* friend, which meant you were a connected guy, but they wouldn't discuss business in front of you, or they'd say you were *our* friend, which meant you were a *made* guy, a person of mutual respect, and someone who could be trusted with business. A person who'd taken the oath.

Levi shook hands with the big man, who stood a good three inches over Levi's six-foot frame. "Frankie's a good man." He gestured to the dingy joint. "You eat in this place?"

Dino smirked. "You kidding me?" He motioned for Levi to follow him out of the restaurant, and they began walking down a busy street in DC. "Nah, I just wanted to make sure nobody saw who I'm talking with, or you'd have the cops tailing you. I'm more a Virginia Beach guy than DC proper."

Levi adjusted his cap, turning it back on. He felt the tickle of barely-perceptible shocks coming off the metal posts inside the cap's liner as it went through its startup diagnostics.

The two of them chatted about the differences between Virginia and New York City, and how Dino had gotten into the rackets. He was surprised by Levi's back story.

"Damn, I've never heard of made guy who wasn't at least part Italian."

"I might be the only one." Levi said. "I've known Frankie and Don Bianchi since they were kids. And the old boss, the current don's father, he'd made an exception. I heard he had to go to the commission to make it happen, official-like."

"Damn." They crossed the street into Penrose Park, and Dino headed for one of the benches that lined the playground. "You must have made quite an impression to have a boss go to bat for you like that. I'm not sure any boss nowadays would stick his neck out that far for anyone."

They sat on the bench and stayed silent for a moment, absorbing the sounds of the nearby traffic, the birds in the trees, and the smell of the changing season.

Levi felt a slight tickle from one of the rear metal posts in his cap. Someone or something behind him was looking his way. But when he turned, he saw nothing but the semi-circle of trees that bordered the park. Then the tickle of electricity stopped.

He cupped his hand, placed it on the side facing the trees, and said, "The former Don Bianchi was a good man. He believed in doing right by people who were loyal."

Dino nodded. "I heard that about him. So, Gino Fiorucci is who Frankie said you needed to talk to. I don't personally know the guy. He's a connected guy, good earner, but I don't really know much more than that. I talked to his friend, and he said he was into shipping stuff. Contacts at the docks, things get lost, you know what I mean." The large mobster turned sideways on the bench and faced Levi. "So what's he got to do with you?"

Working with the feds wasn't unheard of, but it was almost always a death sentence in the Mafia. Something Levi would have to work around.

"Dino, my boss is working a deal with someone, and let's just say someone's granddaughter got kidnapped and there was a black Suburban involved. I got some info about that black Suburban being trashed and set on fire. One of my guys gave me a report saying it had a fingerprint left on the steering column, and it matched a Giancarlo Fiorucci. That's why I want to talk to him. I don't give a crap about the car. Just the kid."

"How old is he?"

"The kid? Well, the kid's five, and she's a girl."

Dino's face scrunched up as if he'd swallowed a lemon. "My baby girl Donna just turned five." He shook his head and glanced around the empty park. "I can't let you rough him up or anything. That's on us. But I'll have to talk to the boss before we can go any further."

"There's a ransom," Levi said, "and we don't have much time." *Eight days.* "When can you talk to your boss?"

Dino dug into his suit pocket and extracted a notebook with a short pencil stuck through its coil binding. He began scribbling something. "I'll talk to him this afternoon and call you with what he says." He ripped a sheet of paper from the notebook and handed it to Levi.

It was an address in DC.

"A friend of ours told me that Gino eats lunch almost every day at this place. Real out of the way from my normal stomping ground, but since it's nearby, maybe you can at least keep an eye out. Remember, I can't let you touch him. He's protected."

Levi folded the sheet of paper and stuck it in his jacket pocket. "I understand. Dino, I appreciate this. And tell your boss that I'm just going on a hunch. It's just when it comes to a kid and a deadline, I can't leave any stone unturned, you know what I mean?"

Dino nodded, and they shook hands. "I'll call you later."

As Dino walked out of the park, a couple of neighborhood kids walked past him and then began playing on the jungle gym.

Levi pulled out his phone and searched the internet for photos of Giancarlo Fiorucci.

He smiled as images of Giancarlo "Gino" Fiorucci showed up on his browser search. Gino had a dark-olive complexion, black hair, bushy eyebrows, and a long hawk-like nose. Not exactly a pretty boy. In fact, the longer Levi studied the man's face, the more he felt a desire to hurt him.

He looked at his watch. He had an hour to get to the restaurant.

That was plenty of time.

THE INSIDE MAN

~

It was almost four in the afternoon, and Levi had observed Gino's every movement for the last four hours. He'd found him at a place called the Cafe Deluxe, just outside of a part of DC called Foggy Bottom. Lots of government types ate there. When Levi came in and took a seat at the bar, Gino was eating at a table by himself.

After lunch, Gino walked along Dupont Circle, and a man approached him. The new guy was dressed in the kind of run-of-the-mill suit the drones in the State Department wore. Probably some middle-level flunky.

Levi immediately pulled out Denny's video pen, and turned it on.

Anyone who was watching Levi would see a man staring off into space, and if they were paying careful attention, he happened to be nervously playing with a pen in his hand.

Levi purposefully faced east while he aimed the pen at Gino and the government worker. An image flickered in front of his right eye and he zoomed in while leaning against a light pole. The whole idea of an image overlaid with what he was seeing still left him a little queasy. It was like a heads-up display, but in real life.

He began recording.

The two men clearly knew each other. Gino pulled from his suit jacket a paper-wrapped package just the right size to be a stack of cash, and in return he received a large manila envelope.

Oh, now that's interesting.

The two men shook hands, and Gino headed east while the other man went north, directly past Levi.

Levi stopped the recording and his phone buzzed as the pen

spooled the video contents to it. After a few moments, a second buzz indicated the transmission was complete. Levi put the pen away and checked the silent video on his phone. The video quality was excellent. He fast-forwarded to the part when the unidentified man was facing him and took a snapshot of the man's face.

He forwarded it to Denny and typed: *Can you get me an ID on him, ASAP? Likely a fed of some kind.*

Denny responded almost immediately with a text, *"Received. Working on it now."*

~

O'Connor watched the surveillance footage of Levi Yoder walking the streets of DC. It was being displayed on a small handheld camera by a CW, a cooperating witness, who was involved with the Calabrian Mafia known as the 'Ndrangheta. The wiry man had been a productive source of actionable data over the last nine months.

"Who is that with him?" O'Connor asked.

"That's Dino Minelli." The CW had a strong Italian accent. "He's a capo from the Marino crime family out of Virginia Beach."

"He's a bit out of his area, isn't he?"

"Yes and no. Most of their business is drugs and controlling labor, mostly in their territory. But I've been hearing they're branching out a bit. Politics is good business."

The agent watched as Levi sat down with the mobster in a kids' park.

Almost immediately he turned and faced the camera with a look of suspicion, and the video shifted away from the target.

"Ya," said the CW, "that Yoder guy has eyes in the back of his head. Every time I focused in on him, he'd get spooked and turn around looking for me. Luckily, I'm quick on my feet."

O'Connor glanced at the wiry man and jabbed his finger in the man's direction. "Be careful with this Yoder guy. He's especially dangerous."

The CW shrugged. "What do you want me to do?"

"I gave you the name of the hotel he's staying at. You'll catch back up with him there. Just keep me apprised of what he's doing and where he's going."

"You got it, boss."

∽

It was late evening when Levi met with Dino just outside a bar on West Great Neck Road in Virginia Beach. Dino motioned to what looked like a brand-new black Cadillac XTS. "I'll drive the rest of the way," he said.

Levi got into the passenger seat of the roomy vehicle, and they started down Shore Drive, with only minor traffic. "So," Levi said, "anything I should know about Don Marino?"

Dino tapped his thumbs impatiently on the steering wheel as he waited at a red light. "Nah, he's pretty old-school. Know your place. Show respect. That's about it. When I talked to him, he didn't like something about what he heard, so he wanted a sit-down at his place."

Soon Dino was pulling past a security gate and following a long curving driveway up to a house on a cliff, overlooking the beach. The place was immense, easily twenty thousand square feet, and it sprawled across a handful of acres of prime coastal property. This guy was no pauper.

A few men in suits were waiting to walk them up to the mansion. Levi surrendered his weapons and went through a pat-down before entering the building.

Two of the men led him and Dino to another wing, past a large dining area that could easily seat thirty people, and an elegant piano room overlooking the ocean. Finally, they entered a library. Books crowded the shelves from the floor to the fifteen-foot-tall ceiling, the higher ones accessible via an attached wheeled ladder that moved along a track.

One of the boss's men knocked on a heavy oak door that was partially ajar. The door looked like it had come from a medieval castle.

A gruff voice sounded from within. "Come in."

Dino entered first, followed by Levi. The boss's man closed the door behind them.

Don Marino was a beefy man in his sixties. He was about Levi's height, but likely outweighed him by at least a hundred pounds. Surprisingly, the man wore it well. He was thick-wristed and the epitome of what someone might have rightfully called big-boned. The same genetics someone would need to be a professional defensive lineman … or a leg breaker.

Dino motioned toward Levi. "Boss, this is Levi Yoder. He's the friend of ours that I talked to you about earlier."

Levi nodded toward the boss. "It's an honor to meet you, Don Marino."

The don motioned to the chairs arrayed in front of his desk. "Both of you, have a seat."

Levi sat in an ornately carved wooden chair that reminded him of furniture he'd seen in museums.

"So," the don said. "Dino's telling me that you think one of our connected guys might be involved in some kind of kidnapping of a little girl?"

"Well, I have some word from the inside that the same man Dino talked to you about, his fingerprint was found in a burnt-out wreck of a car. It's the same model car that we're pretty sure was used for the kidnapping."

The boss frowned. "Whose car is it? Do you know if our guy owned it?"

Levi paused, realizing he had no idea who the vehicle belonged to. A situation he'd soon rectify. "No, sir. I think I might be able to find out, though."

"Well, then it seems that not all of your ducks are in a row yet. I can't give permission for you to question him without a solid, verifiable reason."

It was now time for Levi to pull out what he hoped would be his trump card. He motioned to his suit jacket. "Sir, do you mind if I show you a bit of surveillance video of the man we're speaking of? I took it today. I think you'll find this interesting."

The boss tilted his head and looked at Dino. "Do you know about this?"

Dino looked confused and shook his head. "No, Boss. I didn't know anything about a video."

The boss leaned forward, elbows on his desk and frowned. "Mister Yoder, I don't like it when my people are harassed without cause." He motioned to Levi's jacket. "This better be good."

Levi's heart thudded a bit louder in his chest as he retrieved his cell phone, unlocked it and started the video. He spoke as the video played.

"I wanted to get a feel for his movements. What he did. Who he hung out with. Maybe if I was lucky, he was going to visit a place that was hiding this girl. But he never left DC until after he'd met up with this guy you see now in the video. As you can see, your guy handed him something that looks like a brick of cash and he got a folder full of something in exchange."

The boss's face darkened and his Italian accent grew heavier. "Who is that other guy?"

Thankfully, Denny had come through with the ID. Levi swiped to another screen and displayed a photograph of a State Department personnel file. "His name is John Benson. He works at the State Department in the TIP office. TIP stands for Trafficking in Persons."

The boss motioned to the phone. "May I?"

Levi handed it over, and the man used his thick sausage-like fingers to zoom in. "You'll read in that summary that he's some kind of manager who deals with getting emergency visas and passports for people who are in need." Levi said. "That department has a lot to do with monitoring sex trafficking. It kind of worries me, because the girl that got kidnapped, she's young, young enough to be trained by some of these sick bastards. And of course, she's got blonde hair, and for some of these deviants, that's a bonus."

The don had a grim expression as he handed the phone back to Levi. He jabbed his finger at Levi. "None of my people deal with that kind of stuff. It's a sin beyond nature to do that to kids." He sat back in his chair and took a deep breath.

Levi hoped he wouldn't have to go around these guys. He was going to take care of business with or without the don's permission, but it would be a lot less dangerous for him to if he got it.

Don Marino turned to Dino. "Go get a couple of the boys with you. Have a sit-down with our guy. Get the truth out of him, and if it's a sin, make sure there's penance involved." He gave Levi an approving nod. "You did well bringing this to me. I talked with your don, and he told me about you. I think I'm starting to believe some of what he said. I give you permission to talk to our guy—with Dino supervising."

Levi bowed his head as a sign of respect. "Thank you, Don Marino. I'll find out what's going on."

The don motioned for them to both leave, and as soon as they'd left the boss's office, Dino was on the phone setting up the meet-up.

It was going to be a long night.

∽

Levi walked into a bar with two other made men that Dino had called in. Gino was sitting at a table that would have seated eight, but it was just him making obscene gestures to the TV that was hanging up on the wall.

The three of them sat at the table with Gino, who snapped, "What the hell, this is my table—oh, sorry Tony, I didn't recognize you." Gino had focused in on the mobster to Levi's right, who he obviously recognized. "What are you guys doing in this part of town? You want me to get you guys something off the menu? Lulu makes a really nice veal piccata."

Tony waved dismissively and didn't say a word. He also didn't introduce anyone, and it wasn't Gino's place to ask, though he did shoot furtive glances at Levi and the other made man.

That was the difference between a made man and a connected guy. A connected guy might be a big shot among ordinary people who realized that he had mob connections, but made men were kings of whomever and whatever they surveyed. And a connected guy couldn't even question a made man without risking a serious reprisal.

And if Dino were here … well, Dino was a capo—a captain or organizer of made men—and a connected guy shouldn't even look a capo in the eyes without expecting a slap from just about every made guy in the area.

That's what the Mafia was like. It had a definite hierarchy, and for Levi, it had been all he'd known since he was eighteen.

The TV was broadcasting news about the Palestinians and Israelis, and Gino waved toward it. "You see that shit? Them bastard Israelis think they own that land, but the Palestinian people were there well before them. Those Israeli fuckers need more rockets sent up their asses, not less."

Levi grinned. "What do you know about that part of the world?"

Gino turned to him. "What do you mean?"

"I mean the history. Before 1948, when Israel, the country, was born." Levi had had the privilege of walking both Palestinian-occupied and Israeli-occupied Jerusalem. He'd visited the remnants of the second temple, the mosque built partially on its ruins. "What makes you think the Palestinians have any more right to be there than the Jews do?"

"Because they've been there forever, that's why. What makes you think different?"

"What makes me think different? How about the Holy Koran, specifically chapter five, verses twenty and twenty-one?"

Gino gave Levi a sidelong glance. "How the hell am I supposed to know what the Koran says?"

"Well, I figured if you're going to argue with such a strong opinion, you'd be well-informed about what the Palestinian people's holy book says."

"Okay, smart guy, what does it say?"

In his mind's eye, Levi saw the Arabic script and recited both verses.

"wa- 'idh qāla mūsā li-qawmihī yā-qawmi dhkurū ni 'mata llāhi 'alaykum 'idh ja 'ala fīkum 'anbiyā 'a wa-ja 'alakum mulūkan wa-'ātākum mā lam yu 'ti 'aḥadan mina l- 'ālamīn.
"yā-qawmi dkhulū l- 'arḍa l-muqaddasata llatī kataba llāhu lakum wa-lā tartaddū 'alā 'adbārikum fa-tanqalibū khāsirīn."

All three men stared open-mouthed at Levi.

"What the hell is that supposed to mean?" Gino said.

"Those two verses are about Moses talking to his people, the Jewish people. He says, 'Oh my people, remember Allah's blessing upon you when He appointed prophets among you, and made you kings, and gave you what none of the nations were given. Oh my people, enter the Holy Land which Allah has ordained for you, and do not turn your backs or you will become losers.'

"So," Levi continued, "even though I know this, and I know how complicated the history of that land is, I wouldn't feel right taking a side on this issue. Those two groups need to work it out, and us on this side need to keep our misinformed noses out of things we can't possibly understand."

Tony smirked at Gino's stunned expression. "Gino, let's go somewhere more private. We need to have a talk."

The blood drained from Gino's face as he realized this wasn't a social visit.

CHAPTER TWELVE

The room smelled of copper and piss. Both from Gino. The copper was coming from the drying pools of blood that had been spilled. Splattered on the walls. On Levi's clothes. On the floor. Pretty much everywhere. Levi had had the foresight to strip out of his suit before any of this started. He was wearing blue medical scrubs, and he was sure it looked like he'd just butchered a hog.

Gino had had each of his fingers broken multiple times, his face was a bloody mess, and his left ear had been torn cleanly off by one of the other mafiosos. Levi had taken over after that. He didn't want Gino to die without giving up what he needed. But even Levi had his limits. He was pretty sure he'd felt a cheekbone crack with one of the last hits that had sent the man unconscious … again.

He looked over at Tony, who'd been standing off to one side, watching. "Wake him up." It was almost six a.m., and Levi's mind reminded him that there were only seven days left.

There was an IV tube hanging from a pole behind Gino, left over from the first time Gino had gone unconscious and one of the mafiosos had run a central IV line into the man's neck. Tony plunged a syringe of something into the IV port, and within seconds Gino's eyes were fluttering. "Please, just kill me. I didn't take any little girls in a black car."

The door opened, and Dino walked in, still wearing his suit. "Holy shit. Is he alive?" He stepped up to Levi, avoiding some of the mess on the floor. "What do we know?"

Levi kicked Gino hard in the shin. "Mister Fiorucci, tell me again about that transaction I saw yesterday over at Union Square."

Gino's head lolled back and forth. It looked like he was trying to lift his head up, but couldn't quite manage it. Some of the muscles in his neck might have been torn during his last beating.

Tony grabbed the guy by the hair and pulled his head up so Dino could see.

"I ... I ... what did you want me to—"

"Union Square. Tell me about that guy you paid yesterday. What was that for?"

Gino's eyes flickered and bubbles of blood came out of his nose. "I paid fifty G's for papers and a manifest."

"What were the papers for?"

"Passports, IDs for the girls." Gino moaned, and his right eye began twitching uncontrollably. "They're coming in on a freighter hidden in a dozen shipping containers full of rice."

"What are you doing with these girls?"

"Selling them. I've got buyers already lined up all along the East Coast. These girls are prime stock. How the fuck do you think I bring in five hundred G's a month?"

Dino's face turned red, and he asked in a low voice. "How old are these girls?"

Gino sneered, and for a second he grew more lucid. He smiled, revealing that his two front teeth were missing and several others were chipped. "All ages. None older than twelve, but some are just right. Probably the same age as your Donna."

Before Levi could even react, Dino pulled out a Smith & Wesson revolver and put three shots into Gino's chest.

"Hey!" Tony yelled, jumping back from Gino's body as it went rigid. "You could have hit me!"

Levi's ears were ringing painfully, and he sighed as the smell of crap filled the air. Gino had lost control of his bowels and along with more blood pooling on the floor, there was now a fresh stream of urine dribbling from the chair.

He wasn't going to be getting any more answers out of Gino.

"Son of a bitch." Dino shook his head and turned to Levi. "There's a shower down the hall. You clean up and get dressed. I'll have the boys finish up in here."

As soon as Levi walked out of the room, he took a deep breath of fresh air. His muscles ached from the physical exertion, and he smelled like the room he'd left behind.

He hated this part of the job.

∼

Levi paced back and forth in an empty area of his hotel's parking lot as he talked on the phone. "Seriously, I don't have much time left, Denny. Can you can get those tracking devices to me overnight? I don't trust any of these government bastards as far as I can throw them. I need to be able to track where these rats scurry off to when I drop the bomb on them."

"I'll do you one better. I can get on the train and be there in a few hours."

"No, there's too many eyes on everything. I don't want you taking that kind of risk. I'm not sure who the bad guys even are right now."

"Levi, you do realize that some people might think you're the bad guy, right?"

"I'm okay with that. As long as it saves that little girl, I'll be the nightmare people talk about in hushed voices to scare misbehaving kids."

"Okay, my friend, I've got the stuff packed up. It looks like your hotel is on an early delivery route for FedEx, so this should get to you around eight a.m. if we're lucky."

"Sounds great." Levi realized he'd nearly forgotten something. "Hey, Denny, can you do a quick lookup of the owner of that Suburban? The one with the fingerprint."

"Sure. Hold on a sec, let me pull up the image of the report."

A car pulled past the hotel's guest gate and parked a few dozen yards away. Levi walked farther away.

"Well, it looks like that was a government vehicle."

Levi stopped, standing between a Buick sedan and a Nissan SUV. "Really? How the hell did a Mafia associate's fingerprint get into a government vehicle? Can you track down who that was checked out to?"

"I think so, but I won't know if I can get access to that information until tomorrow. I'll reach out to my guys first thing in the morning."

"Okay, Denny. Thanks a bunch for everything. I'll settle up when this crap is all over with."

"All right, man. I'm out the door with your stuff. Expect it tomorrow morning. See ya."

The line went dead and Levi glanced at his watch. He dialed a number and put the phone to his ear.

One ring … two rings … and the phone picked up just as the third ring started. *"Hello?"*

"Yoshi? Are you by chance in DC?"

"Oh, hey, Levi. Um—yes, I am. What's up?"

"Can you meet me at Union Square, near the fountain?"

"Sure, I guess so. When?"

"Can you meet me in half an hour?"

"I'll get in the car now."

"Okay, see you there."

Levi walked over to his rental and popped the trunk. Inside was the tactical case that he always had with him. One of Denny's little specialties. He slammed the trunk shut and hopped in the car.

～

Levi walked around Union Square, panning his gaze back and forth, looking for Yoshi. Every once in a while, his baseball cap tingled, and he turned to see nothing obvious, or sometimes a scanning security camera. Denny's surveillance detection hat had always had some idiosyncrasies that were unavoidable, but triggering a few too many alerts was infinitely better than not enough. With the hat constantly sending out infrared beams of light in all directions, the signal that bounced back usually wouldn't register anything with Denny's gadget. It was only when the signal bouncing back repeated frequently that it would trigger an alert.

That would only happen if someone was watching him. Their eyes would be following him, and the invisible light would keep getting a signal bounced back, triggering one of the metal posts in the hat to give his scalp a mild tingle. Levi may have looked like a skittish cat in a crowd, but he appreciated the invention.

One of the posts tingled, and he glanced in that direction. A blonde woman was looking at him. As soon as their eyes met, she lowered her gaze and blushed.

"Levi!"

He turned to see Yoshi jogging up to him with a look of concern. "I got here as quickly as I could. Is there some news on June?"

Levi shook his head. "I'm sorry, but not yet. I wanted to ask you a favor, but didn't want anyone else to hear." He motioned toward the far end of the square and they began walking. "Can you call June's mom and arrange for us to visit?"

"Sure, I think so. But, why? And what's this about not wanting anyone else to hear?"

Levi wished he'd have thought of this earlier. "Well, I've been thinking about what happened the night of the kidnapping. How the hell did the kidnapper know the Mom would be ordering pizza? You said that they didn't order out very often. So, how did the kidnapper know to ambush the delivery driver and get past the gate?"

Yoshi's eyes widened. "Shit, I have no idea."

"I want to sweep Helen Wilson's apartment, to see if there's anything unusual."

"I'll see if I can arrange it." Yoshi pulled out his phone.

Levi put his hand on the man's shoulder. "Whatever you say, figure someone's listening. You understand what I'm saying, right?"

Yoshi nodded as he put the phone to his ear. After a moment passed, he smiled. "Hey, Miss Wilson. It's Yoshi. I was wondering if you'd be around this evening. I wanted to do a quick check on the apartment, and I'd rather do it while you're there" He paused, then nodded. "Okay, I'll see you at five."

Levi raised an eyebrow. "Miss Wilson? That seems a bit impersonal. I thought you two were closer than that."

Yoshi shrugged. "On the phone, we've always played the roles of apartment security and tenant. But sometimes, when June was asleep, we'd meet at the apartment's swings and talk."

"Talk? Don't get me wrong, but the way you carried on about her, I figured you two were having an affair. Am I wrong?"

Yoshi's face turned beet red. "I-I'd like to, but it's too early. And too complicated. I could never—"

"You don't need to explain." Levi chuckled and patted the man on the back. It was almost sweet how nervous he was. "Let's grab a bite to eat and then we'll go see 'Miss Wilson.'"

～

Levi watched as Yoshi gave Helen the handwritten note that said, *Don't say anything. He's going to check your apartment for listening devices.* Her eyes widened, and she nodded her understanding.

Yoshi and Levi walked in, and Levi cracked open his case and extracted a wand-like device with a small loop at the end. It not only detected active listening devices, it also triggered passive ones that turned on only in response to motion or sound.

Levi had done this many times for hotel rooms, but doing an entire apartment was going to take some time. He decided to methodically work from one end of the dwelling to the other.

He started with the table next to Helen's bed. Lifting the receiver of the corded phone, he ran the wand over it. A little red

LED flickered over the handset. He retrieved his case and pulled out a container that was lined with a metal mesh. It was both soundproof and signal-proof. He unscrewed the handset, and out fell a fingernail-sized device. He plopped it into the container and continued the scan.

Yoshi scribbled on a notepad and showed it to Levi.

Was that a bug?

Levi nodded. For a second, Helen and Yoshi clasped hands and stared at each other.

It took almost an hour for Levi to cover the entire apartment. He collected all the electronic surveillance devices he could find, and for good measure, he also dusted for prints in the places where he'd found the bugs. He managed to snag a few prints.

He snapped the container shut and breathed a sigh of relief. "This place was bug central. All your phones, above the china cabinet, under the coffee table, in each bathroom, and in June's bedroom. Someone really wanted to keep tabs on you."

"But who?" Helen asked, a look of shock on her face. I don't understand. Should I call someone?"

Both Levi and Yoshi said "no" at the same time.

"It's best to just leave things alone for now," Levi said. He shook the container with the listening devices. "I'll have someone look into this. It's best to just leave things alone for now. Has anyone had access to your house?"

Helen shrugged. "Well, sure. Plenty of people. The cops and the FBI have been all over this place."

"How about before the kidnapping?" Yoshi asked.

"Well, I guess lots of people then, too. We had a birthday party for June. And I had some people over from work. I have no idea how that stuff could have gotten there or how long it's been there."

"It's okay." Yoshi put his hand on Helen's shoulder and she put her hand on his.

To Levi, she said, "Did you talk to June's grandfather?"

"I did."

"And?" She looked up at him expectantly.

"I think he'd do just about anything to save her. He's heartbroken over what's happened."

She motioned for Levi to come closer.

He leaned in, and she whispered, "The kidnapper asked for a ransom. Ten million dollars."

Levi nodded. "What did the FBI say to that? I presume you don't have ten million dollars."

"They said they're doing everything they can to find her, and even if I had ten million, which I don't, they wouldn't recommend paying. They said I'd lose any leverage I had."

"Well, they do have a point. You have almost six days until the ransom is due—"

Helen gasped. "How do you know that?"

Levi smiled as both Helen and Yoshi looked at him with astonishment. "Trust me, we're doing everything we can. Don't tell anyone anything. I'm trying to flush out whoever took her. If I can, then I might have a chance of getting her before the deadline."

Helen's hands began to shake, and Yoshi held them in his. "This is really hard…"

"Actually," Levi said, "I have an idea. We might be able to use one of these bugs. If you don't mind, I'm thinking of putting one of the bugs back by the china cabinet back. We can use it against whoever planted it. Let them think we missed it. Are you okay with that, Helen?"

"I … I guess so. I just have to be careful."

"Good. And if I ever send you a text directly, I want you to come up with some pretense to read it aloud."

Helen looked confused, but nodded.

Levi put a finger to his lips to indicate silence, then he cracked open the container, removed a listening device, and put it back in its spot on the china cabinet.

He put his hand on Yoshi's shoulder. "I'll leave you guys. There's some things I need to follow up on."

Levi left the apartment, looked up the location of the nearest FedEx dropoff that could still ship overnight, and began texting Denny a series of names.

The puzzle pieces were beginning to fall into place. A plan was forming.

CHAPTER THIRTEEN

Six days remaining. As the number grew smaller, Levi's concern over the looming deadline increased. Hopefully, by setting up these dominos, he'd be able to follow where they fell, leading him straight to June Wilson.

Denny's package had arrived at the hotel right on time, and Levi had spent the better part of the day tracking down cars and planting Denny's tracking devices on them. Next up was O'Connor's car. It was a gray Chevy Impala, and even though Levi had only seen it for a second, the image of the license plate was etched in his mind.

The difficulty lay in getting into the underground parking facility where it was parked. His best chance was the Third Street entrance, but the entry was manned by security, and physical barriers prevented anyone unapproved from driving in.

Levi parked on the street, palmed one of the tracking devices, and walked toward the security booth just outside the parking entrance. He wasn't exactly sure what he was going to say.

A car pulled up alongside him. "Hey, Yoder. Are you here to see me?"

Levi couldn't believe his luck. There was O'Connor in his gray Impala staring up at him across the open passenger's side window.

Levi walked up to the passenger window, leaned in, and lied. "I tried calling you, but the call wasn't going through for some reason."

The agent motioned for him to get in. "Well, let's not talk on the street."

Levi got in. Between closing the door and making a production of putting on his seat belt, he managed to stick the magnetic tracking device on the underside of his seat.

"So, what's the status?" O'Connor asked as he pulled into traffic and began circling the block.

"I saw someone who I think works in the State Department meeting up with one of my leads. They exchanged papers and cash, but that's about all that I know right now."

O'Connor slowed to a crawl, and cars behind him began honking. He turned in his seat to face Levi. "Do you have pictures of this State Department person?"

"Yes. I'll send them to you tonight. I've got some things to follow up on in the meantime. Just figured you should know."

The car completed the circle around the block, and O'Connor stopped to let Levi out.

Before closing the door, Levi leaned down and said, "And get your phone fixed. Coming out here wasn't exactly on my to-do list today."

~

"Shit," Levi muttered as he stared at the entrance to Marine Base Quantico. There was no way he was getting in. He'd followed the guy from the State Department and frowned as it became obvious that he was probably heading to the FBI Laboratory today. And for him to get to the FBI Lab, he needed to get past the gate.

He drove up to the main entrance and a marine stepped out of the guard booth.

Levi rolled down his window. "Excuse me, Corporal. I need to visit someone who works at the FBI lab."

"Yes, sir. Can I have some ID and the name of the person who's sponsoring you? They'll have to have called your name in before you can get in."

"They have to call ahead?"

"Yes, sir. It's procedure."

Levi motioned to the turnaround. "In that case, I'll be right back. Let me give him a call."

The marine motioned to his right, and Levi made a U-turn away from the entrance. He did know one other person who worked at the lab, and he called them now.

Unfortunately he got voicemail. *"This is Nick Anspach. Please leave a message with your case number and the phone number to reach you at, and I'll get back to you as soon as I can."*

"Damn it." Levi hung up and dialed another number. Almost immediately, O'Connor's voice broadcast through the car's speakers. *"Yup."*

"Hey, it's Levi Yoder. What would you say if I thought I might be able to get you some answers in the next two to three days regarding who's responsible for the kidnapping?"

O'Connor's voice took on an animated tone. *"You're shitting me, right?"*

"No, I think I have a really solid lead. But I need a favor. Otherwise this might all fall apart."

"What's this favor?"

"I just need you to call up the gate at Marine Base Quantico so I can get in. I swear to you, nobody's getting hurt, nothing is being damaged. I'm just going to take a quick look around, and I'll be back out in like thirty minutes. No harm, no foul. But it might make all the difference."

The line was silent for a full five seconds before O'Connor responded. *"Fine. I'll call right now, but it might take five or ten minutes before the duty officer at the gate gets word. Don't fuck this up for me, I'll make you wish you weren't born if you do."*

"Thanks, O'Connor. I'll owe you."

※

Levi nodded at the Marine as he waved him through. He pressed slowly on the accelerator, and followed the signs that eventually led him to one of the overflow parking lots adjacent to the large three-story building the FBI used for its most advanced forensic analysis.

Scanning the parking lot, he glanced back and forth, looking for the Cadillac CTS the State Department scumbag had been assigned. That seemed like a high-end car for some State Department criminal, but Levi had seen crazier things before. There were hundreds of cars in the lot and he slowly drove up one aisle and down the next when suddenly he lurched to a stop at a black Buick LaCrosse.

The license plate matched one of the ones Denny had sent him. It was for Anspach.

Pulling into an empty spot, Levi snatched one of the devices from the shipping package, hopped out of the car, and walked in the direction of the Buick. Just as he reached the vehicle, he knelt, pretending to tie his shoe, and as he stood, stuck the magnetically-held tracking device underneath the vehicle's rear passenger compartment.

Levi knew that Anspach probably had nothing to do with anything, but he had sent Denny the names of everyone associated with any aspect of this case. The people who'd done the crime scene analysis. The people who'd been sent to investigate the apartment. Anyone even remotely associated with June or Helen Wilson. Levi had even stopped off at the day care and planted devices on both the principal's and teacher's cars.

He got back into his car and continued surveying the parking lot, looking for the Cadillac, when he spied Anspach himself striding down the path that cut through the green landscape surrounding the lab.

As the forensic specialist got into his car and drove off, Levi kept his head low so as not to be spotted.

Levi scoured the entire parking lot without finding the red Cadillac. It wasn't until he tried a second parking lot that he found his target and put his tracker in place.

Moments later, he was waving to the Marine as he exited Marine Base Quantico.

His phone vibrated, and he tapped a button on the steering wheel. Dino's voice came over the speakers.

"Hey, I've got that thing you were looking for."

Levi had asked Dino to look for the folder that the State Department guy had given the now-dead Gino.

"Do me a favor and keep that thing safe. I may need it pretty soon."

"Ya, no problem. The boss is really happy with what you did. We should talk."

"Okay, maybe soon. After I find the munchkin."

"You go do that thing. And remember, if you need anything, me and a couple boys can help out if you need some influence."

"Thanks, that's good to know. Talk to you."

"Ciao."

As Levi got onto the on-ramp to I-95 North, he dialed Yoshi's number.

"Hello?"

"Yoshi, where are you?"

"On my way to Old Alexandria to meet someone for my brother."

"Is it urgent, or can you take some time? I wanted to have a quick talk, but not on the phone." Levi pressed the accelerator, and carefully weaved his rental through northbound traffic.

"I don't think it's urgent. I just got an e-mail from Ryuki asking me to meet someone at the corner of Prince and Strand Street at four."

Levi had studied the DC maps, and he pictured in his mind the intersecting streets that Google Maps had shown him months ago. "There's a restaurant called Chadwick's near there, and there's parking right across from it. Let's meet there. It should be quick."

"Okay. I'm stuck behind some serious traffic, so for all I know, you'll get there before me."

"I'll be there in twenty minutes."

Levi hung up and gritted his teeth in frustration. Yoshi might know more than he thought—if only Levi had thought to ask him earlier.

Checking the rearview mirror, and seeing no cops, he pressed down harder on the accelerator.

～

Levi and Yoshi walked along Strand Street. From somewhere in the distance came the sound of bagpipes.

"What's with the bagpipes?"

"I'm not sure," Yoshi said. "I had to drive around some crazy Scottish parade on the way here. A hundred guys dressed in kilts, all of them playing the bagpipes. Evidently it's some Christmas tradition. Anyway, you wanted to talk."

"Has anyone else from the FBI been to Helen's house other than in response to the kidnapping? I figure you've been watching who came and went."

Yoshi shrugged. "Sure, plenty of people. I remember she had a pool party for June, and lots of her co-workers were invited. Mostly the ones with kids June's age, but some didn't have kids." He pressed his lips firmly. "Actually, I can't remember exactly who was there. Most of those people I didn't know. And that was months ago. Any security tapes of that would have been recorded over by now."

The cacophony of the bagpipes had grown louder as they walked, and now, as they reached Prince Street, it was nearly deafening.

Levi felt one of the metal prongs on his cap tingle—and it was a consistent tingle, not fleeting. He looked down Prince Street in that direction, trying to identify the source.

Right next to the South Union Street intersection stood an old four-story brick building. Light reflected off something in a fourth-floor window.

Levi spotted the muzzle flash just as he dove at Yoshi. He felt a shooting pain in his arm. He grabbed Yoshi by his shirt collar and belt, sent him sprawling behind the corner of a bicycle store as he took another a hit in the back.

With a grunt of pain, he tripped, he fell to one knee and felt a heavy impact to the side of his chest.

And all the while, the bagpipe Christmas parade continued their deafening march past them.

CHAPTER FOURTEEN

Levi nearly bowled Yoshi over as he scrambled for safety.

"Levi! What the hell?" Yoshi yelled as he wiped a smear of dirt from his face.

Levi winced, as he squeezed his own shoulder, checking to see if anything was broken. His arm throbbed with pain as his finger probed the hole in his suit. Something slithered its way down the sleeve of his suit jacket, and a bullet dropped to the sidewalk.

"Holy shit." Yoshi scrambled to his feet and looked from the bullet to Levi. "You got shot?"

Levi moved his arm back and forth. It didn't feel broken, but the fingers on his right hand were tingling, likely from the shock of the hit.

A siren sounded somewhere in the distance, and there was a scent of smoke in the air. Levi peered around the corner of the bike shop and saw licks of flame coming from the roof of the building where he'd seen the muzzle flash come from.

"Levi? You've got a bullet hole in your back, I'll call—"

"I'm fine." Levi turned to Yoshi and shook his head. "I'm wearing body armor."

"But still, it's got to ... I mean, your arm can't be armored, I don't understand. How is it you're even standing?"

Levi ignored the question as he watched the crowd of people backing away from the fire as fire engines came onto the scene. Whoever shot him must have set the fire as a distraction and probably fled the area. He suddenly turned to Yoshi. "How do you know it was your brother who sent you here?" he asked. "Did you try calling him?"

Yoshi shook his head. "No, he's on a plane to Tokyo right now."

"Then how did he send you an e-mail?"

With a look of doubt Yoshi said, "I don't know. I've used Wi-Fi on a plane before, so I figured ... what are you getting at? You think this was a setup? Someone faked Ryuki's e-mail?"

Levi scooped up the bullet from the ground and bounced it in his hand. There was no way *he* was the intended target—the shooter couldn't have known he was coming here. This was almost certainly a setup for Yoshi. But why?

He lifted his arm to adjust his cap—it throbbed with pain, pulsing to the beat of his heart—and turned Yoshi back the way they'd come, toward the parking lot. "Yes, that's exactly what I think. I think you were set up, but I have no earthly idea why."

∽

Levi winced as he removed his vest. One of the bullets that was still tangled in the lining fell onto the hotel's bathroom counter.

He looked at it closely under the light and spotted the sawtooth file markings of the expanded round.

He replayed the seconds of the event in his mind. Even through the cacophony of the bagpipes only twenty feet away, he would have expected to hear the report of the shot. Even suppressed, the crack of the bullet would have made some noise.

Unless it was a subsonic load.

A subsonic bullet would still be plenty deadly, but with a suppressor, and a bagpipe parade … no one would have heard a thing.

That was probably why Yoshi had been asked to be at that particular location at that particular time.

Brilliant.

Turning the bullet over in his hands, Levi was certain that someone had custom-filed it to expand for maximum damage. And for accuracy, since the shot was taken from about one hundred and fifty yards, the rifling on the barrel would need to have been specially adjusted to stabilize the subsonic round.

Levi removed his T-shirt and saw that his right arm was purple from his shoulder almost midway to his elbow. But the tingling in his fingers had subsided, and he was thankful the bullet hadn't done more damage. "Esther, I owe you big for that suit you got me. I approve."

He turned his back to the mirror and saw light bruising from where he'd taken the two chest shots. One he felt whenever he breathed deeply—probably a bruised rib—but the other he didn't feel at all. It wasn't the first time Esther's body armor had saved his bacon.

His phone buzzed from the nightstand. He jogged over to it, picked it up and put it to his ear. "What's up?"

"*Levi,*" Denny's voice crackled across the bad connection. "*I've got news on your bugs. All government made.*"

"What government? Ours?"

"*Yup, and I got lucky. One of them was from a batch of devices I had to track down for another reason. At least one of these bad boys started its life in FBI procurement. The others, probably the same story, but I don't have confirmation yet. However, from the looks of them, I'd say ninety-percent chance.*"

Helen Wilson worked for the FBI. Why the hell would the FBI be bugging one of their own people's apartment?

"Denny, thanks for the data—"

"*Hey, I've got more. Those prints you sent me from the mom's apartment. Only one of them got a hit—the one you labeled 'coffee table.' It's someone out of the FBI, a guy named Nicholas Anspach.*"

Levi nearly dropped the phone. What the hell did Anspach have to do with Helen Wilson?

His mind flashed back to the day he'd first laid eyes on the forensics expert. The platinum-blond hair, the burn on his face, the missing parts of his pinkie and ring finger. In his mind's eye, he scanned the photos on the man's wall—photos of parties and people. He strained to recall the details even though he'd only glanced at those pictures that one time.

Yes. Helen Wilson was definitely in one of those pictures. No, more than one.

"Holy shit!"

"*Levi? Are you okay?*"

"Denny, how quickly can you get me everything there is to know about Nick Anspach?"

"*I can't access the personnel files directly. I've got people for* that. Let me make some calls. It's late, so maybe not until the morning, but I'll see what I can do."

"Do everything you can. If money will help, I'll figure something out. I'll make good on it, somehow."

"I'll do what I can. But I actually had more to tell you. If you still want to hear it?"

"Of course. Go ahead."

"I pushed an app to your phone that will allow you to get a map view of where all of your tracking devices are. I'm looking at the app right now, and unfortunately the devices don't have a sophisticated labeling system. When you pull up the app, you'll just see dots with numbers associated with them. The numbers represent the order that they came online."

"What determines when one of those things goes online?"

"When the magnet connects with an object, it goes online. So, they're labeled based on the order you stuck them onto people's cars. The first device you stuck onto a car would be number one. The next car would be two, and so on, and so forth."

Levi replayed in his mind the cars he'd attached the trackers to. "Thirteen. Anspach was car number thirteen."

He put the phone on speaker, saw the new app on his home screen and tapped on it.

It took a few seconds to load, another few to draw the surrounding area's map. But then dots appeared on the screen, each with a tiny numeric value. Two of them were moving, the rest seemed stationary. Number thirteen was just outside of Arlington, Virginia.

"Okay, I see him, but is there a way to see where those cars have been?"

"Sure, you see the hourglass on the bottom right hand side of *the screen? Just put your finger on that and slide the hourglass to the left, it'll move you back in time, as far back as to when the car first went online."*

Levi slid the hourglass to the left, and the dots scurried about. A clock appeared at the top of the map indicating how far back he'd scrolled. He took number thirteen from Arlington all the way back to Quantico, then replayed the journey from there.

"Anyway, that's all I've got. If you're good, I'll see what I can do about getting info about your guy. If he's ex-military, I know someone on the West Coast who might be able to dig up records for me."

"The guy is missing a piece of his right hand and has got a doozy of scar that looks like it might be a phosphorus burn. You might try EOD or even an ex-cop, probably working as a bomb tech."

"I'll get in touch as soon as I have something." Denny clicked off.

Levi continued to roll time forward on the tracking app.

Anspach's car traveled north on I-95, and Levi's face warmed with anger as he watched the car take exit 177 to Alexandria. By a little after four in the afternoon, Anspach was rolling north on US 1.

"He was the shooter," Levi muttered. "I'd stake everything on it."

But what was the Yoshi connection? Why set him up?

Levi continued scrolling toward the present, and the car tracked toward Arlington, then paused. He zoomed in on the map as far as the app would let him.

The car was parked in front of a Safeway, of all places. Probably shopping for a steak dinner after an attempted assassination.

He probably thinks it was more than "attempted," Levi

thought. He saw me stumble. Those rounds, the way they mushroomed open, they would have been lethal, especially where he hit me.

Anspach thinks I'm dead.

Levi sent a quick text to Dino.

His stomach growled angrily. It was almost midnight, and he couldn't remember when he'd eaten last. He considered room service, but decided against it. He needed sleep more. So he lay back in bed, trying to ignore both his hunger and his desire to do irreparable harm to Anspach.

Those things would have to wait.

With his internal alarm reminding him that there were only five days left, Levi closed his eyes. He felt certain that tomorrow was going to bring lots of answers.

∼

Chains rattled against the door at the top of the stairs. June moved in the darkness and whimpered as part of the vest rubbed against the back of her neck. It hurt like that time she got a sunburn.

The creak of the door and the stomping of heavy feet coming down the stairs announced the arrival of the robot. Or at least the man who sounded just like a robot.

June was pretty sure there wasn't such a thing as a robot person, even though she'd seen one on an old show Mommy said was a classic, whatever that meant. Something called *Lost in Space*. She was pretty sure Robby the Robot couldn't climb down these stairs. His feet were too fat.

"I have your food and milk." The robot spoke with its usual metallic sound.

"Thank you, Mister Robot. Is it almost time to see my Mommy?" June choked back tears. She had promised herself that she wouldn't cry again.

"Soon."

She heard him doing something in the dark, but the tiny red light on the vest was the only thing she could see.

"Mister Robot, can you make the vest stop rubbing my neck? It really really hurts, like bad. I can't sleep when it hurts."

"Hold still." Something tugged lightly on the back of the vest, and a hand pressed against her cheek. A man's hand, not a robot's. But it smelled funny, like when Mommy went to go for shooting practice. It smelled like that.

The robot man let go and said, *"I'll be right back."*

Stairs creaked, and the door opened, and closed. But it opened again almost right away.

Clump … clump … clump were the sounds of the steps as the robot man approached.

A hand pressed against the back of her head. *"Put your chin on to your chest."*

She did as she was asked, and felt something cold and wet on the back of her neck.

"Don't move."

The snap of a stapler sounded right behind her head, startling her.

"I'll be back with more food and drink later."

Clumping footsteps on the stairs, the door opening and closing, and the rattling of chains. Then the light turned back on.

June lifted her head. Something like a rubber pillow pressed against her neck where the vest had been rubbing her. He must have attached it to the vest.

"Thank you, Mister Robot Man."

June scooted toward the cardboard box. Along with her Uncrustables and milk, this time it also contained a banana and an apple. Two things Mommy would definitely approve of.

As she peeled the banana and took a bite, she wished that Mommy could see how brave she was being.

CHAPTER FIFTEEN

As the sun peeked above the horizon outside Levi's hotel room, he flew into a flurry of kicks and punches. Sweat dripped down his face as he maintained his fighting form, throwing lightning-quick jabs at the invisible target and diving low into a leg sweep. His right arm ached from the workout, but he also knew that it would be worse if he didn't stretch and move the damaged muscles. The blood needed to flow through the injured area, and the pain he was feeling reminded him of his goal.

There were five days left, but Levi was pretty sure it wouldn't matter.

After his workout, he showered and dressed. Instead of his customary suit, he wore the dark fatigues Esther had provided. Today was going to be one of those days.

He checked his phone and found several unopened texts from Dino. He hoped they were responses to his texts from last night. As he scrolled through, he nodded with approval at the images

Dino had sent. It was clear that they had come from that folder Benson had given Gino.

One showed a printout containing the manifest of the incoming vessel with the so-called "supplies" along with a series of work visas for a bunch of girls who all claimed to be eighteen, though their photos told a different story. Most looked too young to drive, and some were clearly prepubescent.

The manifest was the key to the illegal shipment. It showed the shipping containers' identification numbers, their publicly advertised contents, and which girls were in which container. The paperwork even listed names and other data associated with each girl, but their validity was clearly suspect. The paperwork claimed that they were from the United Kingdom and Ireland, but they all had dark brown complexions and a very North African look. Probably refugees from Libya or Egypt.

Levi shook his head with disgust and dragged the photos to the "cleaner" application that Denny had provided. One of the lessons he'd learned from the technology whiz was that digital photographs sometimes carried something called EXIF data—hidden data in the image that would allow a forensic examiner to see private information about the photo, like where it had been created.

Levi wasn't about to give up Dino's location if the mobster had inadvertently sent him images that had his private information hidden inside. Who knows what other kind of stuff could be hidden in these things, it wasn't Levi's area of expertise. All he knew was that it was safer for all involved that any picture he ever sent anyone would go through Denny's cleaner app beforehand.

Once done, he typed a quick note identifying the source of

the images as John Benson in DC, put in O'Connor's e-mail address and hit the send button.

His phone buzzed, and a message from Denny popped up. It was a scanned copy of a DD-214, military discharge papers for a Nicholas Anspach.

"Right on time."

Levi scanned the form for the pertinent data: Enlisted and Airborne out of Fort Benning, SFAS and Q-Course out of Fort Bragg, and then seven years as a Special Forces Weapons Sergeant.

Anspach was no slouch. And he was discharged honorably. No mention of why.

Another text came in from Denny, this one with FBI personnel records. Anspach lived in Arlington, which made sense from what Levi had seen in the tracking app. He had a bachelor of science in computer engineering and a master's degree in electrical and computer engineering, both from Georgia Tech. He was thirty-eight, and had worked at the FBI for eight years.

Levi pulled up the tracking app. Most of the dots were moving, as expected—probably commuting to work.

He zoomed in on number thirteen, Anspach. His car was stationary at Quantico. Like most military folks, the man was apparently an early riser. Levi then scrolled to number fourteen, the guy he had just dropped the dime on. His dot was just arriving at the State Department.

Levi grabbed his keys from the nightstand and headed out the door. O'Connor hadn't reached out to him yet, but he suspected that was coming—and he wanted to be somewhere in the center of the action when and if something happened.

Levi sat in his rental, a Ford Taurus with a V6 engine. He'd tried getting something with a bit more oomph, but this was the best the rental place could do at the time. He was waiting for someone to make a move. It was going to be O'Connor or Benson, maybe even Anspach. Today was the day things would turn around, he could feel it.

He was in the PMI parking garage located less than half a mile away from the State Department building and two miles from where O'Connor's car currently was, underneath the FBI Field Office building.

He took the opportunity to review the last eighteen hours of every vehicle he was tracking. If the girl was being hidden somewhere, then they'd have to bring her food every once in a while. Starting with the preschool's principal, and then the teacher, he watched as they took their daily commute.

Nothing struck him as out of the ordinary until he got to Anspach. He'd moved around quite a bit after his trip to the supermarket—traveling north on New Hampshire Avenue a good distance past Arlington, into what looked like a rural area more than twenty miles from home.

Levi zoomed in and the Google Maps feature showed that New Hampshire Avenue was a two-lane road. The tracking app showed him going off the road a good distance. Zooming in, all he could see from the satellite image of the area was trees. No obvious homes or anything else.

His heart began beating faster and he exited the history view and looked back at the current tracking status.

O'Connor's car was on the move.

"Oh shit!" Levi backed out of his parking spot, put the car into gear and floored the accelerator.

Benson's car was moving as well.

Levi exited the parking garage, and the Taurus's engine whined as he accelerated down Virginia Avenue, and then hung a hard right on Twenty-First Street. Based on what the app was saying, his target was somewhere right ahead of him. Scanning the road as he approached Constitution Avenue, he looked for Benson's red Cadillac.

Glancing again at the app, O'Connor must have been flying, because his dot was barreling down Constitution Avenue from the east, faster than should have been possible given the traffic.

Did he have his lights on? That might explain it.

Levi spotted a flicker of red up ahead. Benson's Cadillac was hanging a right on Constitution.

Gritting his teeth, Levi honked and bullied his way through the late-morning traffic in the Capitol. It was a miracle none of the police were on his tail for reckless driving.

As he turned right on Lincoln Memorial Circle, he realized that Benson had to be heading out of DC and across the Potomac, via the Arlington Memorial Bridge.

He weaved in and out of traffic and pressed hard on the accelerator. The car's V6 roared in protest, but it closed the distance ... until the Cadillac's more powerful engine launched it past a scrum of cars.

With a blockade of red brake lights ahead of him, Levi tightened his grip on the steering wheel and swerved up onto the side of the bridge's walkway. People dove out of his way as he passed the slowdown and he plunged back onto the asphalt, accelerating after Benson.

Ahead he saw more red lights—cars were slowing. An accident had somehow managed to get a Corvette spun around on the wet asphalt.

The world seemed to slow as Levi watched Benson's Cadillac accelerate straight for the Corvette—and ram directly into it.

But due to the sports car's low body, it wasn't so much a crash as a launch. Benson's heavy vehicle drove over the Corvette, angling upward as it flew into the air. The front-heavy Cadillac almost immediately tumbled forward, slamming into the concrete guardrail of the bridge, its momentum flipping it end over end as it disappeared off the side of the Arlington Memorial Bridge.

Levi slammed on his brakes.

Lights and sirens blared behind him. Stunned into inaction, Levi stared ahead at where the car had flown off the bridge. Within moments, a half dozen unmarked cars converged onto the scene. Too fast for response vehicles.

More than one FBI windbreaker was visible among those who hopped out of the cars at the scene.

As Levi turned the steering wheel sharply to the left and merged himself into the line of cars that was moving past the accident, his phone buzzed—a DC number he didn't recognize. He answered. "Yes?"

"Lazarus Yoder, I presume?"

"Who is this?"

"We've met before, at a certain FBI agent's funeral."

Levi frowned as he drove past the accident and began picking up speed. The only other person he'd met was that guy named Tim, and this wasn't his voice.

"I've been watching you. I think you and I need to meet. It might be mutually beneficial."

"How'd you get my number?"

"You've just passed a rather unfortunate accident. Keep going north on George Washington Memorial Parkway. I'll be waiting for you at the OHB in Langley. I'll send you the address. Oh, you'll need to go through a metal detector, so to avoid any unnecessary hassle, leave any problem items in your car. Just come into the main entrance, I'll leave your name, and someone will bring you to me."

The line went dead.

At the end of the bridge, signs prompted him to continue on I-66 West or to take the turnoff onto the G.W. Parkway.

For a second, he hesitated, wondering who the hell could know where he was.

Then he turned right onto the parkway.

～

As Levi entered the chilled lobby of the OHB—the Old Headquarters Building as the CIA employees called it—his eyes were drawn to the huge granite CIA logo on the floor, its white shield and eagle head showing prominently against the black-and-gray-flecked granite. He crossed through the turnstile and approached one of the lobby's receptionists—a middle-aged woman wearing a headset.

She looked up at him. "May I help you, sir?"

"Yes, my name is Levi Yoder and—"

"Yes, sir, you're expected. Can I please see some ID?"

Levi pulled out his wallet and handed her his driver's license.

She pressed his ID into a slot next to her terminal. His license was immediately sucked into it, a light shone from within the device, and his ID popped back out. Some red entered the woman's cheeks as she handed his license back to him. She also handed him a visitor's badge and motioned toward the chairs arrayed against the far section of the lobby "Someone will be coming out to escort you, Mister Yoder."

He had no idea why he'd come here, but the way the man on the phone had talked, it made him nervous. How had did this guy known exactly where he was at that moment?

"I've been watching you."

It was a wild card he hadn't planned for.

Levi sat in the lobby for nearly five minutes before pulling out his phone. Him being here was probably a mistake. There was somewhere he really needed to be, and it was only insane curiosity that had brought him here. He texted *Meet me at three* to Yoshi. Yesterday, after the shooting, he'd worried about all of Yoshi's communications being monitored, so they'd come up with a solution.

A woman's voice echoed through the lobby. "Mister Yoder?"

Levi stood and walked over to an attractive brunette, dressed in modest business attire, but with an hourglass figure that was hard to hide. He felt a pang of guilt for looking at someone in such an appraising manner, but then he remembered … he was single. Well, he'd been single for years, then he sort of wasn't, but Madison had made things pretty clear, and he was the type that didn't need to be told twice.

They shook hands and she motioned for him to follow her.

"So, who am I here to see?" he asked. "That wasn't exactly made clear to me, Miss…"

"Kubs, I'm Mindy Kubs, Director Mason's assistant. I'll leave the introductions to him. He'd prefer it that way."

Levi walked through two banks of metal detectors, let someone swipe a cloth over his hands—looking for what he'd assumed was explosive residue—and waited patiently as another security officer waved a scanner over him from head to toe.

After passing the last set of security checks, Mindy led him down what seemed to be the main corridor of the building, took a right, and made a few more turns before stopping in front of a large wood-grained door. She swiped her badge, and they entered a long wood-paneled corridor.

About fifty feet down the corridor a side door opened and a well-dressed man stepped out.

Levi immediately recognized him—the guy from the funeral. The one who'd been staring at him from the other side of the mourners.

He was short—not much more than five foot seven or so. Judging from the fine wrinkles around his eyes, and the frown lines, he was in his fifties. Light brown hair, with a slightly receding hairline, and very pale eyes that looked almost silver.

The man smiled as he shook Levi's hand. "Do you prefer Lazarus or Levi?"

"Only my mother calls me Lazarus."

"Very well, Levi it is. I'm Doug Mason, and I apologize for the cloak-and-dagger stuff, but you're in the middle of something that I think we're both interested in solving."

Levi tilted his head and studied the man. Mason emanated a strong sense of self-assuredness. He didn't get a sense of aggression or hostility in any way, just an air of confidence. But it set Levi on edge. It was as if Doug Mason held all the cards, knew everything, and he was doing Levi some kind of favor. The thing that bothered him was … he wasn't sure that wasn't the case.

"And what exactly is this thing being solved?" Levi asked.

"Let's stop standing around in the hallway." Mason stepped

through the door into a conference room, and Levi followed. Mindy had already disappeared quietly back down the hall.

Levi stopped short as he looked around the conference room. Pictures were tacked to the walls, and more were laid out on the long conference room table. Pictures of people he knew.

Pictures of kids—*his* kids—at play on his parents' farm.

A picture of his mother.

A picture of Levi sitting on a park bench with Dino.

A picture of the front of the Helmsley Arms, where he and many of the made men from the Bianchi family lived.

A picture of Levi standing on the street in Chinatown.

Him boarding a private jet at LaGuardia.

Him handcuffed in the FBI's interrogation room.

Levi flushed with anger.

Mason picked up a remote and turned on a wall monitor. It showed an active video stream of a steering wheel.

Levi's mouth fell open. The steering wheel to a Ford Taurus. The steering wheel of Levi's rental car.

He couldn't believe he was such an idiot. Somehow, this guy had managed to have someone break into his car and bug it without him even noticing. Of course they did. His car was out in the open.

Clenching his jaw muscles, he focused on the man who'd brought him in. He knew he wasn't going to be arrested—if he were, he wouldn't currently be in this room alone with this Mason guy.

"What do you want?" he asked.

Mason picked up one of the photos from the table. It was of Mei. "We worried about what you were doing. With all those kids." He walked over to what looked like a tall clear garbage can with a white slotted lid. He fed the picture into the slot.

THE INSIDE MAN

The sound of a shredder activating echoed through the room, and tiny squares of picture confetti fell into the receptacle beneath the slot.

Mason scooped up more pictures and began shredding them as he talked. "Levi, I represent an organization that's focused on getting some things done, with less worry about the actual tactics being employed. We don't exactly follow the same rules as some of our brethren agencies."

"I don't understand," Levi said. "Obviously, you're in some section of the CIA. You abide by the same rules and—"

"Uh, uh, uh." Mason wagged his finger. "Don't think that us meeting here has anything to do with my agency. Would you have come to me if I said meet me at your local Denny's? I don't think so."

Levi glanced at his watch, anxiety building within him. "On that note, why *did* you ask me here?"

Mason sat at the table and motioned for Levi to sit as well. "I'm the director of a small organization. Each member brings to the table something I can't find elsewhere."

"And what's that?"

"An angel in wolf's clothing."

The hairs on the back of Levi's neck suddenly stood on end. He'd heard that turn of phrase before.

"My friend, you're an angel in wolf's clothing"

Vinnie had said those same words to him. Now Levi really had no idea what he was dealing with.

"What does that mean?" he asked.

Mason flicked an invisible speck of dust from the lapel of his thousand-dollar suit. "It's a very rare thing to find someone who is willing to do terrible things, but is, in actuality, an honorable person. Doing things for the right reason, even if those things are horrible."

Levi shook his head. "I find that hard to believe."

"Well, it's more than just that. Sure, maybe we'd find a gas station attendant in Des Moines with similar attributes, but they're likely to end up in jail. They're not streetwise. They'd get tripped up by a polygraph." Mason gave him a knowing smile. "They don't have the skills needed to survive in this type of business. They're also not in a position to think strategically. My organization doesn't onboard the run-of-the-mill. We look for a very specialized type of people.

"For instance, I can count a dozen laws that you've broken by kidnapping those kids, acquiring illegal papers, falsifying federal records, interfering with police investigations, assault, the list goes on and on. But in the end, the good you did for those kids far outweighs the bad. And the way you did it, nobody will be the wiser.

"I also know that you're preoccupied with saving Shinzo Tanaka's granddaughter. And you're not being paid for it."

Levi's words were stuck in his throat. He couldn't believe this average-looking fed knew about his arrangement with Tanaka. How was that possible? Could Vinnie be involved with this guy? A Mafia boss for one of the New York families involved with the feds? No chance.

"How can you know anything about that?"

Mason drummed his fingers on the conference room table, and a sly grin creased his features. "I know more than you think. But I do have a question about that. Why are you doing it?"

Levi shook his head. "She's a five-year-old kid. You never answered my question. Why did you ask me here?"

"Well, I thought that was rather obvious." Mason smiled. "I want to recruit you into service."

Levi snorted. "Me, a fed?"

"No, not a fed. The people who work for me … correction, let's instead say that we work together. Anyway, my people don't carry IDs, and you won't be part of the system. The system is compromised, as you know all too well. Too many fingers in those pots.

"Think of us as kindred spirits. We both want the same thing, and my organization can help fund some things that maybe would be hard for you to do on your own. In return, we'd ask for an occasional favor. Over time, maybe we could steer some of your energy in certain directions."

Levi had heard this kind of scam before. The Mafia bosses did it all the time. A favor given now, means a favor requested later, and over time, you're obligated and they own you. No chance.

"There's no way—"

"Before you say anything, I've got someone for you to meet. You actually know them already." Mason pulled a pen from his front pocket and spoke into it. "Come on in. He's here."

Levi's heart began to race as a million thoughts rushed at him at once. Was Vinnie about to walk through that door? No way! Maybe Madison?

When the door opened, it was neither. In walked a statuesque Asian woman with long black hair.

As Levi's mouth dropped open, so did hers.

Mason stepped in between them and smiled. "Lucy, I believe you've met Levi. He's a fixer for the Bianchi family, also a polyglot, and he trained under one of the best martial artists ever to walk the earth. Levi, this is Lucy. She's the widow of the founder of one of Hong Kong's largest triads, she's also a martial artist, and she has an IQ that's off the charts."

Levi held out his hand, but she backed away with a look of revulsion. "I told you not to touch me." She glared at Mason. "Doug, you know I don't like being touched."

Mason motioned for Levi to back away with a somewhat apologetic expression. "Sorry, I guess you two would have gotten off on a better foot."

Levi eyed the woman with confusion. *This is the same chick who kissed me in the middle of the street.*

Still glaring at Mason, she pointed at Levi. "He grabbed my shoulder."

"Hey," Levi said, "that's not exactly how it went—"

She switched her glare to him, and he almost expected lasers or something to shoot out from her eyes.

"Okay, I guess I did grab you, and for that I apologize. But come on, I was worried you were endangering everyone I cared for. Think about it: if you found someone you don't know is at your mom's place with your kids, you wouldn't be very happy either."

Her expression softened and she glanced back and forth between Mason and Levi. Then she sniffed loudly. "Apology accepted." She pulled out a chair, sat, and crossed her long legs. Turning to Mason she asked, "Why are we here, Doug?"

Mason pulled a set of photos from his inner suit pocket and tossed them on the table. "Here."

Levi took a seat—making sure that there was a chair between him and the temperamental woman—and peered at the photos.

They were the same photos he'd sent to O'Connor. Did

O'Connor forward them to Mason? Or was Mason so deep into the system that he plucked it from O'Connor's inbox?

"It looks like Levi uncovered one of the rats in the State Department," Mason said. "This man was helping some of the traffickers with their jobs."

Lucy slid the photos closer to her and frowned. "So, this is pretty much what I'd expect. Actually, this is a smaller operation than the kind of stuff I've been hearing about crossing in from the Canadian border and the West Coast. But maybe it's just a smaller delivery than normal ... I presume you tracked down the buyers?"

"Yup. And with Levi's help, we've uncovered a rat's nest of scheduled deliveries coming in within the next two weeks."

Levi felt more confused than ever. "How exactly did I help you uncover anything?"

Mason turned his attention to him, and Levi felt Lucy's gaze on him as well, an amused expression barely hidden. "Remember how I said I've been watching you? Well, that wasn't a lie. I knew about Benson, but I didn't know about his East Coast contacts. As soon as you figured out Giancarlo Fiorucci was the bag man for a bunch of buyers, well, I was able to put two and two together." Mason raised an eyebrow and said in a conspiratorial tone, "You know, this Fiorucci character ... I've been trying to track him down, but he's gone missing for some reason. Interesting, don't you think?"

Gino was likely chopped up into fertilizer and spread across a good part of the Atlantic, but even if Levi knew that for sure, which he didn't, he would never talk about it. "I didn't really have any thoughts on that guy."

Lucy put her hand over her mouth as she laughed and pointed in Levi's direction. "When I first saw you, I really thought you were some tourist way out of your element. That's just too funny." She turned to Mason and hitched her thumb at Levi. "I'll bet you a steak dinner he killed him and that guy is buried somewhere nobody'll find him."

Levi glanced at his watch. "I know this isn't what you want to hear, but can I take a rain check on all of this? I—"

"Need to save a little girl," Mason said.

"Well, I don't know if … fine, I guess that's what I'm trying to do." He glanced back and forth between the two strange characters in the room. "Can we pick this conversation up later?"

Mason wagged a finger at Levi, "Just realize, what I'm going to ask you right now isn't about only *one* little girl. We're talking about hundreds of boys and girls. Innocents that our country is allowing to be enslaved. And I need the two of you to help. From what I can tell, you both have the exact skills and relationships we need to put a dent into this trafficking. Go take care of the Tanaka girl, but can I count on your help?"

"You know I'll do it," Lucy said without hesitation.

Levi wouldn't have believed it was possible for his life to get more complicated than it already was. "Hundreds of kids coming in to be enslaved? Pimped out?"

"And worse," Lucy and Mason said at the same time.

With a deep sigh, Levi shook his head. "I can't believe I'm saying this. Fine, I'll try to help. *After* I find the Tanaka girl."

CHAPTER SIXTEEN

Before Levi had left the enigmatic Lucy and Mason behind, he agreed to stand in front of a device that took a three-hundred-sixty-degree scan of his head and flashed lights in his eyes. Mason said the scan would serve as his ID from now on, whatever that meant.

Now Levi pulled into the parking lot where he'd last met Yoshi. The ex-FBI agent hopped out of his car and started to walk over, but Levi parked and motioned for Yoshi to turn around. "We're not taking my car."

"Okay. But why, what's up?" Yoshi asked.

He didn't have the tools to remove whatever Mason had put into his car's headliner without making the rental look like a bunch of alley cats had had a fight inside his car, so Levi pressed a finger to his lips, motioning for silence.

He popped the trunk to his car and shoved his gear into a backpack. He then ran his handheld bug scanner through the interior of Yoshi's car, along the undercarriage, and in the trunk. He found nothing. Finally, he and Yoshi got in Yoshi's car.

Levi turned to his companion and gave him the intersection to plug into the navigation system. "We've got about an hour's drive north, take US 1 and once we get there, we'll be navigating by feel."

"Okay," Yoshi backed the car out of the parking spot and began driving. "Are you going to clue me in on what's going on?"

Levi was still processing what he'd learned in the last twenty-four hours, and he didn't want to admit he was running mostly on instinct. "I don't want you to get your hopes up, but I have a lead that might be fifty-fifty on figuring out where our little princess is."

Yoshi tightened his grip on the steering wheel and pressed a bit harder on the gas. "You're not serious, are you?"

Levi noticed the subtle signs of emotion on Yoshi's face. He was blinking rapidly; his breathing was deeper than normal and his face was slightly flushed. Good.

"I don't joke about these kinds of things, Yoshi. I've been monitoring someone, and I saw them take a ride up into what looks like a rural area late at night and turn right back around." He pointed to an offramp, "Actually, let's ignore your navigation. Take I-29 North and then the New Hampshire Avenue exit. We'll follow that almost the entire way."

Yoshi followed Levi's instructions and they drove in silence for a long time.

Levi motioned to the right. "Georgia Avenue. Cut off over there."

"How do you keep this straight in your head?" Yoshi asked.

Levi wasn't about to explain his near-perfect memory, since

he had no rational explanation for it. "I studied the maps for the trip." Which was true, if incomplete. "Hang a right on this street."

Thick woods hugged both sides of the road, and a dead-end sign loomed ahead. It was colder here by a few degrees, maybe they were at a slightly higher elevation? Snow dotted the ground. Then the asphalt ended abruptly, and there was nothing but a dirt track crowded by woods.

Levi looked at his phone. There was no signal, but oddly enough, his GPS seemed to be working. He pulled up the history of Anspach's car as they followed the dirt road. When they were in the exact spot where the forensic analyst had stopped, he held up a hand.

"Stop here and turn the car off. Let's take a look around on foot." Levi hopped out of Yoshi's car and surveyed the area. "Our bad guy stopped right here and this seems like a good place to hide something."

"Like a little girl," Yoshi said with a grim expression.

Levi pointed to the edge of the woods where a hunting trail led off from the dirt road. "Let's see what we find." He glanced at Yoshi. "You packing?"

Yoshi lifted his shirt and jacket to show an in-waistband holster with what looked like the butt end of a .45.

"Good," Levi said. "Watch your six. I have no idea what's back here. It could be bears, deer, or bad guys. Just be ready."

Levi had spent almost two years learning about tracking game, looking for the signs of things that had come before him. Crushed blades of grass, a bent or broken twig, even the smell in the air—they were all clues.

But Yoshi's footsteps behind him were like a hammer slamming on an anvil.

"Shh." Levi motioned for Yoshi to stop.

Levi focused and reached out with his senses. He could almost feel the world breathing.

He heard squirrels high up in a tree to the northeast. Breathing in deeply, he detected something in the air … it was the musky scent of a black bear. The wind shifted slightly from the east, and the scent grew stronger. He closed his eyes, and the scent of the bear grew more distinct. He heard a slight grunt … and then the sound of deep breathing. The bear was hibernating.

Levi turned to Yoshi, motioned to his left, and whispered, "Bear." He pointed at Yoshi's feet. "Be quiet."

Yoshi's eyes widened, and he walked more quietly as they continued.

After another fifteen minutes of following the trail, Levi spotted a clearing about fifty feet off to one side. He pulled out his Glock—in which he always kept a round chambered—and heard Yoshi do the same behind him. Together, they left the trail and moved toward the clearing.

At its center was an isolated cabin. From the roof of the cabin there was a set of cables running up a nearby tree, and from Levi's angle he couldn't quite make out what the cables were attached to. Certainly, it was some kind of platform, but it was too flimsy to support a person.

Yoshi pointed at the tree and whispered, "Solar cells. The cabin is getting electricity from up there."

Levi put his hand over his brow as the sun glinted off a black square pattern, confirming Yoshi's assessment. Hitching his backpack higher on his shoulder, he whispered, "Stay here, I'm going to scout this out."

He pulled a laser pointer from his pack, activated the green laser, and panned it back and forth across his path. It was an old trick his cousin had taught him years ago after he'd joined the Army and become a Ranger. A laser's beam would flare brightly if it crossed the path of a tripwire. It wouldn't be the first time that that trick saved him from a deadly booby trap. But in this case, he found nothing.

As he approached the front porch, Levi saw that some of the snow had fallen unevenly on the wood slats. Aiming the laser at the slightly raised section in front of the door, he back away from the porch and shrugged away the tension he felt building in his shoulders. He shrugged off his backpack, pulled out a metal detector, and extended its telescoping arm to its maximum length. Turning it on, a red LED blinked once, twice, three times. It was ready.

Levi put his backpack on and looked back at Yoshi. The man was squatting with his gun drawn, panning his gaze back and forth from the path they'd been on, to the house, and back. Just like Levi would have done as a sentry.

Levi moved once more to the porch, all the while swinging the metal detector's rounded loop back and forth. When he got to the uneven plank that had drawn his attention, the red light flickered on and off.

A tingle raced up and down the middle of Levi's back.

Quietly, he returned to Yoshi.

"The front door looks like it's booby-trapped."

"Shit," Yoshi said. "So what are you going to do?"

Levi took a deep breath. "I'm thinking of doing something really stupid."

"What?"

"Stay here." Levi unlocked his phone and handed it to Yoshi. "If something bad happens, call your brother from my phone. I think yours is being monitored by whoever kidnapped June."

Levi motioned for Yoshi to stay as he walked back toward the cabin. Sweeping the path ahead of him with the metal detector, he walked the entire perimeter of the cabin. The cabin had no windows, and he saw no other signs of disturbed ground. The front door was the only way in.

Cringing, Levi stepped up onto the porch, skirting past the suspicious plank. At the front door, he knelt and examined the locking mechanism. It looked simple enough—a typical pin and tumbler lock. He set aside the metal detector, pulled out his lock picks, and selected what he needed.

He stuck a torque wrench into the slot and probed with his pick. Scraping the pins while putting just a little pressure on the tumbler, he felt the pins begin clicking into position. Finally, the lock turned.

Levi pushed open the door ever so slowly.

Nothing happened.

From within the cabin, he heard the whir of a compressor, and he felt a slight warmth coming from within. This place was heated with some kind of furnace and forced air.

He once again picked up the metal detector, passed it over the suspicious plank, verifying that there was some form of metal object beneath it, and pushed the door open with the detector.

Finding no obvious metal in the entryway, Levi stepped inside.

What he encountered was not what he'd expected.

He'd expected a bare cabin with maybe a cot, and hopefully with a little girl. What he found was some kind of workshop. The room was barely fifteen feet square, and along the far end were two workbenches with what looked like electronics hobbyist tools: meters to measure current, batteries, tubes of epoxy, breadboards for wiring circuits, all variety of wires with alligator clips

… and two blocks of something in olive-drab mylar wrapping. On the wrapping were the words. *Charge Demolition M112 with taggant (1 1/4 lbs Comp C-4)*

Military-grade explosives.

This was an explosive expert's hideaway.

A partially peeled-off red stencil had been used to label a gray plastic device as a *Voice Changer*. Levi picked it up, held down the button, and spoke into it. His voice came out sounding like a robot.

Exactly like the robot he'd heard on that ransom audio.

A tingle of excitement rushed through him.

He panned his flashlight across the walls, found a light switch, and flicked it on. Nothing happened, but somewhere he heard something move. He held his breath and listened.

He heard whimpering.

"June Wilson!" Levi projected his voice at the walls, unsure where the sound was coming from. "Can you hear me?"

For a couple seconds, the silence that greeted him felt oppressive. Then a tiny muffled voice responded. *"I heard you!"*

"What's your mom's name?"

"Helen! Please help me!"

Every inch of Levi's skin tingled with the realization that this was the place. He'd actually found her.

He calmed his breathing and listened. The girl was crying. And the sound was coming from somewhere below him.

Panning the flashlight along the floor, he spotted the outline of a trap door under one of the work benches.

"I'll be right there!" he shouted.

A beeping noise came from one of the devices on the workbench.

"Please turn the light back on. I'm scared."

Levi flicked the light switch back to its original position and slowly backed out of the cabin. He motioned for Yoshi to join him out front.

"It's her," Levi said. "She's here."

Yoshi's eyes filled with tears, but his smile couldn't have been bigger.

"I want you to come in with me so she has a familiar face she trusts." He motioned toward the suspicious plank. "Just watch out for the wood plank on the left side of the door. It wouldn't surprise me if this guy has some kind of land mine for unexpected visitors."

The workbench was holding the trap door down, so Levi carefully moved it aside. It made a horrendous metallic clanking noise as it scraped across the floor of the cabin. He opened the trap door, and there she was. At the bottom of an inclined ladder was the tear-streaked face of a little blonde girl.

June.

She began to climb up the ladder. The device on the workbench started beeping faster.

That's when Levi noticed what she was wearing.

"Wait!" he shouted. "Go back down, I'll come down to help you."

Levi had seen vests like June's in his journey through the northern Kashmir region of India as well as Afghanistan. He'd seen what they could do to both the wearer and the people around them.

He climbed down the ladder, and Yoshi followed.

"Yoyo!" June jumped into Yoshi's arms and began bawling.

Yoshi held her tightly. "You'll be okay. We found you. Nobody's going to hurt you again."

Levi waved at Yoshi to get his attention, then mouthed the words, *Suicide vest.*

Yoshi's face paled and he nodded grimly. As the girl buried her face in the crook of his neck, he whispered, "Can you disarm it?"

Levi hesitated for a moment, but slowly nodded his head to give Yoshi some reassurance. He knew Yoshi had no experience with explosives—Denny had pulled the ex-FBI agent's personnel file for him—but the truth was, Levi didn't have much more. He'd read up on it, and he was probably only one of a handful of people alive who'd ever disarmed a fifty-year-old nuke. But that was under Madison's guidance. But a suicide vest? He'd never even studied one.

Yoshi whispered, "Baby, I'm going to put you down so Mister Yoder can take a look at what you're wearing, okay?"

"No." June shook her head and began sobbing all over again. "Yoyo, it hurts so, so bad."

"What hurts?" Levi asked.

She pointed at her neck and sniffed loudly. "The robot man made a pillow, but it fell off when I was asleep."

Levi glanced at the floor and saw a rolled-up bundle of foam rubber sheets, held together by black electrical tape. A few fragments of the torn rubber sheeting remained at the top of the vest.

Her vest was making a beeping noise, similar to the one upstairs. And its frequency was increasing.

June said in a quavering voice, "That noise started happening as soon as I climbed up the stairs. Oh, I promised the robot man I wouldn't go near them, but when the door opened, I forgot."

Levi glanced back at the ladder and wondered if she'd triggered some kind of proximity sensor. Were the beeps some kind of countdown?

A trickle of sweat dripped down the back of his neck as Yoshi set the girl on the floor and assured her everything would be okay.

Levi lifted up her shoulder-length hair and saw the red raw skin and blood blisters that had formed from the chafing. Of course the vest was hurting her. "Okay, honey. Let me turn you around so I can see what you've got on."

June cooperated as he turned her, looking at the vest from every angle. It was made so it couldn't be removed without being unclipped, and the connections each looked like wired contacts. It was a classic design he'd seen in some of Madison's sketches.

"June, stand with your feet spread wide, I'm going to look at the vest from underneath. I need to see which spot I can use to get you out of it."

She followed his instructions, and using a flashlight, Levi followed the two straps that looped around her legs. He pressed his fingers on the material and felt some wires running along the length of the straps. Following the straps to the main part of the vest, he peeked under the vest and saw a box-like protrusion.

He pulled out a folding knife. "Don't worry, June, I'm just using the knife to get a better look at what you have here."

The girl nodded and put on a brave face, even though her chin quivered.

Using as little pressure as he could, Levi cut a slit in the outer fabric, shined the flashlight in the hole, and saw a plastic box with wires coming out in several directions. Solid epoxy sealed the unit so that it would be almost impossible to tamper with. It also probably held more than enough C-4 to blow up June and anyone within a ten-foot radius.

There was really only one choice.

Levi cupped the little girl's face in his hands and looked her in the eyes. "I promise you we'll get you to see your mommy. But right now, I need you to be brave. Yoyo and I are going upstairs just for a minute, and he's going to go back to our car and call your mommy while I come back downstairs to help get this off you. Okay?"

June looked up at Yoshi.

He placed his hand on her head and nodded reassuringly.

She turned back to Levi. "Okay. I can be brave. I've been brave before."

Levi smiled. "Just stay right here. Don't move a muscle."

Yoshi kissed the girl on the cheek and whispered, "It'll be okay."

When they returned to the workshop above, the device on the workbench was beeping even faster than before. Levi scanned the benches for a remote, or maybe some kind of tool to disable the damned vest. He saw nothing.

"What's the plan?" Yoshi asked.

Levi motioned toward the door. "Remember the booby trap. Get back to somewhere where we have signal and call O'Connor. Call the cops. Call everyone." He held out his hand. "Give me my phone."

Yoshi handed it back to him, and Levi sent a series of quick texts. He then handed it back.

"Just keep my phone with you, so as soon as it gets signal, my texts should go through automatically. By the time you get back here, we'll be done here one way or another."

"Um, Levi?" Yoshi's worry was obvious. "Don't you think we should wait for the bomb guys?"

Levi frowned. "I'll be honest. I'm not sure. That beeping could be anything—but if I were trying to make sure my kidnap victim didn't escape, I'd put a proximity sensor on the vest so that when she got either too close or too far…" He left the rest of the sentence unsaid.

Yoshi nodded grimly. "I'll be back as soon as I can."

∼

Levi set up a workspace on the floor of the hidden basement, using the items from the workbenches upstairs and an extension cord he'd found coming off the solar panel array.

He sat cross-legged in front of June and gave her a reassuring smile. "Okay, I'm going to explain what I'm doing, that way you can maybe learn some cool stuff, okay?"

June nodded and looked curiously at everything he'd brought from upstairs.

Levi found himself sweating as the beeps on the vest were practically on top of each other. He had no idea if that meant he had a few seconds, or a few minutes—or if the beeping was something completely innocuous.

He wiped the sweat from his forehead and grabbed his knife. "Okay, the goal is to get you safely out of this thing the bad man put on you. First, I'm going to take a look inside the strap on your left shoulder."

June looked to her right.

"Your other left, sweetheart." Levi carefully slit open the canvas strap on both sides, revealing a red and black wire. "Okay, I'm seeing two wires. But do you know what a ring is?"

"A ring?" June asked. "I think so. Isn't that like a circle?"

"Exactly. The wires in that strap are making a big circle. Let's go ahead and call that circle a circuit. Right now, that circuit has electricity going through it—"

"Like in a TV?"

"Exactly like in a TV. But if I cut the wire, the circuit will collapse. It won't be a circle anymore."

"Like unplugging the TV," June said, the fear in her voice replaced with curiosity.

"Yes, the circuit collapsing would be like unplugging the TV. What we don't want is to turn the TV off. All the electricity is coming from that little box on your chest. And since I can't look in that box, I'm going to have to use some special tools to see how much electricity is coming through those wires. I'll need your help, if you don't mind."

She nodded.

Levi switched the multimeter to measure the current, plugged in one end of the probe into the multimeter, and clamped the alligator clip to the black wire.

"Okay, it looks like this wire has seven hundred microamps running through it. Can you remember that number for me?"

"Seven hundred."

"Great."

The little girl was watching closely, and Levi figured that was infinitely better than her squirming while he worked.

He switched the setting on the meter and saw that it was pulling 1.4 volts. He switched the alligator clip to the other wire and tested the current. It had the same readings.

"Okay, so now what I'm going to do is take this wire and plug it into this thing called a power supply. Can you tell me what the number was I asked you to remember?"

"Seven-hundred," June said confidently.

Levi adjusted the power supply to match the current flowing through the wires, then attached four probes to the power supply. "I'm going to take these wires and attach them to the wires on your vest. This box will help the circuit stay active so it won't collapse."

"I don't understand."

The beeping now sounded almost like a monotone.

Levi clamped two live patch cords to each of the vest's wires. "Imagine the wires are a big loop. Now this box is holding hands with the wires in your vest. I'm going snip the wires between where the box is holding hands, so even though the wires in the vest won't be connected together, the circle won't be broken because this power supply is still holding hands with each end of the wires from your vest. Do you understand?"

"I think so. But it won't be a circle anymore. It's more weird shaped, right?"

Levi grabbed a set of wire cutters. "You're right. It is weird shaped. Okay, here it goes."

He placed the wire cutters between the patch cords, clamped down on the wires, and…

Nothing.

No boom.

Levi grabbed his knife and cut through the rest of the canvas strap. "Okay, let's be very careful. We don't want to stop the box from holding hands." He pulled June close and carefully slipped one shoulder out of the vest, then the other. Within seconds he was holding her around the waist and lifting her out of the vest.

Gripping her tightly, he scurried one-handed up the ladder, dodged past the board at the entrance, and jumped from the porch.

A heavy thump shook the ground behind them. The girl's eyes went wide, and Levi's heart nearly beat out of his chest.

Taking a deep breath, he slowly walked away from the cabin,

the girl cradled in his arms. The smell of smoke reached his nostrils.

Yoshi jogged into the clearing and smiled when he saw June. She scrambled out of Levi's arms and jumped into Yoshi's. Levi heard the wail of sirens somewhere off in the distance.

"They're on their way," Yoshi said. "Locals followed by the feds out of DC."

Flames began licking at the doorway to the cabin.

Levi took his phone back from Yoshi. "Can I borrow your car? I need to do something."

Yoshi tossed Levi the keys. "Sure. I'll catch a ride with one of the FBI guys."

Levi rubbed June's head, which was buried in the crook of Yoshi's neck, "June was a very brave girl." The he turned and raced toward the car.

He had an appointment to keep with June's kidnapper.

CHAPTER SEVENTEEN

Levi shook hands with Dino as one of his men backed a dingy car onto an abandoned dirt and gravel path that intersected with New Hampshire Road. The car was an old Cadillac Fleetwood Brougham, one of the land yachts of the seventies.

"Is the engine solid?" Levi asked. "The last thing I need is for this stalling out when I floor it."

Dino gave him a lopsided smile. "Oh, that engine will go. One of my guys had a mechanic who owed him something, and this was his baby. It's got a 425 V8 big block in there, and it purrs like a kitten." He chuckled. "Kind of a shame, actually."

Levi strapped a brace around his neck, and one of Dino's men handed him a motorcycle helmet. He glanced at the app, it was almost time. "We've got less than five minutes guys. Who's the lookout?"

"Me," a mean-looking dark-haired man waved. "I got it. It's a black late-model Buick LaCrosse, right?"

"That's right. Call me as soon as you're in position."

"You got it." Lenny turned and jogged out of sight. His lookout position was about a quarter mile up the road.

Dino called out to the rest of the men and pointed to the large Cadillac Escalade he'd driven. "Okay, guys, pile in. We've got business coming in a couple minutes."

Levi clasped Dino's hand. "I owe you and Don Marino, big time."

"Naw, man. The boss wanted this done. And for me, I'm just thinking of what I'd do if someone did that to my Donna. No way. We did this 'cause it's the right thing."

Soon, Levi was alone in the empty dirt road with the land yacht's engine purring next to him. He climbed in, put on the helmet, and fastened the chin strap. He was ready.

His phone buzzed, and he put it on speaker.

"Hey, it's Lenny. I'm in position."

"Good. It looks like he's about a minute out. Keep your eyes peeled and let me know when you first see him, but tell me exactly when he passes your position."

"Got it."

Levi looked again at the app. Anspach had to be doing nearly sixty down the two-lane road. He smiled. Helen must really have gotten Anspach's attention when she read aloud the text Levi had sent to her.

Helen, I've gotten information that I think will lead us to June. She's being kept in a cabin twenty miles north of Arlington. I'm flying in and will be there this evening. It should be over tonight.

. . .

Anspach was probably thinking he needed to do something with the kid. And who knows what that might have been?

Whatever it was, the bastard wouldn't get his chance.

Levi gunned the engine, put on the seatbelt and got ready. He glanced at the phone sitting in its cradle. "Anything yet, Lenny?"

"No, the road's totally—hold up, I see a car. It's black. And it's flying this way."

Levi began to coast forward slowly, hoping to avoid fishtailing in this giant rear-wheel-drive monster he was in.

"Okay, he just passed me, and it's our guy."

Levi slammed his foot onto the gas. The back wheels spun in the gravel and dirt, and the car only fishtailed a bit before the tires got traction.

Levi started the countdown in his head.

Fifteen seconds for a quarter-mile at sixty miles per hour.

At four seconds, Levi tightened his grip on the steering wheel and the car finally settled into a straight path.

At eight seconds, the trees on either side of the road became a blur as the street approached.

At twelve seconds, Levi saw the intersecting road—and the black car. The world seemed to slow as he noticed Anspach's hands were at ten and two, his eyes focused on the road ahead of him.

With a slight turn of the steering wheel, the Cadillac, weighing two thousand pounds more than its target, launched itself at the side of the black Buick LaCrosse, hitting it dead center.

Glass shattered all around Levi as his body was launched against the seat belt.

The steering wheel cracked, and the shriek of metal came from all around as the Buick was launched from his view.

Levi slammed on the brakes—by some miracle, they still worked—and it was all over.

His ears buzzed. He heard a voice yelling, the pinging sound of his engine stalling. The smell of burning rubber brought him to his senses.

The entire dashboard had collapsed in on itself, yet from beneath it came a voice.

"Levi? Levi!" It was Lenny. Levi's phone must be somewhere down there.

"Ya, I'm here," Levi shouted. "Just trying to get myself free of this mess."

"Holy shit, man. I heard that from over here. You're a fucking lunatic!"

Levi wasn't sure he disagreed as he tried unlatching his seatbelt.

"I'm calling Dino to get you. I've got the other car coming for your guy."

Levi finally managed to undo his seat belt. He felt around under the collapsed dash and found his phone. Miraculously, the screen wasn't even cracked.

Levi futilely tried opening the door with the door handle, but it was jammed closed by the impact.

Wiping the beads of glass from the window frame, Levi crawled out, *Dukes of Hazzard*-style. He removed his helmet and neck brace and stretched. To his shock, he felt fine, apart from what was almost certainly going to be a painful bruise from the seatbelt, he didn't seem to have any other issues.

Dino's Escalade arrived as Levi was surveying the damage to the Buick. It was a mess. It had rolled onto its side and the airbags had deployed, obscuring Levi's view of Anspach.

One of Dino's men hopped into the ditch, climbed up onto

the car, and looked into the driver's-side window. "Holy shit, the guy's still alive."

Lenny arrived with a tow truck and almost immediately began hooking the Buick up to large winches attached to the truck.

Dino's focus shifted to Levi. "Are you even bleeding, you crazy son of a bitch?"

Levi chuckled and surveyed himself once again. "Other than some pearls of tempered glass probably still in my hair and down my pants, I'm no worse for wear."

"Okay, then, let's get you out of here and back to your car." Dino opened the passenger side of the Escalade and Levi hopped in. "The boys will take care of your friend."

Levi leaned back in the leather seat and smiled. He had done it. And depending on what happened next, he might actually be done with DC for a while.

∽

"What do you mean June and Helen are in protective custody?" Levi asked. An FBI agent drove away, leaving Yoshi and him alone in the same parking lot where they'd parked earlier in the day.

Yoshi shrugged. "I don't know. That's all O'Connor would say—that they're keeping Helen and June in a safehouse until they sort all of this out. I know O'Connor really wants to talk to you."

"Do you know where this safehouse is?"

"No clue. I didn't even get a chance to talk to Helen before she went silent."

Levi looked at his tracking app. Helen's car had been one of the ones he was tracking, just in case. "This says her car is still at her apartment."

"I tried calling her place, her cell phone, everything. Couldn't reach her. But that jibes with what O'Connor said. When people are taken into protective custody, they're not allowed to have any items that someone might use to track them. That includes phones, cars, and any electronics whatsoever."

"Well, I suppose that's going to be temporary." Levi sighed. "This isn't going to make your brother or Mister Tanaka very happy."

Yoshi nodded and looked very uncomfortable. "I probably shouldn't admit this to you, but I'm a bit worried that Mister Tanaka might try to kidnap June, now that we know where she is … or at least we will."

Levi imagined what Tanaka might do in this situation. He wasn't welcome in this country, but it was obvious to him that the mob boss saw June as his sole heir, and for his only blood heir he'd be willing to move the earth and sky. Maybe even kidnap her for her own so-called safety.

"I don't know, Yoshi. I can't get in that man's head. I do know he loves that girl and wants her safe. He asked me to call him directly when I got news, so I'm going to have to do that. We'll talk afterwards and see what happens."

They shook hands, then Yoshi suddenly pulled Levi into a hug. "Thank you for everything you did. If it weren't for you, June would probably still be in the kidnapper's hands. Or dead."

Levi patted Yoshi on the back and smiled. "Listen, things like this tend to work out. The worst is over for June and Helen, and that's what's key."

Yoshi gave him a weak smile. "I know, and thanks again."

Levi felt sympathy for the man, he had to have a bunch of

conflicting things brewing in his head. But Levi had only one thing on his mind: talking with the head of the Tanaka syndicate.

∽

Levi walked along the cold shore of the Potomac, with his phone to his ear. The international connection was a poor one, and odd pops and random echoes made it hard to understand what was being said.

Levi repeated himself in Japanese. "Yes, Tanaka-sama, I found your granddaughter. She's alive and well."

Even though Tanaka was on the other side of the planet, Levi heard him take a deep breath and let it out slowly. *"Thank you, Levi. I'd prepared myself for the worst. So, I'd like to speak to my granddaughter."*

Levi winced, knowing this explanation wasn't going to go over well. "Unfortunately, the FBI has June and her mother in protective custody. They're now hiding them."

"But why? I don't understand. I thought you said you found her. Why did you let them take her again?"

"I apologize, but it's complicated. I wasn't given any choice in the matter. It will only be temporary. The FBI is still trying to piece things together. As far as they're concerned, the person who took June is missing. So I think they're truly trying to protect your granddaughter and her mother from further harm."

Tanaka's voice sounded menacing. *"And the kidnapper? What happened to him?"*

"He'll never bother anyone again. That I can promise you."

"Good. Very good. I'm sorry to be so upset; it isn't you that I'm upset with. I would like to ask you to keep watch over this

situation. I will have Ryuki call your Don Bianchi and arrange it. As soon as June is free, I want to be told."

"I'll do everything I can."

The phone line went dead, and Levi figured that conversation could have gone a lot worse than it did. He didn't know the infamous mob boss, not really, and when it came to a person's family being in danger, it was hard to guess how that person would react. In Levi's experience, that reaction was almost never logical.

Levi glanced at his watch and figured Denny would be at the bar. He dialed him up and listened to the phone ring several times and it then went to voice mail. It was a Friday night—Denny was probably swamped.

His phone buzzed almost immediately, and he put it to his ear. "I'm guessing you're busy tonight."

The voice that responded wasn't Denny's, but Doug Mason's. *"It's not too bad, I was looking into where Nicholas Anspach disappeared to. You really kicked a hornet's nest with that kidnapping rescue you pulled off. The FBI folks are buzzing around looking for you; you might want to throw them a bone. But I wouldn't tell them that Potomac Metals over in Springfield has Anspach's car and is in the process of shredding it. You'll be answering questions until you grow old."*

Levi stared at the phone and couldn't fathom how Mason could know any of this. Even Levi didn't know what Dino was doing with Anspach's car.

"I'm sure you're wondering what my deal is. Let me make it really simple. I'll clear up this FBI thing for you. All I want you to do is take a quick flight over to Seattle for me."

"Seattle? What for?"

"Don't worry about the Wilson girls. They're going to be fine."

"Do you know where they are?"

"That doesn't matter. Focus. Seattle."

"Why do you want me to go to Seattle?"

"Remember those kids I talked about? Anyway, let me help you out before someone gets a wild hair and puts you on America's Most Wanted. Think of this as getting what you want by helping me out with this child trafficking problem we have. We have a lead for a West Coast drop, but the drop isn't the issue. We need to know both who ordered these kids, and who's responsible for smuggling them into the country."

"How am I supposed to even know where to start?"

"Lucy will meet you at the terminal in Seattle. She's spent the last two years prepping for this assignment."

"And you want me to start after, what, a couple minutes of talking on the phone with you?" Levi replayed the conversation he'd just had with Mister Tanaka. "I have responsibilities I need to take care of, here."

"First of all, I wouldn't put you out there unless I knew you could do it. Remember, I've been watching you for a long time. And as to your so-called responsibilities, I'll watch the Wilson girl for you. She'll be fine. Besides, this shouldn't take long."

"This is messed up, and you know it. I barely have an idea who or what you are, and you're expecting me to just go on your word, buy a ticket, and just see what happens?"

"Ah, you've got a point. I've been monitoring you for so long, I sometimes forget that you haven't run a mission yet. This is how it will work. It's almost eight in the evening. You'll have an American Airlines ticket waiting for you at Dulles, leaving at five a.m. By then I'll have smoothed things over with the folks who are looking for you. Lucy is already in the air and will meet you at baggage claim in Seattle. I'll take care of the rest. It's as simple as that."

Levi breathed in the salty air and panned his gaze across the shoreline. "You said the FBI is looking for me? Why hasn't O'Connor given me a call?"

"His phone accidentally got wiped, and so did your records on the high side computers."

Levi had heard the term "high side" before. It was what the intelligence community called the computer system that held classified material.

"So, you've made me invisible?"

"Not really. Wiping the records on a computer is simple enough, but people have memories. They know you're out there. I need to make a few calls. Oh, and don't go back to your hotel. It's being watched. I assume you didn't leave anything there you needed, right?"

Levi paced back and forth. "No, I never do. It's all in my trunk."

"Good. I've got you a room next to the airport. I'll text you the information. It's prepaid and they won't ask for ID."

Levi stopped, stared at nothing in particular, and shrugged. "Okay, Mason. I'm not sure I believe any of this is legit, but I'll play. If this works out, I may have some favors to ask."

"Of course you will. You don't even have to ask. I'll work on it and see what can be done."

The phone went dead, and Levi wondered if Mason could read minds, was nuts, or something in between.

Levi squeezed his way through the crowds in the SeaTac airport, following the signs to baggage claim. It took him nearly ten minutes to get through the hordes of people, and it was only then that he realized that it was the weekend just ahead of Thanksgiving. A busy time for travelers, and a time he'd much rather be at home.

Finally, he got to the end of the main terminal and passed a lone security guard in the hallway watching to make sure nobody tried going the wrong way, breaching security.

The baggage claim area was mobbed with people, and just as Levi began wondering how he'd ever find Lucy in this place, the crowd parted. Standing not more than twenty feet away was the tall Asian woman whom he'd now encountered in a handful of different states.

As she walked toward him, he caught the scent of jasmine. He offered to shake her hand but she refused. "I don't like to be touched. No offense. Did you have any luggage?"

"Hold on a second," Levi said. "I have no problem with the no-touch thing—that makes things very simple—but I didn't imagine you kissing me and grabbing my arm back in New York, did I?"

Embarrassment flashed across Lucy's face, and was quickly replaced by a cocked eyebrow and a frown. "You seem to remember that incident much better than I do. Like I said, I don't like being touched."

"But you touching others is okay?"

She ignored the question. "Do you have any luggage you're waiting on?"

Levi shrugged the black canvas backpack off his shoulder and held it up by its strap. "Everything I have is in here."

"Then follow me."

She led him across a sky bridge that eventually brought them to the light rail station. Lucy bought two tickets, and within minutes, they were standing on a crowded train heading north.

Holding onto the loop hanging from to the metal rails bolted onto the ceiling, Levi noticed that Lucy looked distinctly uncomfortable among the people jostling one another in the crowded cabin. Well, at least her no-touching issue wasn't specific to him.

But he could tell she was genuinely uncomfortable, so he tried distracting her from the inevitable unwanted body contact everyone experienced on a crowded train. "Where are we heading?"

"International District. Into Chinatown. My car is there, and I'll show you the office."

"The office?"

Lucy gave him a sly grin. "You'll see. Doug said he'd have some stuff waiting for you."

Levi's interest was piqued.

A voice over the intercom announced Othello Station, Columbia City, then Mount Baker. With each stop, the train grew less crowded and Lucy looked less stressed.

Eventually, the train began to slow and Lucy motioned to the door. "International District, Chinatown" was announced, and when the train doors slid open Levi followed his new partner out of the train and across a business park full of modern buildings.

They were in downtown Seattle, a place he'd never before explored, at least not beyond the airport. The smells and scenery were completely different than those in New York. Everything looked new and clean.

They walked past a store called Uwajimaya, where an older Asian man was outside roasting nuts in front of what looked like a Japanese supermarket. But then they stepped into Chinatown, and that's when things began to look a bit dingier—a bit more like home.

The buildings were older. The streets narrower. The streets signs were all written in both English and Chinese—though as far as Levi could tell, he was the only Anglo in the neighborhood. Still, it was a pleasant area, mostly middle-aged or elderly could be seen walking back and forth for groceries or whatever else people did in this neighborhood.

"You said there's an office here?" Levi asked in Mandarin, the only Chinese dialect he knew.

Lucy gave him a sidelong glance as they walked through the old neighborhood. She held an amused expression and responded in rapid-fire Mandarin, "I'm impressed. Unlike Mason, who seems to know everything about everyone, I have to wonder why you speak Mandarin. And why do you speak it with a German accent?"

"Well, I might ask why you have a slight Russian accent when you speak English."

"You first."

Levi chuckled. "Well, I'm Amish, or at least I grew up that way. And my first language was Pennsylvania Dutch, which has many of the same intonations as German."

"Huh. I've never heard of one of our kind coming from an Amish background. Aren't you pacifists or something?"

Levi shook his head. "I'm not exactly something my community would approve of. And what about you? It *is* a Russian accent, isn't it?"

They crossed Weller Street and ducked into a very narrow side path called Canton Alley.

"I suppose the accent comes from when I was first brought

into my husband's home. He acquired a Russian tutor for me. She taught me English and Japanese."

"A tutor? How young were you?"

"My parents were very poor farmers in Guangzhou. That was when the construction cranes came in, consuming much of the farmland to sacrifice it for the city. My parents couldn't afford to feed everyone, so I was ten when my husband bought me."

Levi was about to say something, but she waved him off.

"It was a good arrangement. My parents could then afford to feed my brothers and sisters, and I had a good life. Especially when we moved to Hong Kong. A life of privilege. Of tutors and training. Little did I understand how useful that would become when my husband was killed by a rival gang member."

Lucy stopped at a five-story red-brick building that looked abandoned and run-down. Trash littered the alleyway to one side, and the whole area gave off a faint smell of urine. This place looked like any number of locations Levi had been in when he was in Asia. Lucy whispered, "Do you see those three marks on the bricks?"

Levi looked where she pointed. Three small divots marked the age-worn bricks at eye level. Two of the indentations had a glassy sheen to them.

"This is the entrance to the office. Using both eyes, look into the lenses."

Levi put his face up to the wall, almost as if giving the bricks a kiss. And as soon as he was within inches, he saw something flicker behind the clear dime-sized glass lenses and heard a metallic click.

Lucy pushed at the bricks, and they swung open noiselessly on a hidden hinge. They stepped inside, and the wall closed behind them.

Levi found himself at the end of a long, brightly lit, white corridor. An armed guard stood at the other end of the hallway behind what looked like bullet-proof glass with a slit for his MP5 submachine gun.

"Follow me," Lucy walked past the guard whose face was frozen into an expression of indifferent malice.

They both stood side by side in front of a blank wall while a series of lights scanned them both from shoulder to forehead and back down again. With a soft metallic click and a whir, the wall in front of them lowered until it was flush with the floor, revealing another short corridor. This corridor led to a plain room with a table and a row of tall, gym-style lockers.

Lucy motioned toward the lockers. "One of those is for you."

"What is this place?" Levi asked.

Lucy sat at the table and stretched her arms above her into a languid and alluring pose. "It's kind of hard to explain. We're part of a thing that doesn't have a name, but over the last couple years, I've learned that Doug's reach is kind of astounding. In fact, I've never met another person who works for him, except for you. But"—she motioned toward the lockers—"it seems he has more than just us. I've only met with Mason in person a handful of times, including yesterday. Usually, when he needs to get me something, he texts me and I'll go into the local office and something will be waiting for me in my locker."

"So there's lockers in New York as well?"

Lucy crossed her legs, and Levi struggled to keep his eyes on her face. "So far, I know about the offices in DC, New York, and here in Seattle. For all I know, that's the only drop-off points there are, or maybe he has them everywhere. I just don't know." She motioned toward the lockers. "Anyway, let's get a move on. We're just here so you can pick up whatever he left for you."

Levi turned to the wall of lockers. Each had a digital nameplate on them that was full of X's, except for two: one with Lucy's name, one with his. As he stepped toward his locker, a light flash on either side of the nameplate, and with a metallic snick, the door opened.

On the shelf at the top lay a pair of night-vision binoculars, a Glock 19 with an in-waistband holster, two fifteen-round magazines, a few boxes of nine-millimeter ammo, a manila folder, and a money clip.

Levi thumbed through the wad of cash, then held it up. "This pretty normal?"

"Twenty-five hundred dollars, each and every time."

There was one more thing in the locker. In the open space below the shelf was a large guitar case. "A guitar?" Levi said.

"I doubt it. Open it, and let's see."

Levi pulled the case out of the locker, popped it open and smiled.

It was a rifle—and not just any rifle. The barrel was twenty inches long, and it came with a heavy bipod attached to the front, a muzzle brake, a long silencer, and a top-of-the-line Leupold scope. A sticky note on the barrel said it was zeroed to one hundred yards.

Levi ratcheted the bolt action on the rifle. "Did you hear that?"

"Hear what?"

"Exactly. This action moves like it's slicked down with butter." He gave Lucy a crooked smile. "This is a top-grade sniper rifle." He checked one of the boxes of ammo and noted the handwritten characteristics. "It's a .308, and Mason's given us subsonic rounds."

Lucy walked over and gave an approving nod as she dragged

her finger lightly over the gun's barrel. "This'll be useful. I figure since part of this trip will be in the woods, we might need something to kill a bear, moose or maybe Bigfoot."

Levi admired the gun one last time before putting it back in the case. "Well, I don't know about Bigfoot, but this rifle is a beauty."

"Smart that it was packed in a modified guitar case," Lucy said. "On the Seattle streets, even in Chinatown, it would be a bit much to be seen carrying that slung over your shoulder or even in a normal gun case."

Levi turned his attention to the manila folder. Inside was a single sheet of paper: a photocopy of an incident report. Levi skimmed through it.

Approximately one-hundred surveillance photos of a woman who has been identified as Helen Wilson were found in Nicholas Anspach's residence, located in the nightstand of the master bedroom. These photographs were taken with what we believe to be a long-range zoom from an elevation of approximately fifteen feet.

A Bushmaster .223 rifle was also found in Anspach's garage. It has a sixteen-inch barrel with a one in nine-inch twist. Several boxes of fifty-five grain .223 subsonic ammunition were also found. One box is missing ten rounds. The magazine in the gun has seven rounds.

In the attic, a box of ballistics gel finger molds was found. Prints were taken and run through IAFIS. Most had no match, but one print came back with an identification hit: Giancarlo Fiorucci.

. . .

Levi gritted his teeth. It now made sense why Gino had looked at him like he was crazy when he squeezed him about the black car. So many things made sense, now.

He closed his eyes and replayed in his mind what Anspach had said when he brought up the black SUV.

"Levi, I'm not at all familiar with the case, but if you have those security tapes, we have people here who specialize in enhancing video images. You never know, we might be able to get a license plate."

The bastard must have gotten cold feet, trashed his own car, and laid the blame on some random guy who just happened to be a Mafia associate. It made a good story. But the pictures of Helen at his home and in his office told a different story. He was obsessed with the redhead.

Levi flipped the report over and continued reading.

Approximately 1350 grams of C-4 were recovered from a toolbox in Anspach's garage. Trace composition analysis confirmation is pending, but preliminary results show it to be a match for the explosives used in the Wei/Nguyen bombing.

He grabbed the phone out of his pocket, dialed a number and almost immediately Dino answered. *"Hey, what's up?"*

"How's our guy?"

"He's ready when you need him."

"Good. It'll be soon."

"Gotcha."

Levi hung up and smiled.

"That's a smile that tells me someone's going to die," Lucy remarked matter-of-factly.

He turned to her. "So, what's our next move?"

Lucy picked up the guitar case by its handle. "We're off to Frost Creek, which is about three hours by car. Then we've got some off-roading to do."

Levi couldn't remember seeing that name on any map of this area. "I assume you're going to fill me in on the details on the way there?"

Lucy waved dismissively. "Come on, let's get going. I'd rather get there before nightfall."

As Levi followed Lucy toward the exit, he asked, "Where exactly is Frost Creek?"

"It's on the US and Canadian border. Believe me, it's in the middle of nowhere. And it's the perfect place for the first exploratory incursion by the smugglers. It's going to be a long night."

CHAPTER EIGHTEEN

Levi watched the road pass as Lucy drove them north on I-5. After nearly an hour of silence, it was obvious this woman wasn't the talkative type. But as they turned off the highway, taking exit 236, and continued north, he couldn't take it anymore.

"How in the world did you and Mason get acquainted?" he asked.

"I win."

He turned from the window. "What do you mean, you win?"

She motioned dismissively with her right hand. "It's a game I used to play when I was a kid. I just wanted to see who'd break the silence. You want to know how Mason brought me into this thing of ours?"

"Is that what you call it? 'This thing of ours'?"

La cosa nostra, or LCN—otherwise known as the Mafia—literally translated to "this thing of ours."

Lucy gave Levi a half-smile as if she knew what he was thinking. "No, it's not called that. It doesn't really have a name.

At least none that Mason ever shared with me. And what difference does it make what it's called? It's not like we've signed any employee contracts. The only thing that's different about it and our regular lives is that Mason can pull strings for us, get intel from who knows where, and do some things with the feds or the military that might otherwise prove to be difficult for us to accomplish."

"Okay, so I know Mason saw me at a former soldier's funeral, or at least that's the first time I noticed him. And eventually, he called me out of the blue. How about you? How did you get sucked into this?"

Lucy pressed her lips tightly together for a few seconds before responding. "It goes back to when my husband was killed. I fled Hong Kong on the same day that it happened, and Mason was there when I arrived at LAX. At the time, I knew him as one of the customers that I'd failed to deliver to."

"What were you supposed to be delivering?"

She turned right on Bow Hill Road, a lonely stretch of road with one lane going each way through a heavily-wooded area. "This isn't something I've really ever talked about." She glanced over at him. "This goes no further?"

He nodded. "It won't." Levi was many things in life, and if there was a hell in his future, he probably deserved it, but if there was anything he could be counted on to do, it was to keep his promises.

"Well, before I talk about the failed delivery, I suppose you need to understand how things worked back then. My husband was into many things as he built the business. And believe me, it was a business, run by him with an iron fist, and it had a very hierarchical structure like a normal corporation. It was just that our business dealt with all things illicit. Gambling, drugs, prostitution, all of those were certainly fair game.

"And when I'd arrived in his household, I wasn't sure if I'd been brought in as a wife or as something to be sold. But my husband quickly figured out that I had an uncanny ability to remember things. Facts, figures, names, almost anything. My mind is like a steel trap. I don't forget anything."

Could she really have an eidetic memory like him? What were the chances of that? He focused on the woman sitting two feet away and was intrigued. By the way she acted and her lived experiences, he'd have had trouble believing she was in her twenties, even though she could easily pass for it. She had a mature beauty, yet Lucy had an odd ageless quality about her. She might even be in her forties, it was impossible to tell.

"Anyway, I was still a teenager when my husband began involving me in the business. Giving me responsibilities, all of which I took seriously. I helped where I could, and eventually, I became his second—the most senior person, the most trusted, and I'll be honest, the one who helped make it grow to a multi-billion-dollar enterprise. We branched out to the rest of Asia and made inroads into the US.

"And that's when I began trying to shift the business away from what I felt were some of the dirtier things. Things that I felt were beneath my husband's honor."

"Like what?" Levi asked.

"Dealing with kids," Lucy held a sour expression as she turned onto WA-9 North. "It was a small portion of our business, but it was growing quickly. We had buyers lined up all over Canada and the US, and a growing market in the Middle East. But it was wrong."

She took in a deep, shuddering breath, and began tearing up.

Levi would never have expected that from a put-together and businesslike person such as herself.

"It was my doing. I convinced my husband to pull out of those business dealings and to cancel the transport of anyone under fifteen. But because I'd managed to sway my husband to do something against our business interests, he was ambushed and killed by one of his lieutenants."

Levi put two and two together. "So you fled to the US and Mason met you upon your arrival. Was he one of the buyers you'd canceled on?"

Lucy nodded. "I didn't know his name at the time, but somehow, he knew what I'd done. He knew that my husband had just been killed, and he knew why."

"How could he possibly know?"

"No idea, but he did. He's got eyes everywhere."

"And is this how you make your living? Through missions for Mason?"

Lucy took her foot off the gas and looked at Levi with amusement. "Why in the world would you think that? My husband and I had quite a lot of convertible assets stored all over the world. Do you seriously think I'd have left all of them to those vultures who killed him?"

Levi felt admiration for this self-reliant woman. "I suppose not. But then, I don't understand why you're still doing things for Mason. Why aren't you on a beach somewhere, relaxing?"

Lucy turned right on Mount Baker Highway. "It's pretty simple, actually. If I'd simply disappeared, after they were done picking clean whatever they could find of my husband's wealth, they'd rightfully assume I had taken a lot of his wealth to hide out with, and I'd have to be looking over my shoulder forever. Instead, I decided to play the role most women in my society have played for centuries: the helpless widow who escaped with just enough to get by. After all, they did reclaim a huge amount of my husband's wealth."

Levi pictured her place in New York. It had to have cost a small fortune to retrofit an old building with such a richly appointed apartment. "But if they reclaimed your husband's wealth, how do you get by?"

"I'm not an idiot. I've got enough money hidden away for several lifetimes. But I don't show it off. I played dumb, but not so dumb as to be useless. I'm still in the business; I helped the current boss consolidate his power, and I curried favor to ensure I wasn't mistrusted. I'm at a much lower rank than before, but that's okay. This way, I can still keep my ear to the ground.

"And that's how I learned that the child trafficking spigot had been turned on once again. And yes, that's something that I shared with Mason. I've been helping fill in some of the gaps in the intel he's received from his other sources. But I have plans for my husband's business."

"Take it over again?"

She shook her head. "Burn it to the ground."

∽

Levi stared at the deepening shadows cast by the woods that surrounded them. Even though it was only five in the afternoon, it was getting dark quickly as Lucy stopped the car at the end of the dirt road. His phone buzzed and he glanced down at the screen. It was a text from Mason.

. . .

Spy satellites confirm a large truck has arrived at the compound two miles north of the intercept point.

Expect exploratory maneuvers tonight. The real deal tomorrow tonight.

Be careful.

"Did you get the text?" Lucy asked.

"Yup." Levi climbed out of the car, shrugged himself into his backpack, slung his rifle over his shoulder, and followed Lucy as she headed almost directly northeast, along a game trail.

After about fifty yards, she stopped and tore away some snow-covered pine branches to reveal an all-terrain vehicle. "You'll drive, I'll sit behind you."

"Shouldn't you be the one driving?" Levi asked. "I have no clue where this intercept point is. All you said is Frost Creek, which doesn't help."

"I'm sorry, but you need to be in front. I can't let you touch me." Lucy pulled out her phone and showed him a digital image of where they were and where they were going. She pointed at a line crossing what looked to be a stream. "Right up against the Canadian border is where we expect them to come. It's only a couple miles from here as the crow flies. We should be able to get there in an hour or so."

"If it's only a couple miles, we're better off just walking the path."

"No. I'll need the ATV tomorrow for when I go across the border."

Levi examined the ATV and saw that it had no exhaust system. "This is electric?"

"Yes. This whole operation is going to be dependent on us not attracting attention."

Hitching the rifle up higher on his shoulder, Levi smiled. "So, that's why the ultra-smooth bolt action and subsonic rounds." This was going to be what the Russian KGB would have called a wet operation. Someone was going to die. The trick was making sure it wasn't him or his partner.

"Anyway," Lucy continued, "There's an easy walking path along Frost Creek that we're expecting them to follow. Like Doug's text said, tonight, they'll scout the path out to make sure there's nothing unexpected, and tomorrow, they'll smuggle in the kids."

Levi kicked away some of the brush in front of the ATV and mounted it. Lucy hopped up onto the seat right behind him and wrapped her arms around his stomach. He pressed the starter button, and the ATV started up without a sound. The only sound he detected was her breathing as she leaned into him. He twisted the throttle and began weaving them toward their destination.

Levi panned his gaze across the clearing. A slight mist rose from Frost Creek, giving the forest a somewhat eerie look. He glanced at Lucy as she pressed something into her ear and then handed him an identical object that looked almost like a blackened piece of putty.

"Just press that lightly into your ear, it'll harden in a minute once it's in there."

Levi pressed the rubberized device into his ear and it immediately began crackling with static.

Lucy aimed a small wand-like device at his ear and the static immediately vanished. She handed him a throat mic, which he strapped around his neck, adjusting the mic so that it was positioned properly.

Lucy took a few steps back and covered her mouth. *"Testing, one ... two ... three."*

"You're coming in loud and clear."

"Same here, you're coming in fine."

Lucy knelt next to Levi and, using a stick, spent the next five minutes drawing out the night's plan.

∼

Levi hadn't planned for the cold. His dark fatigues had kept him warm enough when it was in the forties, but now it was almost midnight and the temperature was falling. It was certainly below freezing.

Lucy's voice came over his earbud. She sounded breathless. *"Levi, I'm about two klicks north of the border and I just saw an SUV heading south. It's probably our guys. Keep your eyes peeled."*

With a throat mic strapped to his neck, he whispered, "Roger that. I see headlights."

He was in the woods, about twenty feet from the edge of the clearing that marked the Canadian border, and backed away even further into the trees. Positioning himself behind a thick pine, he peered through the scope mounted on the rifle and zoomed in on the incoming vehicle. A full moon cast an eerie silvery light across the snow-patched landscape.

Enveloped by the forest all around him, Levi's heightened senses strained to catch a hint of his quarry. They were about one hundred yards away, but he easily heard the opening and closing of the SUV's doors.

There were four men. He couldn't quite be sure, but judging by their relatively short stature, dark hair, and darker features, he'd guess they were Asian, which of course was what he'd expected.

The one in front held something that briefly lit up his face—maybe a cell phone.

Definitely Asian.

The other three had rifles slung over their shoulders, as if they were a hunting party.

The leader motioned toward the stream known as Frost Creek, and the group entered the woods, following the still-flowing creek.

Levi stood still as they crossed his field of view. They all wore sidearms, and two of the men had a set of binoculars hanging from their belts.

One of them lifted his binoculars and panned his gaze across the forest. Levi stayed hidden behind the pine tree, but it dawned on him that the man wouldn't be using those binoculars unless they had some form of night vision or thermal detecting capability. Likely the latter.

A shot rang out, and even though he was easily one hundred yards away, he heard the sound of a body fall.

Then there was coughing.

Almost like the sound of a cat hurling up a hairball, it was something Levi had heard a few times before.

A deer had been shot, likely in the lungs.

The men walked toward the animal, and after verifying it wasn't a threat, they followed the path of the stream.

"Levi, I'm outside the warehouse. Using the FLIR, I see a

bunch of bodies huddled together inside a freight container. I'd say between fifty and a hundred kids."

FLIR was a thermal imaging system that Levi had used in the past when looking for people in the woods. With one of those, a human body showed up like a matchstick in the dark. Evidently, Lucy had something that could see into a metal shipping container.

Levi crept toward the sound of the hacking deer, all the while, keeping his gaze focused on the four men moving south along the waterway.

"Our guys here look like they're pretty paranoid. They're scanning the woods for thermal signatures. One of them just shot a deer. They're currently moving further south."

"Be careful they don't detect you."

Levi drew a razor-sharp knife from a sheathe on his belt, bent down and put the deer out of its misery. "Don't worry about me. If these guys are paranoid, then so are the ones you're watching."

"Not so much. They've got campfires going along the perimeter. Probably to keep the sentries warm. Either way, they're blind to anyone watching them."

Levi shook his head at the idiocy. He'd never been in the military, but the years he'd spent with lifelong trackers, hunters, and survivalists had taught him to think of nature in a different way than most. Predator versus prey. If he was worried about someone sneaking up on him, the last thing he'd want is to have campfires giving him night blindness and advertising his position.

"Okay, just watch yourself. I'll meet you at the car in about three hours, like planned."

Levi crouched at the edge of the woods, his eyes on the rental car that they'd arrived in. He heard the crunch of snow somewhere to his left and he whispered, "Is that you approaching."

"You've got good ears."

Less than a minute later Lucy emerged from the woods, looking like a shadow in the mottled backdrop of the snow-covered woods. Levi dropped from the observation point he'd built between two intertwined trees.

Lucy gasped, and he heard her voice in his ear as well as across the clearing. "Holy shit, where the hell did you come from?"

Levi motioned toward the car. "Let's talk in the car, I'm freezing my dangly bits off."

~

After about thirty minutes, they were finally driving on pavement again and heading back to Seattle.

"Do you have everything you need for tonight?" Levi asked.

"I'll need to call Doug in a bit. I think I might need a few special things delivered to the office."

"What do you know about these kids? Their situation..." Levi hesitated. "I really don't know much about this trafficking thing other than what I heard from the girls I'd found."

Lucy's expression turned dour as she stared ahead at the highway. It was a full thirty seconds before she replied. "I'm sure you know the basics. These kids may have been abandoned, orphaned, kidnapped, or sold. It really doesn't matter so much how they got into this situation, it's the nightmare that they have to look forward to if someone doesn't intervene."

Images of Mei lingered in Levi's mind. So young, and

dressed so provocatively. He couldn't bring himself to imagine in detail what she may have already been through, but Lucy drew the mental picture with a stark sense of reality.

"These kids, if they're lucky, are brought to illegal work camps," Lucy said. "Taught to sew, farm, whatever is needed. It's the unlucky ones that I worry the most about. The ones who have pretty features, especially the girls, they're the ones that die quickly or live through a hell few can believe.

"Imagine being thirteen and you're raped thirty times a day for five years straight. A body isn't made to undergo that level of abuse. Most don't make it to eighteen. Some escape and try to reclaim their lost lives, but they almost never do. Others are so scarred by their ordeal, they go crazy. They're broken for the rest of their lives. Still others, after countless abortions, are left sterile, or they catch a disease that can't be cured, and they disappear."

Levi balled up his fists in anger as he listened to Lucy clinically describe what really happens to the victims of human trafficking. "When you say 'disappear,' I assume you mean they're killed and buried somewhere?"

Lucy shrugged. "Killed, yes. Buried? That implies some level of dignity. Usually not. Let's be honest, your people dispose of bodies in ways that are probably similar. Dissolved in acid, burned into ashes, shredded and spread across the ocean for the fish to eat … there's plenty of ways to get rid of evidence."

Levi hitched his thumb back the way they'd been. "Well, let's see what we can do about helping out the few that we know about."

"That's why we're doing this."

Levi sifted through what she had just described. He knew so little about this topic. He'd only been tangentially aware of this through the handful of kids he'd rescued, and he'd never been privy to the details. Part of him didn't want to know that people were capable of such depravity.

The Mafia was many things—even the Bianchi family were almost certainly doing things he'd never do himself—but they still had some vestige of honor. Honor even amongst the most ruthless. Families, and especially kids, they were off limits.

It was hard for him to imagine that only a short time ago, this whole thing started with the unrelated kidnapping of a Japanese mob boss's granddaughter.

He looked at his watch. It was almost four in the morning, and they'd be heading back in about twelve hours after hitting Seattle. "Do you think Mason can get stuff in your locker today?"

Lucy turned onto Mount Baker Highway. "I don't know how he does it, but he's pretty quick."

Levi dialed Denny's number.

"Hey, Levi. I'm about to close up for the night. What's up?" Denny was almost always at the bar fiddling with things in his workshop past closing time, but it was three hours later in New York, so Levi had gotten lucky catching him while he was still there.

"That wet suit you were showing me, do you still have it?"

"You mean the dry suit? Ya, I still got that. You interested?"

"I think so. But I need it, like, now."

"Okay, when you say now, I'm assuming you're picking it up?"

"That's the thing. I'm in Seattle. Any chance you can get it to me here today, like the earlier the better?"

"Damn, man. Hold on, let me get to the computer and see." Levi heard tapping on the keyboard. *"Okay, if you're serious, I*

can rush this over to LaGuardia right now using Delta, and as long as I can it get there by eight, it'll land in Seattle at just before five in the afternoon your time. That looks like it's about as good as it gets. Will that work?"

Levi turned to Lucy and cupped his hand over the mic. "You know the traffic around here better than I do. If I have something arrive at the Delta Cargo terminal at five p.m., will we have enough time to make it?"

Lucy frowned, then nodded. "We should make it."

"Okay, Denny. I'll owe you big time. Send it over. I'll pick it up in Seattle."

"You got it, my friend. Okay, enough jibber-jabbering, is that it? I have to rush out with this thing if I'm going to make it."

"Ya, that's it. Thanks."

As Levi hung up, Lucy asked, "What in the world do you need a wet suit for?"

Levi leaned back and smiled. "I'd rather be invisible when it's time to start killing the bad guys."

CHAPTER NINETEEN

Lucy lurched up into a sitting position, her heart racing as she shoved the all-too-familiar memories of being suffocated aside. She forcibly slowed her breathing, then switched off the alarm that was about to go off. It was time to get ready.

Throwing back her covers, she padded over to the bedroom door and slowly opened it. Levi was laying on the sofa in the living room, eyes closed. A relaxed expression had replaced the tension he usually carried around his mouth and furrowed brow.

He was a disturbingly handsome man, with dark brown hair and rugged features that she could easily imagine being on a magazine cover. But at the moment, while sleeping, he looked so different … so innocent. She pictured the boy in the man. The same boy that his mother would have watched over as a child.

This man was much more than what he seemed.

Levi stirred and opened his eyes. He turned in her direction and gave her a wave. He then stretched, letting out a loud yawn for good measure. Then he sat up, gave her an appraising look, and smiled. "Do you always stand around naked in front of strangers?"

Lucy looked down at herself and shrugged. After what she'd been through in her life, nudity was not something she gave much thought to. She harrumphed and went back into the bedroom to get dressed.

As she got dressed, Lucy began questioning what she'd just done. Was she giving Levi the wrong impression? Sure, being naked in front of someone didn't exactly mean anything to her, but it might mean something to him. In fact, it probably did, especially since he mentioned it.

And she'd already been naked in front of him twice. Today made a third time. Until Levi, nobody had seen her naked since her husband was killed. What the hell was wrong with her?

Lucy frowned, knowing that there were plenty of things wrong with her, things nobody would be able to understand or accept.

"Hey, Lucy," Levi called from the living room. "What's the story with this apartment? It looks like an exact copy of your place in New York."

Lucy slipped a brace of throwing knives over her shoulder, shrugged into a Kevlar vest, and walked into the living room. "It's actually a copy of my penthouse suite when I lived in Hong Kong. It's hard to explain, but I can't sleep unless I'm in a familiar setting."

Levi was lacing his boots, and looked up. His electric blue eyes made her feel self-conscious. As if he could see things about her that she didn't want anyone to know. He nodded. "I know what you mean."

He couldn't possibly.

Levi's phone buzzed, and he put it to his ear. "Yes, this is

Levi Yoder … okay, I'll be there." He slipped the phone into his pocket. "My package is on schedule."

Lucy nodded. "Okay, we've got some time. Let's head over to Chinatown and grab a bite. That way, it'll be easy to buzz by the office, then back to the airport to get your stuff. And then we'll be in business."

Levi hopped to his feet and asked in near-perfect Mandarin. "Will it be authentic Chinese food?"

"Authentic enough for a white boy," she said with a smile.

∼

Levi held the restaurant door open for Lucy, and as she walked past him, she felt his hand touch the small of her back. She hopped forward, trying not to show her revulsion.

"Oh, I'm so sorry," Levi whispered. "I wasn't thinking."

She motioned dismissively. She knew her reaction was irrational. He didn't mean anything by it. He was trying to be nice.

An elderly waitress with a big yellowed smile approached. She'd been working in the Shanghai Garden ever since Lucy had discovered the place.

"Two for here lunch?" the waitress asked in broken English.

"Yes. Just two for lunch, thank you." Levi responded in Mandarin.

The woman's eyes widened. It was definitely a novelty for the older woman to have a handsome Anglo man speaking to her in her native tongue.

She led them to a table that was set apart from the other customers, then came back to serve them water and hot tea.

Levi pointed at a spot on the menu. "I see here that you have shaved spicy beef tendon. Is it served cold?"

The waitress nodded and responded enthusiastically in Chinese. "Yes, we cook it for a very long time, and then, when it's done, we cool it so it can be shaved thin enough so that you can see through it. It's very good for joints and skin."

"Well, given how lovely your skin is, it's obvious you must eat it often," Levi said with a smile, and the waitress gave an embarrassed laugh. "I think I can use some of that magic." He patted at his stubble-covered cheek. "I'll take one sliced beef tendon. And…" He looked over at Lucy. "Do you like pickles?"

She nodded. Lucy smiled as she observed the way this mobster charmed the heck out of the waitress, and he was inadvertently doing a number on her as well. When Levi wanted to, he knew just the thing to say to get a girl's attention. If the waitress was a few decades younger, she'd probably be inviting him over to spend the night.

"Also," Levi continued, "one order of your spicy cucumber, and your house special hand-shaven noodle soup, and that's it for me."

The waitress turned to Lucy.

"I'll take vegetables with barley green hand-shaven noodle chow mein."

The old woman pointed at the pot of tea. "Anything else to drink?"

They both shook their heads and the waitress scurried away.

Almost as quickly as she disappeared, the waitress reappeared with a silver bucket of pickle spears laced with red peppers, and a tray of gelatinous beef tendon. Lucy had never liked the consistency of the latter, but it was clear that Levi had no issues with it. She watched with fascination as he expertly used his chopsticks to grab the thinly sliced rubbery appetizer and pop it into his mouth.

She grabbed a pickle and nibbled on it. Unlike the pickles served in a typical New York deli, these had a slightly spicy tingle and tasted of the ginger they were fermented with.

Levi leaned forward a bit and whispered, "I don't want to pry as to why, because I'm sure there's an important reason that's probably none of my business, but I wanted to understand. It isn't a germ thing, I don't think. You seem to be fine touching things that I've touched. It's only if I or someone else touches you directly, right?"

She studied Levi's face. Something about his expression pained her intensely. He wasn't poking fun at her, like so many people in her life had about this problem of hers. He looked like he was sincerely trying to understand. She only wished she had an explanation that made any sense.

Blowing out a deep breath, she forced a neutral expression on her face. "That's pretty much it. I remember my mother saying to someone that I was even like that as a baby. I hated being touched."

Levi's looked thoughtful as he nibbled on a pickle. "That had to be particularly tough when it came to getting married."

Lucy flashed back to a happier time when her husband was still alive. It truly had been a good time in her life, despite the unusual circumstances of their arrangement. "He knew about it from the beginning. I made it work to his satisfaction. He never had a reason to complain."

Levi's face turned dark red with embarrassment, and she barely suppressed a laugh.

Soon the waitress arrived with their food. As Levi ate, Lucy wondered who this guy was that she was sharing a meal with.

∽

The cold breeze that filtered through the woods didn't make things any easier for Levi as he put on Denny's dry suit. The moon cast a silvery light, and Levi had exceptional night vision, but even so, Lucy's form was well-hidden. She was dressed from head to toe in a very dark camo pattern that blended well with the mottled backdrop of the woods.

Levi wasn't quite at the same level of readiness for tonight's task. He felt Lucy's gaze boring into him as he stood in the woods, wearing only underwear and trying to squeeze into the thick-walled dry suit. The inner lining of Denny's suit threatened to pull out every hair he had as it dragged over his skin.

"My kingdom for some talcum powder."

Lucy looked amused. "Do you want me to help you put it on?"

"No," he barked. He pressed his bare back against a tree and managed to squeeze his lower half into the heavy suit. Once he finally wedged one shoulder in, the other slipped right through the other armhole. Now only his face was visible, and that would disappear as soon as he lowered the face mask with the attached rebreather.

"Do you think that outfit will really help?" Lucy asked. "I just hope it doesn't interfere with your ability to move."

Levi set the thermostat of the suit to automatically match the external temperature. "The whole reason I got this is so I at least have a chance of not being spotted on a thermal camera. If I'm having to move quickly, there's probably something else going wrong."

Lucy hitched her dark canvas backpack up onto her shoulders and flipped down a night-vision monocular over her left eye. "Okay, I'm going over the border to scout things out. I'll let you know what I see when I get there, but I'd expect these guys to follow the same path as they herd the kids south."

Levi motioned toward the ATV, which was still hidden under a blanket of branches and snow. "Aren't you going to take that?"

"No. It turns out that the forest presses up right against their compound, and it's too dense for me to maneuver that thing. I'm better off without it."

Worried, Levi took a step closer. "No offense, but do you think you're—"

"Listen to me." Lucy stepped even closer, so only inches separated them. "I'm not questioning your skills. Don't question mine."

Levi winced at the aggressive tone in her voice. She was right: he needed to have his head on straight. He couldn't worry about what she was doing without compromising his own effectiveness.

He was about to apologize when she patted him on the cheek and smiled. "Go do what you need to do." She turned and jogged north, in the direction of the Canadian border.

∽

Levi was perched on a slight, snow-covered rise with clear visibility to the meandering stream known as Frost Creek. He was approximately seventy yards from where his targets would be.

He was surprised at how well he was able to see through the liquid-lined facemask of Denny's suit, and the night almost disappeared as he peered through the rifle's high-quality scope. He shifted his aim toward a fist-sized clump of grass sitting on the bank of the river. He focused his aim, and pulled the trigger.

The clump of grass swayed as a bullet traveling nearly one

thousand feet per second and slammed into the muddy bank—right on target.

Levi smiled. Not because he hit the target—any moron with a properly zeroed rifle should have been able to make that shot—but because the sound that had escaped his weapon was no louder than a soft ping.

"Levi." Lucy's voice came through clearly in his earpiece.

"I hear you. Send it over."

"You've got a caravan heading straight for you. I count sixty-eight kids. They're all roped together, ankle-to-ankle, wrist-to-wrist, in two columns. They'll be snaking their way toward you. Two men leading, two men in the back, and two more walking alongside. They're all carrying rifles."

Levi took a deep breath and slowly blew it out. This was going to be a challenge. How to take all six out without them triangulating on him?

He chambered the next round in the rifle. "How much time before they cross the border?"

"They're about two klicks out, and judging by their pace, figure about twenty minutes. You okay with this?"

Levi sorted through the lessons he'd learned wandering the Outback with an aboriginal trapper. He smiled as he realized he already had what he needed in his pack. "No worries," he said. "I think I have a few ideas on how to handle our guests. How about you? You've got your end all buttoned down?"

"Not quite yet, but I'll probably be done with what I need to do before you are."

"Okay, my dear, keep your eyes peeled and let's do this."

"See you on the other side."

Lucy focused on the "compound"—which was little more than a single concrete building about fifty feet square, surrounded by a chain-link fence topped with barbed wire. A light pole next to the building lit up the entire area.

She pulled a heavy pair of binoculars from her pack. Evidently, the binoculars were being developed for the military and not yet deployed. According to the label, they used multi-wavelength infrared imaging sensors, whatever that meant.

Pressing the power button, the device hummed to life and she peered through it at the building. She smiled. Whatever these things were, they were able to actually penetrate the walls of the building.

She spotted two body heat signatures located in the same section of the building, plus one guard, in glowing detail, walking the perimeter of the compound.

Lucy put the binoculars away and pulled a .22 caliber pistol from her in-waistband holster. She screwed on a long-barreled suppressor and crouched just inside the woods, out of sight of the one-man patrol.

Crouching low, Lucy watched as the guard walked from the southeast corner of the compound toward the southwest corner. Slung in front of him was a gun; its size and shape suggested a submachine gun with an extended butt-stock. The last thing in the world she needed was to get into a firefight with that.

Patiently, she watched as the man crossed no more than a hundred feet in front of her. Still, he was walking slowly, panning his gaze back and forth, looking for anything out of the ordinary.

Lucy shifted her gaze to the top of the light pole next to the main building.

It painted the grounds of the compound with enough light to show anything within the borders of the property.

She glanced once at the guard just as he hit the southwest corner of the compound and turned his attention to the north. She racked the slide of her pistol, took aim at the light and fired two quick shots.

The high-pressure sodium floodlight blew apart, bathing the compound in darkness.

Lucy flipped down her night-vision monocular as she advanced from the edge of the woods. The world through the military-grade device was a hazy green and black.

The guard turned in her direction and cursed as he stumbled on a rock. He was completely night blind.

Two quick shots from her pistol, and he was down.

With her gun still aimed at the guard, Lucy drew a pair of wire cutters from her pack and cut an opening in the chain-link fence. Then she walked over to the guard, pressed the muzzle of her suppressor against the top of his head, and pulled the trigger. A soft thump and a dribble of blood from the nose confirmed he wouldn't be getting back up.

Lucy smiled as she took from the guard what turned out to be a Heckler & Koch MP5 submachine gun. She checked the magazine, it was full. The weapon had a four-position trigger group, so she set the trigger select to a three-round burst, then slung it over her shoulder.

As she walked toward the entrance of the building, she said a silent prayer.

It was time.

CHAPTER TWENTY

Looking through the rifle's scope, Levi saw the beginning of the snaking line of kids. It was exactly as Lucy had described. The two men leading the stumbling kids were about twenty feet ahead, and on their belts they each had activated glow sticks, presumably to make it easier for the kids to follow them in the dark.

Levi adjusted the scope to zoom in on the kids. They were struggling, their eyes were as wide open as they could make them, each of them concentrating on the person ahead of them, and Levi saw the glint of tears on some of their cheeks. Most of them had terrified expressions, and he forced himself to look away.

Clouds had swept in, and the bright moonlight from earlier was now a muddy glow that barely extended to the shores of Frost Creek. The two men leading the kids wore what looked to be some type of night vision equipment, but Levi needed no assistance.

Levi's vision was completely adjusted to the dark and he'd always been able to see much better than most in very low light conditions. So much so, that with the help of the muted moonlight, he had no problems seeing at all.

The men headed south, followed by a train of bedraggled kids that was long enough that he hadn't yet spied the trailing end. But Levi's aim focused on the two men that were leading the group.

The chances of him being able to take out six armed men without further endangering the kids or himself was practically nil, but he'd prepared for them. There was a plan.

And these two men were about to act as unwilling diversions.

Levi had prepared a surprise on both shores of the creek: shallow pits covered by sticks, snow, and scattered pine needles.

The first of the men crunched onto the snow-covered sticks, plunged three feet, and screamed.

He shifted his aim toward the man's partner, the one who'd managed to just barely skirt the pit trap. Levi aimed and fired.

Without a sound, the bullet connected—a head shot—and the second guard collapsed in a heap.

Levi chambered another round.

Chaos erupted in the front of the line as the one guard, who'd likely been impaled by at least one of the inverted wooden spears in the pit, gave off a blood-curdling scream of pain.

The front of the line of kids stepped back as two other guards rushed forward, rifles drawn.

Levi took careful aim at the guard on the far side of the kids. He held his breath and felt the slow rhythm of his heartbeat as he focused on his target. Compensating for bullet drop and horizontal movement, he put the very slightest pressure on the trigger, waited between heartbeats, and fired.

The bullet whizzed at the target at nearly a thousand feet per second. When it connected, it was like someone had snipped the strings from a marionette. The guard tumbled face first, arms and legs splayed in every direction.

Levi soundlessly chambered the next round, smiling at the attention being paid to the front of the caravan. Now the two other guards from the back were rushing into view as well.

Panning his rifle toward the one remaining guard from the middle group, and just before he could reach his screaming partner and raise further alarm, Levi released another round.

The man fell face forward, twenty feet from the impaled guard in the pit.

A chunk of bark exploded near Levi's head, and he ducked behind the trunk of the pine he'd perched himself in.

How...?

And then he realized. His gun, and especially his suppressor, they'd built up a significant amount of heat from the shots he'd just fired. If those guys had put on any thermal imaging equipment, his rifle would be standing out like a torch.

Levi threw the weapon twenty feet to his right and dove to the ground.

He heard several shots as he scrambled away from the heated weapon and pulled out two balanced, razor-sharp bo shurikens, a type of throwing spike. Rushing through the woods, he ignored the crying of the kids and the screaming of the impaled guard. Instead, he focused on the two men he was closing in on.

They both wore headgear with monoculars.

As Levi approached, one of them took a shot at the discarded rifle.

A loud metallic ping rang through the forest, and Levi threw the first of the spikes.

It slammed into the soft tissue under the man's chin, and before his first target could even emit a choking gurgle, Levi threw the second spike.

But this one ricocheted off the second guard's rifle as he spun toward him.

A shot rang out just as Levi swept the man's feet out from under him, plunged his stiffened fingers at the man's exposed neck, squeezed, and pulled.

Levi snatched away the man's weapon before sending a devasting kick to the side of his head. He heard the snap of vertebrae as the guard's neck broke.

He then raised his newfound AK-47, pulled back and released the charging handle, and then put a bullet in the other man's head, just to be sure.

Finally he rushed toward the line of kids and said in Mandarin, "Don't be scared. I'm here to help you."

Several of the kids stared wide-eyed at him and backed away. That was understandable, seeing as he had just appeared out of the shadows and killed their escorts. He was also covered from head to toe in a black thermally isolated dry suit, and held an automatic weapon. To them he probably looked like a creature from a nightmare.

He unlatched his face mask, flipped it up, and repeated the message.

One of the kids said something in another dialect of Chinese, and the nearest kids began to cry and give him a thumbs up.

Levi reached out to the nearest kid—a girl who couldn't have been more than twelve. He cupped her chin in his hand, gave her the warmest smile he could manage, and said, "You'll all be fine. I'll be right back." He looked toward the man in the pit, who was still yelling. "I have something to finish."

THE INSIDE MAN

~

Lucy peered through the binoculars and saw that the heat signatures were now in two different parts of the building. That was fine. What was important was that her outside activity hadn't brought either of them scrambling for the door.

She skirted around the building, spotted the electric meter, and hurried over to it. Her formal education had stopped at the age of ten, when she moved in with her husband, but that hadn't stopped her from learning—and one of her interests was electricity. She'd become interested in the subject when an ox that her father owned rubbed against an electrical transformer and was electrocuted.

It scared her, and she hated to be scared of anything.

So over the years, she'd tinkered, and she learned. And she knew what her next steps were going to be.

Canada had the same type of electrical grid that the US had, and spotting the power meter made things very easy. She had no transformer to deal with, and she knew that the building's power was running through the single meter.

From her backpack, she pulled out a modified electrical transformer that she'd salvaged from a microwave. Normally it would only put out about one amp, so she'd disassembled it, salvaged the coil, and removed some of the metal shunts from within the transformer's core. It now would put out over eight hundred amps. Plenty for what she needed.

She placed the device at the base of the meter and wrapped two silver leads around the thick cable where the utility's electrical line met with the building's wiring. All too often these junctures used copper, which was a poor choice, due to oxidation. It increased resistance at the joint points. But she was counting on that. She turned the dial on the timer, setting her device's activation for two minutes from now and hustled to the building's entrance.

She crouched at the door, twisted the doorknob, and waited.

She'd planned this all ahead of time. She knew what was about to happen. As soon as the timer went off, the power supply built into her box would feed the modified transformer, and the metal leads from her contraption would surge with current. The slightly oxidized metal in the utility's connection would act as a resistor, heating up to the point of melting.

Tapping her finger on her knee, she kept count of the time.

Five ... four ... three ... two ... one ... *now*.

She imagined the cable beginning to smoke, a red glow from the heat building within the wires and then suddenly she heard it.

Electric sparks buzzed from the lamp post she'd shot, and someone yelled inside the building.

Lucy went in.

The lights were out, and there were no windows or other sources of light, but her night vision monocular projected a wide but invisible beam of infrared light. In her left eye, she saw the world bathed in a green hue.

"I can't see a damned thing!" yelled a man in Cantonese. He was up ahead and to Lucy's left.

Another voice, this one a woman's, yelled through the darkness from somewhere to her right. *"Don't move—you'll just break something. I'm looking for the flashlight. It's in here somewhere."*

Lucy slung her MP5 over her shoulder, drew her silenced .22, and moved down the hall toward the woman's voice. She passed several open doors leading to small offices.

Then from just ahead came the sound of someone opening

the drawer to a file cabinet. She followed the sound and stepped into the office.

A dowdy Asian woman looked blindly toward her. "Gao Jie?" Her eyes shone brightly in the reflected infrared light, almost like a cat's.

Without a word, Lucy aimed and fired twice.

Two pings, and the woman grabbed at the file cabinet as she fell backwards. The metal cabinet fell on top of her, making a tremendous crashing sound.

"Chen Bao! Are you okay?"

Lucy slipped her .22 in the carrying loop of her backpack, wielded the MP5 once again, and stepped out into the hall. A man stumbled from around a corner, blindly feeling his way.

He had no idea what was waiting for him.

Lucy pulled the trigger.

Three shots fired in less than a third of a second. All three direct hits, center mass.

The man staggered, murmured something unintelligible, and collapsed to his knees. Blood trickled from his lips.

Without a shred of remorse, Lucy shot another burst of three rounds. The man fell backwards, his face an unrecognizable mess.

Lucy turned from the corridor and went back to the dead woman's office to look through the operation's files.

"Lucy, you there?" Levi's voice crackled in her ear.

"I am. I've secured the shipping outpost. How goes it with you?"

"Six down. Kids are spooked as hell, but they're all fine. Isn't someone going to be looking for these kids if they don't show up wherever they were going in a couple hours?"

"Yes, I'm sure someone's probably waiting at a handoff

point. That's why we need to get the kids away from there." Lucy grunted as she lifted the file cabinet off of the dead woman's body and was about to go rummaging through the files when she turned to the file-laden desk. "Listen, we don't have much time. Doug's got limits to what he can call in for assistance. Start walking them toward our car."

"Roger, that."

She heard Levi giving instructions in Mandarin, and most likely, some of those kids would understand him.

Lucy opened up a file folder that was laying on the desk. It was information about the children: contact names, phone numbers, age, height, virginity status, and more. She pulled out her cell phone and took pictures. Lots of pictures.

"Lucy, we're heading to the car. Be there in about half an hour or so. But then what? Obviously we can't all pile into your car. If people come looking for these kids, we're not exactly going to be able to hide which way we've gone."

Lucy sent the first batch of photos to Doug's inbox, then texted to him a set of GPS coordinates.

"Levi, we've struck the motherlode here. I've got location of origin, recruiter, purchaser, kids' names, prices, everything." Her phone buzzed with a text from Doug. "And I just got word from Doug. I don't know how, but he's got a pair of Chinooks lifting off from Lewis-McChord near Tacoma. He says they'll be there in about forty minutes."

"There where? At your car?"

"Those are the coordinates I sent him."

"I'll believe it when I see it. Anyway, I'll make sure the kids get on the choppers, and I'll wait for you at the car."

Lucy felt something warm up inside of her that reminded her of times that were long gone. "No, go with the kids. The military guys will need you at least until a translator gets there. I'll be driving back south by the time you guys land."

"Lucy, please be careful coming back, and don't walk along the shores of the creek. There's a couple of fresh pits with spikes on the bottom. One of them's occupied, and I removed the undergrowth hiding the other, but it's dark and you know…"

"I'll be fine. We're done now. Maybe we'll meet up again on some other occasion. Bye, Levi." Lucy removed her earpiece and ripped off the throat mic.

Knowing there'd be people arriving soon, she raced from the office, jumped over the dead trafficker, and focused on getting home in one piece.

Things were about to get very ugly for one of the triads.

CHAPTER TWENTY-ONE

Pacing back and forth in his New York City apartment, Levi dialed a number and crossed his fingers. He needed this to work.

"Hey, Levi. I was about to call you," Mason sounded like he was next door.

"I did what you asked. I helped Lucy with the kid situation. From what I hear, you got what you needed. So, remember how we talked about a favor?"

"No," Mason responded, an amused tone to his voice. "Why don't you remind me."

Levi frowned and tightened his grip on his cell phone. "I said that if this works out, I may have some favors to ask, and you said, and I'll quote, 'You don't even have to ask, I'll work on it and see what can be done.' Do you remember now?" He tried to keep the anger from his voice. He hated when people didn't deliver on a promise.

"I suppose I do remember something along those lines. I'll deliver. But I have one small thing to ask of you."

If Levi were within spitting distance of Mason, he wasn't sure if he could hold back from tearing him apart. "What is it?" he growled.

"There's about to be a fairly large crackdown coming down on the area where you first met Lucy. Unfortunately, she's managed to slip onto the FBI's watch list, and I need a day or so to clear it up. Which isn't enough time. The fireworks will start before that."

Levi's anger bled out of him, replaced by a feeling of concern. "What do you want me to do?"

"If I have Lucy get to the Flushing–Main Street terminal, do you think you can get her somewhere off the streets without her being tailed? Things will get difficult if she's put into the system."

"Flushing–Main Street, yes I think I can arrange some chaos to waylay any tails. When?"

"Pick her up in two hours."

Levi hesitated as he thought of all of the people he'd have to call. He'd have to arrange for fabricated traffic jams, set up blockers for any cop cars or feds … this would definitely take a bit of coordinating. "Okay, let's do this. And then we'll settle up?"

"You do this, I'll make sure you get what you need."

"Done."

Mason hung up and Levi spent the next two hours on the phone with almost a dozen different members of the Bianchi network of friends and family.

～

It was late in the evening as Levi stood in front of the Helmsley Arms, waiting and waiting until he spotted the car. Feeling the tension leak from his body, he blew out a breath he hadn't realized he was holding as a limo pulled up to the Park Avenue address. Without waiting for the driver, the rear door popped open, and out stepped Lucy. She looked up at him and her eyes widened. "You?"

"Me what?" Levi asked with a smile.

"I guess I didn't realize you'd be involved." She tilted her head, and an uncharacteristic emotion slipped through a crack in her neutral demeanor: she almost looked pleased.

She walked up to him, whispered, "Remember, don't touch me," and wrapped her arm around his.

The two beefy men who were manning the doors to what would end up being Lucy's safehouse for the night smiled at them both as they walked toward the elevators.

When the elevator doors slid closed, Lucy let go, took a step back, and eyed Levi from head to toe. "You clean up nicely. It's the first time I'm seeing you in a suit."

Levi shrugged. "This is more my day-to-day apparel, to be honest." The elevator doors slid open and Levi escorted Lucy to his apartment. "You've pretty much only seen me in operator mode, which is a bit different than the way I am normally."

Lucy raised an eyebrow. "I'm thinking you're not that much of a normal anything. I saw what you left behind over there by the creek. Nice work with those six. But then again, do you always leave such a mess and expect others like me to clean up behind you?"

Levi gave her a puzzled expression as he swiped his finger on the biometric lock to his apartment.

She smiled and shook her head. "Then again, maybe you are

a regular guy, and always leave a mess for others to clean. That was definitely my husband's modus operandi."

He rolled his eyes, but smiled nonetheless at the dry needling she was giving him.

With a wide sweep of his arm, he opened the apartment door and said, "Judge for yourself."

Lucy walked into the apartment, looked around, and nodded in approval.

Not a thing was out of place, and even though Levi was by nature a neat person, he wasn't about to say that a maid came in daily to dust, vacuum and keep things spotless.

"You probably have a maid, anyway." Lucy waved dismissively and plopped herself down in a leather armchair.

"Are you hungry? Thirsty?"

Lucy shook her head. "I already ate." She looked around the apartment. "Where am I staying tonight?"

Levi motioned toward a door that stood ajar on the far end of the living room. "I have a guest bedroom. It's all set up. It has its own bathroom, with fresh towels." Levi picked up a candy from a crystal bowl on the coffee table. "I can even put a mint on your pillow."

"No need." Lucy shrugged her shoulders and sighed. "I probably won't get much sleep anyway." She motioned toward the windows. "I'll be thinking about what's happening out there."

Levi took a seat across from her on the other armchair and asked, "Do you want to talk?"

She shrugged again. "What's there to say? I've delivered enough evidence to wipe out most of what my husband did in the States. And with the evidence I gave Doug, the folks in Hong Kong probably won't make it."

"I thought that was your plan all along, wasn't it?"

"It was." Lucy pursed her lips and held a troubled expression. "It still is, but you have to understand, this is all I've known since I was ten." She looked across the coffee table at Levi, and her eyes shined with unshed tears. "I need to get my mind off of this. How did *you* get on this path? Where'd the Amish kid go astray?"

Levi leaned back, kicked off his loafers, and began to talk about when he first came to the city.

∽

Levi had talked nonstop for nearly an hour. He talked about the early years. How Vinnie's dad, the former boss, broke all the rules to stand up for him and make him a made man. He covered his marriage, his wife's death, his bout with cancer, and his unexpected recovery. He spoke of his wandering of the world and his eventual return to the family.

Lucy asked insightful questions and seemed thoroughly interested in every detail. She even noted when she suspected he left something out. And he did leave out a couple small details—things he'd sworn to never speak of again. And she let them go.

It was almost midnight, and when Levi yawned loudly, Lucy stood and said, "Go to bed. I'll lie down and probably watch TV or something."

Levi stood and motioned toward the kitchen. "If you're hungry or thirsty, kitchen's right there. Just make yourself at home. There's nothing to worry about. Nobody's coming, especially into this building."

∽

Levi lurched up into a sitting position, feeling a sudden sense of panic. The apartment was deadly silent, but his heartbeat was like a pounding drum beat echoing in his head. He felt a chill race up his back.

He knew something was wrong.

He grabbed the .45 from his nightstand and padded slowly toward the living room, his senses tingling and alert.

And then he heard it.

Slowly, he approached the guest room. The door was slightly ajar. He tightened his grip on the gun, finger hovering over the trigger. He slowly opened the door and walked in.

There was a crumpled pile of clothes on the floor.

His tension evaporated when he spotted Lucy asleep on the bed, curled into a fetal position—and naked once again. The sound he'd heard was her snoring.

He slowly backed out of the room and closed the door behind him.

It was four a.m.—no point in trying to go back to sleep. He needed a shower.

A cold one.

∼

Levi stood with Ryuki and Yoshi on the tarmac, waiting for Shinzo Tanaka's plane to taxi in.

Ryuki wrapped his arm around Levi's shoulder and squeezed. "I can't believe you made this happen."

Levi nodded and said nothing. He couldn't tell the man that it was actually a guy who worked for some secret part of the US government that had pulled the strings to remove the visa restriction for the Tanaka syndicate's boss.

"So," said Yoshi, "are Helen and June really are coming out of protection today?"

Levi nodded. "Yes. I got word from my contact and they're setting up a private meetup for the release. In fact, I think they've both already talked to Mister Tanaka while he was in the air."

"Mister Tanaka speaks English?" Yoshi looked surprised.

Ryuki shrugged. "I've never heard him speak any other language, and I've known him for more than twenty years."

Just then, an unmarked Gulfstream turned toward them. Its two massive engines whined as it taxied slowly forward. It stopped, the engine noise quickly subsided, and the door to the plane opened. Stairs unfolded, and customs and immigration officials boarded the plane for inspection.

Moments later, the officials departed and Levi smiled as he saw Shinzo Tanaka emerge from the plane—a legal visitor to a country that had banned his presence for almost three decades.

∽

It was nearly an hour-long drive from Dulles to the high school gymnasium where the first meeting was going to be held. Levi had arranged for a neutral place to meet that also gave everyone some privacy. The two men who had come with Tanaka were in the front of the limo, while Levi, Yoshi, and Ryuki were in the back with Mister Tanaka.

Tanaka smiled wryly as he looked out the window of the speeding vehicle. "I still can't believe I'm here. Levi, this is very important to me."

Levi could hear the emotion in the man's words. He could only begin to imagine what it must be like to meet your only living heir for the first time. That would pull at anyone's heartstrings. "I'm just glad that this all worked out."

Tanaka nodded and looked out the window.

Yoshi seemed tense. Probably nervous because he'd likely never met the mob boss before. Ryuki stared stoically at his own knees. The result was a weird and awkward silence that made Levi uncomfortable. Was it the normal Japanese stoicism or something else? Italians couldn't resist cracking jokes or exchanging stories if left to their own devices. This quiet and somber feeling put him on edge.

"Tanaka-sama," Levi said in carefully measured Japanese. "I heard you've spoken to June. Is that true?"

"*Hai*. But it's difficult for an old man like me to learn a new language. I know only a few words." Mister Tanaka's smile broadened as the limo pulled into a large parking lot.

They'd arrived.

Levi hopped out of the limo, assisted Mister Tanaka out, and led the group toward the gymnasium. Several FBI agents waited at the entrance to the building. They'd probably been in charge of the Wilsons' protective custody.

One of the agents held up his hand. "Mister Yoder?"

"Yes, that's me."

"Okay, you and Mister Shinzo Tanaka will be escorted in. Nobody else is cleared."

Levi relayed the message to Mister Tanaka in Japanese. Tanaka nodded and motioned for the other men to hang back.

The agent opened the door, and Levi and Tanaka walked inside.

Levi followed the mob boss into the well-lit gymnasium. He heard the sound of a basketball bouncing and a soft chuckle escaped from the older man.

It was the first time he'd seen his granddaughter.

Helen waved in their direction, her red hair shining like a beacon against her drab outfit, then she grabbed June's shoulder and pointed her toward them.

The girl's face lit up and she raced toward them yelling, "*Sofu! Sofu!*"—the Japanese word for grandfather. She practically tackled Tanaka, and he lifted her up into a bear hug.

Seeing the two of them stirred emotions within Levi as he watched tears stream down the old man's face.

June stuck out her lower lip and wiped at his tears. "*Sofu*, don't cry. It's okay. I can see you now."

Helen walked over to the two of them, gave a slight bow, and said in not too horrible Japanese, "It's nice so to meet. Spoke Jun very fondly you."

Tanaka held out his arm, and the three of them hugged. Tanaka said in not too horrible English, "Sorry taking long me to come here."

Levi felt a tap on his shoulder. He turned, and for some reason, he wasn't surprised to see Doug Mason standing there like a cat that had just eaten a canary.

"Really?" Levi said. "You pop up now?"

Mason put his index finger to his lips and whispered, "I've got two things for you. First, this." He handed Levi a sheet of paper. It was a copy of a classified FBI report about the Anspach investigation.

Nicholas Anspach, whereabouts unknown.

The Anspach residence has been sealed since the initial report of malfeasance. A second round of evidence collection revealed very little that was new, with one exception: behind a hidden panel in the master bedroom closet were old newspaper clippings having to do with the killing of a Georgetown student named Jun Tanaka.

The hairs on the back of Levi's neck stood on end. Helen's words, even though it seemed like she said it ages ago, they rang out loudly as he replayed them in his head.

"June's father died before she was born. He was a graduate student at Georgetown, and as he was walking to his car, he was killed in a drive-by shooting."

Levi blinked as he realized what it all meant.

He looked over at Helen and Tanaka. They were both trying hard to communicate; both had a poor grasp of the other's language, but somehow they managed. June rested her head on her grandfather's shoulder and hugged him around his neck.

Levi turned back to the printout.

Anspach did it. That jealous bastard killed June's father and … he tried taking out Yoshi too—likely because he'd learned that Yoshi and Helen were involved. All those pictures in Anspach's house…

He whispered to Mason, "Be right back."

Levi walked to the far end of the gym, pulled out his phone, and dialed Dino's number. The mobster picked up on the first ring. *"Ya, what's up?"*

"Is our friend still around?"

"Oh, yeah. No doubt about it. For some reason, he's unhappy, that ungrateful asshole."

"If you can do me a big favor, remember the plans we talked about for him?"

"Oh, yeah."

"Let's put the package in the mail."

"No problem. It's a done deal. When do you want the package to arrive?"

Tanaka only had a seven-day visa.

"Let's say two weeks."

"It's done."

"Thanks. I'll be in touch."

Levi felt a surge of satisfaction as he walked back to the Wilsons and Tanaka. He whispered in Tanaka's ear in Japanese. "Can we talk in private for a second? I have three things to tell you. The first will definitely upset you, but the second I think will make up for the first. And the last, I'm not sure if it's a good thing or not, but I'm honor-bound to tell you."

Tanaka's expression turned serious, as he nodded. To Helen, he said in halting English, "Excuse for me a second."

June had fallen asleep on her grandfather's shoulder, so he continued to hold her as Levi led him away from the others.

"What is it?" Tanaka asked.

Levi told the mob boss what he'd just learned about Anspach, Jun's assassination, the pictures of Helen, and his theory that the little girl might have been kidnapped by Anspach in a sick attempt to curry favor with Helen when he "rescued" her.

Tanaka's face turned red but he maintained control. "And the second thing?"

Levi grinned. "The man who had kidnapped your granddaughter? I told you that he would never bother anyone again, and this is true. But what I haven't told you is that some friends of mine are holding him for me. I've arranged for him to arrive in Tokyo on a cargo ship in two weeks. I'll get you the details. You'll be able to do with him whatever you like."

An icy smile bloomed on the man's face, and he nodded his

approval. "Very nice. Thank you for the gift. I owe you once again. And the third thing?"

Levi wrinkled his nose and hesitated. "This is complicated. First, let me explain that both people are innocent, and that nothing untoward has happened. But … I can tell Yoshi, Ryuki's brother, he's in love with Helen, your granddaughter's mother. And I believe the feeling is mutual."

Tanaka betrayed no reaction. "How do you know this?"

Levi shrugged. "Mostly, I can just tell. Several things tipped me off. And Yoshi was willing to sacrifice himself for June. He was there with me when I rescued her. When she saw him, she went running to him. Anyway, I just felt that you should know. And you should also know that Yoshi would never dishonor his brother by pursuing a relationship without approval or blessing. Nor would he ever ask for that blessing, for fear of you saying no."

June stirred on the mob boss's shoulder. "*Sofu*, down please."

Tanaka set the little girl down, and she ran back to her basketball and started bouncing it.

The mob boss patted Levi's shoulder. "Thank you for sharing this information. Can Yoshi be brought in?"

Levi smiled. "I'm sure he can."

He spoke with Mason, and moments later Yoshi entered the gym, looking very nervous.

"Yoyo!" June screamed with delight. She raced over to Yoshi and threw her arms around his waist.

Levi noted that Tanaka was intently watching the interaction between the two.

When the little girl went back to playing with her ball, Yoshi approached Tanaka and gave a low bow. "You wished to speak with me?"

Tanaka put his arm over the nervous man's shoulder. "Tell me what you think of my granddaughter and her mother."

Yoshi suddenly took on a quintessential deer-in-the-headlights look as his eyes widened and he froze, uncertain how to respond.

Levi said softly in English, "Just tell the truth."

Yoshi blinked rapidly, looking as if he was trying to will himself to disappear. But after a few seconds of silence, he barely whispered in Japanese, "I love them both very much."

"And you've been keeping watch over them for years now, isn't that true?"

Yoshi nodded vigorously.

"It must be difficult to do this, because I understand you live in a different place. It would be very hard to always watch over June or her mother."

"Well, yes, but I tried to do both. I worked at night as a security guard to watch over them both at night, and then during the day, I volunteered at June's school so I could be around her. And then I would go home to sleep."

Levi strained to hear as the mob boss whispered to Yoshi, "Have you considered maybe it would be easier if you lived in the same place?"

Yoshi nodded. "I tried, but the apartment complex had a policy against people living on property also being in charge of security. It's a ridiculous rule, but—"

Tanaka laughed. "No, I didn't mean that. You love them, and June seems to like you a lot. Does her mother?"

"Does she … like me a lot?" Yoshi looked nervous again. "I think so, but I never—"

"Okay, let's fix this." Tanaka beckoned to Helen, who walked over.

"Yes?"

Tanaka looked at Levi and motioned for him to get closer. "Translate for me." He then faced Helen. "I know Yoshi is in love with you. This I approve of, but only if you approve of it."

Helen glanced back and forth between Levi and Tanaka as Levi translated. Her eyes widened as the message became clear, and she looked at Yoshi with surprise.

"So," Tanaka said. "What are your feelings?"

Helen's face turned red, Yoshi had long before turned all sorts of darker colors. "I care for him a lot."

"Would you be willing to get married, and provide my granddaughter with a stable home?" Tanaka asked bluntly.

Yoshi looked like he was about to pass out from lack of oxygen.

Levi whispered to Tanaka, "This isn't how such things are done in—"

Levi was cut off by the mob boss's stern frown. Instead he translated the message for Helen.

Helen's mouth dropped open for a moment and tears glistened in her eyes. "If he's willing, I would be."

Tanaka seemed to understand her response, because he turned to Yoshi and raised an eyebrow.

Yoshi cleared his throat and looked Helen in the eye. In English, he said, "I would love to ask for your hand in marriage."

"And I say yes to your proposal." Helen smiled, a bit wide-eyed.

Tanaka pulled a ring of keys from his pocket and held them out to Yoshi. "This is my wedding present."

They all stared at the keys, unsure what to make of them.

The mob boss explained. "I have for a long time maintained a house in this area. In fact, it was intended to be a college graduation present for my son. I've decided to instead make it a wedding present."

Levi translated and Helen gave the older man a hug and said "thank you" in Japanese.

Tanaka tapped on his watch. "I have six days left in the US this year. During that time, I would like to attend my daughter-in-law's wedding. It can even be an American-style wedding, if you insist."

Helen and Yoshi looked at each other and began to laugh.

June raced up to them, her mom's waistband and dangled while she asked, "What's so funny?"

Helen knelt in front of June and asked, "What do you think of Mommy and Yoyo getting married?"

June hopped up and down with excitement. "Can I help you be married?"

"How about being the flower girl?" Yoshi suggested.

Levi moved away from the family scene. He could see that things were going to be just fine with the Tanaka-Wilson-Watanabe clan.

CHAPTER TWENTY-TWO

When Levi stepped out of the gymnasium, Doug Mason was waiting for him. The man motioned for them to take a little walk. "What's up?"

"Have you heard from Lucy?" Doug asked.

Levi shook his head. "Should I have? She left my place four days ago, just after your guys tore up most of Flushing—which somehow never made the news, by the way. I haven't heard from her since. Why?"

Mason frowned. "Her phone has been offline since she left your place. Did she say anything before she left? Where she was going?"

Glancing at the spook or whatever he was, Levi wasn't feeling a lot of sympathy for his plight. "Is she in some kind of trouble?"

"No. As a matter of fact, I've got her records completely expunged. She's clean as a whistle."

"And the triad? What happened to them?"

Mason grinned. "We've arrested nearly two hundred would-be purchasers and another fifty traffickers, and we're tracking down another one hundred suspects, all domestic. The Hong Kong Security Bureau has put away nearly one thousand direct members of the offending syndicate, included the top echelon who ran the whole thing."

"You cut off the head of the snake. Congrats."

The fed nodded and sighed. "It's a start. But where one trafficking organization ends, it seems like two sprout up. It's a never-ending problem."

"Is there anything else?"

"Anspach. We still can't find him. You don't—"

"Don't have a clue."

Mason stared at him. "You sure?"

Levi stopped and returned the man's gaze. "Would I lie to you?"

Mason made an exasperated sound and muttered, "You probably ground him up and served him as a Bolognese sauce."

Levi cocked an eyebrow. "You know, that's not a bad idea."

∼

Though his taxi cab driver cursed at traffic snarling the streets of Manhattan, Levi smiled contentedly. Nothing was going to wreck his good mood. He was done with DC. No baggage, no pseudo-girlfriends, no obligations, nothing.

The taxi rolled past East 86th Street and pulled up to the familiar building with two marble columns on each side of the entrance. It was still hard for Levi to get used to having a Park Avenue address, even if it was a mob building. The words "The Helmsley Arms" emblazoned in gold leaf above the ten-foot doors showed a little bit of Vinnie's style, and it somehow all just worked.

It was home.

As Levi hopped out of the car, the cool damp of the city hit him. The muted scents in the air, the humidity, the cloud cover overhead ... it was going to snow tonight.

The doors opened as he approached the building's entrance, and Frankie greeted him with a smile. "He's back!"

Levi gave him a quizzical look as they hugged and walked into the building. "Where else would I be?"

Frankie looped his arm over Levi's shoulders as he walked him onto the elevators. As soon as the elevator doors slid closed behind them, he said in a lighthearted tone, "Vinnie was figuring after you got that Jap mob boss's granddaughter back, they'd be trying to lure you away. You know, to work for them. Kind of half expected to get a 'Dear Don Bianchi' letter in the mail."

Levi turned to face the security chief of the Bianchi family as Frankie pressed the button for the top floor. People in their type of business never joked about switching alliances. That's how you found yourself at the wrong end of a bullet.

"Why the hell would you even joke about that?" he said.

His friend laughed and patted him on the shoulder. "He didn't mean anything by it. You'll see soon enough."

Levi's warning radar suddenly kicked into overdrive.

They stepped off the elevator and walked down a short hallway. Two more mobsters hopped up from their chairs and opened a set of double doors to Don Bianchi's parlor.

As Frankie and Levi walked in, Levi's heart thudded loudly. His senses were tingling. It was almost as if he could hear the crackle of the electricity running through each fiber of his muscles.

The room was unchanged since the last time he'd been there. The same two fireplaces, both lit and crackling. Vinnie's large desk, wet bar, chairs, ornately-carved wood paneling, paintings, and even the replica of the *Venus de Milo*.

Nobody else was there.

Trying to keep his breath calm, he was half-expecting the worst when the door at the far end of the room opened.

Don Vincenzo Bianchi, head of the Bianchi crime family, and Levi's lifelong friend, walked in. Their eyes met, and Vinnie's smile told him everything he needed to know.

The man was nervous.

"Levi!" Vinnie walked quickly across the room, and they hugged and kissed each other's cheeks. Like always, especially when the don was nervous, he poured himself an amaretto sour. "Can I pour you a seltzer?"

"No, I'm good."

Frankie went to the far side of the don's desk and came back rolling a large expensive-looking travel trunk. Levi's anxiety shifted toward bewilderment.

"You know what, Vinnie, maybe I'll take a spritz of seltzer." Levi walked over to the bar just as Vinnie squeezed a CO_2 cartridge into a large metal canister, and moments later the three of them were sitting around the fire, sipping their drinks.

Levi waited patiently, knowing that he'd been brought up here for a specific reason. Occasionally glancing at the shipping trunk sitting on casters between Vinnie and Frankie. It had no markings on it whatsoever.

"I know you delivered on your contract with the Tanaka syndicate." Vinnie sipped at his amber drink and then pointed at Levi with his drink hand. "They were particularly pleased with you."

"To be honest, I didn't think we had an actual contract. All I ever promised Mister Watanabe was that I'd do my best in trying to find his boss's granddaughter."

Frankie uncrossed his legs and leaned forward, his drink on the arm of the wingback leather chair. "Trust me, Vinnie set up a doozie of a deal. Lucky for us, you actually pulled through."

Levi pointed at the trunk. "Is that part of the deal?"

Vinnie shook his head and cleared his throat. "I got a call from that Watanabe guy this morning. His boss was on the line and he was translating for him. Basically, the way this guy talked about you, it was like he was talking about his own son. Levi, I don't know if he had a screw loose or something, but it was the strangest thing. Anyway, he asked me to grant him a favor for you."

Puzzled, Levi pointed at himself "A favor for me?"

"Get this. He wanted to know how much it would be to buy you out of this thing of ours, set you on a path to being free."

Levi didn't understand. He and Tanaka had barely met, yet the old man wanted him out of the business. Out of danger. *Why?*

And then it made sense.

To Levi's surprise, a warm feeling bloomed in his chest. He clamped it down and took a deep breath.

"Levi…" Vinnie's voice was low, and had developed a sudden rasp. "It doesn't matter what you do, if you're cut, I bleed. I'd never hold you back from anything. When you left after Mary's death, no questions. I understood.

"When you came back … no questions.

"You want to go, I'll understand. No questions."

Levi took in another deep breath and blew it out. He shook his and was about to say something when Vinnie motioned to Frankie.

Frankie rolled the heavy shipping trunk toward Levi.

"Open it, Levi," Vinnie said. "Whatever's in there, it's for you. A gift from Tanaka, a sort of tip."

Frankie snorted as Levi flipped open the metal latches holding the trunk closed. "Yeah, this morning, we had four of the biggest Asian muscle-heads I'd ever seen outside of a zoo bring that over."

Levi flipped open the last latch and lifted the lid—and his mouth dropped open. Inside was a fortune in dollars, yen, and euros. Hundreds of pounds of cash. "That's some tip." He tried doing the calculation in his head, it was easily millions of dollars, maybe ten million? Twenty?

Frankie whistled. "Man, that's just not something you see every day."

On top of the giant pile of money was a black lacquered wooden presentation box about eighteen inches long, held closed by a shiny gold clasp. Levi picked it up and opened it.

Inside was a scroll held closed by a red silk ribbon, and underneath it was an object wrapped in a green cloth.

Levi untied the ribbon and unrolled the scroll.

It held a freshly inked message in Japanese, drawn with precision, but without artistic flair. It wasn't Ryuki's handwriting. Tanaka's?

Levi,

My plane has just crossed over US territory and we are to meet again within a handful of hours. I cannot begin to express my gratitude for all that you've done for me and for my granddaughter, who is more precious to me than anything I possess.

I have spoken to your Don Bianchi, and realize now that

you and he are not truly kohai and senpai, junior and senior. At least, that is not how his heart knows it to be. He thinks of you as a dearest brother, even though that isn't something he said. Ryuki translated, but I heard his voice. Felt his emotions, read his meaning.

Levi glanced at Vinnie and kept his breathing steady. Focusing on the paper in his hand.

As you can likely see, I have provided for your use a new start. I can only wish for you what I had hoped to accomplish for my son: the means to live a healthy, prosperous, and long life.

It is my most sincere wish that you consider an alternate path to the one which we've both chosen. With this, I hope you can. But, even if you continue in this business, know that you will have an ally and a friend in me and in those loyal to me.

I wish you only the best.

I have also included something that I think you alone will appreciate. It had been my son's most prized possession from before he went to America, near the time you knew him. It is yours to use as honor would dictate.

Shinzo Tanaka

Curiosity flooded through Levi as he carefully unwrapped the green cloth. He gasped as he revealed a shiny dagger—a *tanto*.

With his heart racing, and nobody else existing in the world at that moment, Levi's memories flashed back to a dozen years ago when he'd been given just such an item from Master Oyama, his martial arts teacher.

The balance was the same, the weight, and of course the

maker's mark, Jun's knife was as near an exact duplicate of his as was possible.

Levi's own *tanto* had been stolen over a year ago. He looked up at Frankie and Vinnie who were quietly watching him. He lifted the dagger to his lips, kissed it, put it back into its case, and closed the lid with a smile. "Well, that was definitely unexpected." He set the box back on top of the money. "Any guesses as to how much money is in here?"

"It's about thirty million, give or take." said Frankie.

"So, what do you think?" Vinnie asked. "Off to Hawaii, buy a decent house and play with the hula girls for the rest of your life?"

Levi stood and rolled his eyes. "I got enough girls back at my mom's place that need college educations, clothes, books, and other stuff when the time comes." He stepped around the trunk and gave the don a bear hug. "I'm not going anywhere."

Vinnie embraced him tightly and whispered, "You've always been my brother, never forget that. I'd die for you, Levi."

"Right back at you." Levi stepped back and looked Vinnie in the eyes. They were wet, and slightly bloodshot, likely from the emotion of the moment. "Remember when you called me an angel in wolf's clothing?"

The don wiped his eyes. "I guess, maybe." He patted Levi's chest and chuckled. "Though that fits you to a T, my friend." He turned to Frankie and pointed at the trunk. "You'll need to talk to the Rosenbergs about getting this kind of cash into the system so that Levi doesn't get the feds breathing down his neck for their share."

As Vinnie and Frankie talked shop, Levi replayed in his mind Vinnie's reaction to his mentioning the phrase.

There's no way that Mason would have picked up on that

same phrase, was there? Yet Levi couldn't imagine Vinnie being involved with anything that had to do with Mason or any fed. Vinnie had always had a visceral disdain for all authority but his own.

Levi looked down at the cash. It suddenly dawned on him what such a staggering amount of money actually meant to him. He'd always had a nagging worry about how he'd take care of his mother and the kids, especially if something happened to him. But with this, he'd be able to set them up so that no matter what happens to him, they'd be fine.

He closed his eyes, took a deep breath, and smiled.

With no complicated relationships, no feds breathing down his neck, and nobody expecting anything from him at the moment, life was finally getting back to some semblance of normalcy.

∼

Levi was sound asleep when the phone rang. He lurched into a sitting position, snatched up the phone from its cradle, and said, "Yes?"

"Sorry, Levi. It's Tony from the front. We've got a lady named Lucy here. She says she knows you and it's important, but she made it pretty clear that she ain't letting us frisk her."

Rubbing the sleep from his eyes, Levi saw it was only three in the morning. He chuckled. "Asian lady, right? Pretty hot, but if looks could kill, you'd all be dead?"

"Smoking hot, and ya. Exactly that."

"Okay, send her up. I'll talk to her."

"You got it."

Levi stumbled out of bed, and by the time he walked over to the door, he heard the first knock.

He opened the door, and there she stood, as lovely and statuesque as always. A few snowflakes sparkled in her jet-black hair.

She took a step toward him. "Remember, don't touch me."

Then she looped her arm around his neck, pulled him in for a kiss and pressed herself against him.

Before he knew what was even going on, she walked past him and took a seat in the same leather armchair she'd sat in before.

Levi looked at her with utter bewilderment. "What was—"

"I wanted to make sure I got your attention." Her slight Russian accent became more pronounced. "I have a proposition for you."

"Oh?" Levi stood by the coffee table. "Is this something I should be sitting down for?"

Lucy smiled—an unusual expression for her. She seemed excited about something. "Yes, you'll probably need to be sitting."

Levi sat, but couldn't help but replay in his mind what had just happened at his front door.

"Okay, what's up?"

Lucy leaned forward, her smile widening. "I think you and I need to start our own business."

PREVIEW OF NEVER AGAIN

"If all you drink is seltzer, how am I supposed to seduce you into seeing reason?"

Levi took another sip of his seltzer and stared across the table at the attractive thirty-something Asian woman. They were sitting in Gerard's, his favorite hole-in-the-wall bar in New York's Little Italy. A few customers chatted amiably at the bar, and the smell of garlic and marinara wafted in from the kitchen.

"Just because you think you're right doesn't mean I'm going to agree," he replied. "I'm not this angel you think I am."

Lucy Chen was nursing a scotch and soda. She leaned forward and shook her head. "I never called you an angel," she said with her slight Russian accent. "I just know you. You're willing to do whatever it takes to get the job done, but you're picky about the kind of jobs you'll take on. Too picky." She motioned discreetly toward two beefy men digging into heaping portions of pasta. "You're loyal to your family, I get that. I admire it. But I want you and I to work together on this. We can do so much good in this crappy world if we cooperate. I need a partner in this."

They'd been having this debate for over a month. Lucy wanted Levi to go into "business" with her, but he had other obligations. Besides, he wasn't sure what to make of her. The smoldering behind those dark brown eyes was… intense. In fact, everything about her was dialed up to eleven. The widow of a Chinese gang leader, she was the epitome of the dragon lady stereotype. And through a strange twist of fate, Levi had managed to get himself entangled with her.

He did trust her. To an extent, anyway. After all, she knew more about him than most. Few outside of his normal mob connections knew he was a member of the Bianchi crime family.

Denny, the owner of the bar, walked over and knelt so that he was eye level with the two of them. "Can I get you guys something to eat? The girls in the kitchen are using Gino's recipes." He hitched his thumb toward the two mob enforcers devouring their food. "It's pretty good stuff, even if I say so myself."

Levi smiled ruefully as he realized how much Gerard's had expanded over the last year. Once a small, some would say cozy, neighborhood bar that only served drinks, it was now a mob hangout complete with a dinner menu. He'd preferred it as a quiet place, because Denny wasn't just a bar owner, the skinny black man born and bred in Brooklyn was Levi's main intelligence contact. He was a gadget man, a genius with electronics, and had his ear to the ground about nearly everything.

Lucy shook her head. "Levi and I are going out on a date, so it's best we don't ruin our appetite."

Levi worked hard to keep his frown from showing.

The front door's bell jingled as it opened, and with a smile, Denny turned away to greet his newest customer.

Lucy smiled as she stared back at Levi … and he felt as though she could read his mind. She leaned forward and whispered, "You know damn well that anyone who knows I'm staying at your apartment figures we're a couple. And if they know we're not, that can bring up some awkward questions I'd rather not answer."

Levi sat back in his chair and nodded. Of course she was right, which annoyed the hell out of him. She'd been living with him for the last six weeks, ever since the FBI cracked down on the local Chinese gang she'd been affiliated with and ended up taking down of one of the major Triads in Hong Kong—the same one that Lucy's deceased husband had headed. He couldn't be sure how much she'd been involved in orchestrating that revenge. But one thing was certain: she was a marked woman, and he'd offered her whatever protection he could until things calmed down.

Denny walked back over with an odd expression. He leaned down and hitched his thumb toward the door. "Levi, that lady says she's looking for you. But I get the distinct feeling she doesn't really know who you are. Do you want me to send her away?"

Levi turned in his chair. Standing by the door was a woman in her fifties, dressed all in black, wringing her hands and looking very uncomfortable. He waved at her, caught her attention, and motioned her to the empty seat at his table.

Denny shrugged and went back to the bar.

The woman's look of discomfort was obvious as she skirted past tables and patrons, trying not to touch anything. She pulled out the proffered chair, sat, glanced at them both and said, "I was told to come here, and that Mister Yoder would help me with my problem." She looked at Levi. "Are you him?"

Levi extended his hand. "I'm Levi Yoder. And you are…?"

The woman looked at his outstretched hand and shook her head slightly. "I'm Rivka Cohen."

Lucy extended her hand and said, "*At hassidi?*"

As soon as the woman nodded and shook hands with Lucy, Levi understood. He didn't speak Hebrew or Yiddish, and he was mildly surprised that Lucy knew any, but he knew enough to realize this Cohen woman was very much out of her element. A Hassid was a follower of an ultra-orthodox Jewish movement. Not the type of people Levi often crossed paths with, but there were plenty of them in Crown Heights, only twenty minutes away. And it explained why she wouldn't shake his hand, but would shake Lucy's.

Because he was a guy.

Levi smiled, trying to make this woman, who was clearly a bundle of nerves, more comfortable. "I'm sorry, I would offer you a drink, but I know you won't take it, so how can I help?"

The woman's eyes grew shiny as if she were about to start crying. "My Uncle Menachem, he's a jeweler at a place on Franklin Avenue. He said that you once bought something from him and left with him a promise. Do you remember that?"

Levi pulled in a deep breath as his mind raced back many years—to when he'd been looking for an engagement ring for his now-deceased wife. "Menachem Shemtov?" he said. "The same Menachem who worked at a jewelry store at Franklin and Park Place?"

The woman nodded.

"My God, that was ages ago. Your uncle did this *goy* a great favor on a purchase. I'm surprised he remembers me. I promised to return the favor someday. What can I do for you?"

Rivka wrung her hands together with a pained expression.

"My husband died four months ago. The police say it was a suicide, but I know that he'd never take his own life." She screwed up her courage, even though tears began dripping down her cheeks. "They said he was having an affair, but I know that's impossible too. I have evidence that says so. Can you help me clear his name? It's very important to me, to our kids, to our family. I don't have much money, but I can help pay expenses, I think."

Levi tried to keep what he was thinking from showing on his face. This wasn't what he did. And what she'd described made sense. Religious guy has sex with some random, or maybe some not-so-random person, he feels guilty about it, and he kills himself. This situation had disappointment written all over it.

"What do you mean you have evidence?" Lucy asked.

Rivka looked back and forth between Lucy and Levi.

Lucy waved dismissively at Levi and explained, "Don't worry, we work together."

Levi was about to retort when Rivka turned to him and asked, "Do you mind if I just talk to her? This would be much easier for me."

He opened his mouth, then closed it.

Lucy motioned him toward another table. "Give us girls a little space."

Feeling slightly annoyed, Levi took his glass of seltzer and sat at another table. He sipped at his drink, focusing his better-than-most hearing on what was being said. Unfortunately, there was just enough background noise in the bar, particularly from a rowdy group at a nearby table laughing and having a good time, that he couldn't make out what was being said.

After a minute of whispered conversation between the two women, Lucy clasped hands with Rivka and gave her a sympathetic look. The Jewish woman pulled out an envelope and slid it toward Lucy.

Levi raised his eyebrows as Lucy peeked into the envelope, nodded at the woman and tucked the envelope inside her jacket pocket.

What the hell is she getting us into?

Rivka then stood, kissed Lucy on both cheeks, and walked out of Gerard's without giving Levi a second look.

Drinking the last of her scotch and soda, Lucy strolled over to him and planted a kiss on his cheek. "It's all taken care of."

Levi stood. "What's taken care of? What did you agree to?"

Lucy dismissed the question with a flippant gesture, then waved at Denny and started toward the door.

Levi followed. "Lucy. Seriously. What did you just agree to with that woman?"

She opened the door for him and smiled. "I believe her story, and I told her we'd help."

"We?"

Lucy wrapped her arm around his as they walked out of the bar. "Don't worry about it. We'll talk over dinner."

~

Having set up a breading station on his kitchen counter, Levi dusted the sliced and peeled eggplant with flour, dipped it in egg, and then the seasoned bread crumbs. He glanced at Lucy as she sliced fresh Roma tomatoes for the dinner's salad. He'd promised to keep her safe, but the only safe places were his apartment building and Denny's. So instead of a nice dinner out, it was the Amish fixer and the Chinese dragon lady cooking and eating in a mafia-protected apartment—again.

"So, are you going to tell me what's up with this Cohen woman? Why did you take her money and agree to help her? The story has loser written all over it."

Lucy met his gaze as she laid out the tomatoes on a serving dish and began slicing fresh mozzarella. "Why do you think her case is such a loser?"

Levi shook his head as he carefully laid the breaded eggplant slices into the hot oil. "I don't care if he's a religious guy, when someone's eye wanders, they can succumb just like anyone else. I'm wagering he shacked up with some lady he worked with, probably not even Jewish, and he felt a huge amount of guilt and offed himself. It happens all the time. That's why I don't get why you don't see that. Guys can be like that. I should know."

"Tell me the truth," Lucy said. She'd put the cheese over the tomatoes and was now thinly slicing red onion. "I'll wager you never cheated on anyone in your life."

Levi's mind raced to the few times he'd ever been with a woman that wasn't his wife. He pursed his lips and gave Lucy a sour expression.

"See!" She laughed. "You haven't, have you?"

Levi fished the golden-brown eggplant slices out of the oil and began frying new ones. "No, but I suppose I've never been accused of cheating on anyone. If the cops think he was having an affair, there's probably a reason."

"You're right, but it can't be sex."

"Why's that?"

"Rivka and her husband have seven kids, and the only reason they don't have more is because her husband's diabetes caused him to not be able to get it up anymore. Rivka said they'd even tried Viagra, and it didn't work." Lucy scattered the onions onto the tomato and mozzarella. "She says she has the medical reports to prove it."

Levi frowned as he fished the last of the eggplant from the oil and turned off the stovetop burner. "And the cops didn't take that into consideration? What about the person he supposedly had an affair with? Did they get her testimony?"

Lucy shrugged as she sprinkled shredded basil over the food she'd just prepared and grabbed a bottle of aged balsamic vinegar. "Like I said, there's lots of unanswered questions. She's invited us over for dinner tomorrow. Rivka said she'd give us copies of everything she has, let us look over his home office, and field any of our questions."

With a harrumph, Levi picked up the platter of fried eggplant and a pot of freshly made marinara, and headed for the dining room. "Just because it sounds suspicious doesn't mean we can help with any of it. Don't I get a say in any of this?"

Lucy set her plate on the table and began dishing out servings of the caprese salad. "Of course you do. But you just pointed out there's lots of unanswered questions, this is possibly having to do with a murder cover-up, and it sounded like you owed her family a favor. You're not the type to go back on your word, so do I really need to ask you if you're in?"

Levi put two pieces of perfectly fried eggplant on her plate and spooned some marinara on it. As he served himself as well, he glared at her. She was one of the most frustrating people he'd ever met. "It would be nice," he said.

She poured herself a glass of Mondavi white zinfandel and poured him a glass of Perrier. "So? Are you in? Or am I going by myself?"

They clinked glasses. "When are *we* supposed to head over there?" he asked.

Lucy smiled, and for a second he forgot that she was a former mobster who was trying to turn over a new leaf. Instead he saw an attractive woman who was intelligent, assertive, and very idiosyncratic. He was never able to guess what was going to come out of her mouth next, and it was exhausting.

"Before sundown. I guess we should get there at about five-thirty."

Levi took a bite of the salad. It needed a sprinkle of salt.

Lucy nibbled at her own salad and frowned. "I forgot the salt." She pushed back from the table, got the salt shaker from the kitchen, and sprinkled salt on her salad as well as his. "Try it now, it'll be better. Oh, and you'll need to wear your suit."

He shook his head and tried to keep the smile from reaching his face. "Yes, ma'am." He glanced at the tight-fitting white floral dress she was wearing. It hugged her slender curves, and didn't exactly seem appropriate for a dinner event full of religious people. "And what are you going to wear?"

"We'll go shopping in the morning. I know just the outfit. I've been eyeing it at Bergdorf's."

∽

Paulie opened the rear passenger door to the Lincoln Town Car and both Levi and Lucy stepped out.

Levi shook hands with the huge mobster, who was just a couple inches shy of seven feet tall and built like a bodybuilder. Beside him stood Tom, the mobster who'd ridden shotgun.

"It'll probably be a few hours," Levi said. "You guys can go get dinner or something, I'll call you when we're done."

Paulie smiled and shook his head. "Not happening." He

pointed at an empty spot on the side of Lincoln Place. "We'll park there and keep watch on things. The don's orders."

"Okay, I understand. I'll call when we're about to finish." Levi knew better than to argue. Vinnie, the head of the Bianchi family, was aware of the Lucy situation and was taking every precaution possible.

Levi looked over at Lucy and for the first time took in the details of the outfit she was wearing. She'd said it was a Kay Unger mikado gown, which meant nothing to him, but the long form-fitting dress had an Asian look to his eyes. It was a dark shimmering affair with colored sequin embroidery that reminded him of her dragon tattoo. It had a long slit up the side, revealing hints of her athletic build.

"You're going to make some of the rabbis faint with that outfit of yours," he said.

"If they are truly godly men, they won't be looking. And besides, I've been eyeing this thing forever, and it finally went on sale. I'm glad you like it." Lucy wrapped her arm around his and winked. "Let's go. I'd like to help Rivka with the setup for dinner if she'll let me."

With Paulie and Tom watching, they walked up the steps to the townhome.

Levi pressed the doorbell, and soon he heard the sound of footsteps. The door opened and an older man with a full white beard greeted them with a curious expression. "*Oy vey*, Mister Yoder, you haven't aged a day in what must be twenty years. God has truly blessed you. Do you remember—"

Levi smiled as he spotted the younger man in the old man in front of him. "Menachem, please call me Levi. Of course I remember you."

They hugged and then kissed on both cheeks. Levi motioned to Lucy. "This is my business partner, Lucy."

Menachem smiled at Lucy and bowed his head while stepping aside for them to enter. "It's a pleasure to meet you."

"Lucy! Mister Yoder!" Rivka's voice echoed in the hallway as she rushed toward the door, a smile on her face. "*Gut Shabbes* to you both. It's so good that you came, and just in time."

Within moments, Rivka had taken Lucy with her to the kitchen, and Menachem had led Levi to the living room where nearly a dozen men had gathered ahead of dinner.

Menachem cleared his throat and addressed the men. "This is Levi Yoder. He's the guest I spoke about earlier."

The men introduced themselves, and Levi took a seat on one of the wooden chairs.

The men were dressed in traditional black Jewish garb, fringes of their prayer shawls peeking out from under their formal jackets. All wore a head covering, which Levi knew was called a *kippah*.

Levi patted the top of his head and asked, "Should I be wearing a *kippah*?"

Most of the men's eyes widened, but the oldest of the group chuckled and said, "If you wouldn't mind wearing a *yarmulke*, I think that would be very nice." He fished from his pocket a hand-sized circular head covering with Hebrew letters sewn into it and handed it to Levi.

"I might be a *goy*, but I've lived in New York long enough to know there are some traditions I should respect." Levi put the prayer cap on, and the mood lightened as the men began talking about their day.

Suddenly, what seemed to be an endless stream of kids raced through the room with an older child chasing after them and yelling, "Get cleaned up for Shabbat, we only have fifteen minutes!"

Menachem pulled his chair up alongside Levi's, patted him on the back, and whispered, "We'll talk more after dinner."

###

The main dining room wasn't big enough for everyone to be seated, so the tables spanned past the dining room, into the kitchen, and into the next room as well. Levi had been seated beside Zalman, the eldest of the Cohen family, and the one who'd handed him his kippah, who sat at its head. Lucy was at the far end of the table—still in the dining room—smiling as she interacted with the other women, many of whom were helping with the nearly two dozen kids gathered.

Zalman stood, and all three rooms quickly quieted. "We have guests today who might otherwise be confused by the significance of this day, so it is a *mitzvah*, a blessing, for us all to help them at least understand why we do what we do.

"Tonight is the beginning of Shabbat, the seventh day of the week. The prayers that follow will recount how the Almighty rested on the seventh day and sanctified it. We will then have a blessing over the wine and a blessing thanking the Almighty for giving us this day of rest."

Zalman lifted a cup of nearly overflowing wine and focused on the sabbath candles flickering on the table. They'd been lit by Rivka earlier. In a deep voice he began to say some prayers.

"Yom Ha-shi-shi. Va-y'chu-lu Ha-sha-ma-yim v'ha-a-retz, v'chawl^ts'va-am.

"Va-y'chal e-lo-him ba-yom ha-sh'vi-i, m'lach-to a-sher a-sa

"Va-yish-bot ba-yom ha-sh'vi-i, mi-kawl^m'lach-to a-sher a-sa.

"Va-y'va-rech e-lo-him et yom ha-sh'vi-i, va-y'ka-deish o-to ki vo sha-vat mi-kawl^m'lach-to a-sher ba-ra e-lo-him la-a-sot."

The man next to Levi showed him a prayer book written in English, and pointed to the translation of what Zalman was saying.

The sixth day. And the heavens and the earth and all their hosts were completed. And God finished by the Seventh Day His work which He had done, and He rested on the Seventh Day from all His work which He had done. And God blessed the Seventh Day and made it holy, for on it He rested from all His work which God created to function.

As Zalman's prayer rang through the home, Levi looked at everyone around the table. They were all mouthing the same words, with their heads slightly bowed.

They then prayed over the wine, and finally over the bread. And then it was time to eat.

He glanced at Lucy, and their eyes met. She smiled and gave him a wink.

There was a wholesome feel to this gathering. It reminded him of his Amish upbringing in some ways. Even though he'd left his Amish community when he was eighteen and had never really looked back, he'd also never outright rejected formal religion as a groundwork for beliefs. These people believed in what they practiced, as did his family, and that was something he could relate to, even if he didn't share in the day-to-day practices of either of them.

Menachem handed him a piece of the braided egg bread that was traditional for the Sabbath. "I wonder," he said, "do you like gefilte fish?"

Levi shrugged. "I don't know what a gefilte is, but I like fish. I'll try anything that you put in front of me."

Zalman leaned over with an amused expression. "It's okay if you don't like it. I'm not a fan either."

And that started a heated debate over gefilte fish that led to other amusing discussions that occupied the better part of two hours.

～

After dinner, Rivka led Levi, Lucy, and Menachem up the narrow stairs to a closed door. She pulled a key from a hidden pocket in her dress and unlocked the door. "This is Mendel's office. It hasn't been touched since the break-in. Please, have a seat."

Lights automatically turned on as they entered the room. Levi had learned during his visit that this was a feature in some Orthodox Jewish households.

Levi followed Menachem and Lucy into a cramped study filled with a large desk. It was a working office, that was obvious. Two of the walls had built-in shelves crammed with books. Nothing fancy, just lots of books on random topics, including an Encyclopedia Britannica from 1969 that occupying one entire shelf. Many of the books had Hebrew letters on their binders.

Levi turned to Rivka. "Can you start from the beginning? What exactly did your husband do?"

She closed the door to the office. "He was a consumer reporter. It was his passion." She smiled, looking much calmer than she had at the bar. "It was how we met many years ago."

"What kind of things did he report on? And where? Was it for TV stations, the newspaper…?"

"Mostly newspaper, but sometimes he'd be interviewed on television. When he started, he had a column in the local papers." She blushed and pursed her lips. "You'll probably think it's silly, but back then he would investigate kosher restaurants and report any violations or questionable behaviors so that others would be warned. That eventually led to him reporting on international food imports and exports, and that's when the *Intelligencer* picked him up."

The *Intelligencer* was a huge newspaper with millions of daily readers. "Is that where he worked most recently?" Levi asked.

"Yes. And he became agitated about things at work, and I suppose that's what you want to know about. He told me about some of it. Over the last couple years, he'd noticed how some of his work was being edited to remove names, or it was not being run at all, even though the local editor had given his approval."

"Isn't that pretty normal?" Lucy asked. "From what I understand, there's usually more stories than there's space to print, isn't there?"

Rivka nodded. "True, but Mendel's been doing this for over twenty years... I mean... he had been doing it for that long." She sighed. "And even though it was his job to warn people about problems, he always gave the targets of his stories the benefit of the doubt. It would ruin him professionally if he wrote anything that was inaccurate or misleading.

"But he confided something to me that he wasn't yet prepared to put into print. In fact, he wasn't sure if he ever would be. He was almost convinced that the company he was working for was purposefully trying to deceive its readers. To shape the narrative, if you will."

Levi frowned. "I don't understand. Isn't that a newspaper's job? I see outlandish stuff in the papers all the time."

"That's the editorial sections. My husband worked in what people in the trade like to call *hard news*. It should involve no opinions, just the facts. But Mendel was convinced that the management at the paper wasn't interested in telling their millions of readers the truth."

"Okay," Levi said. "I understand why that would upset your husband. But do you really think that would be cause for him to be murdered?"

Menachem cleared his throat. "My brother-in-law was a very righteous man. He felt it was his calling to bring the truth to the people. You need to realize that to him, what the paper was doing was a sin. I also heard plenty from him in the last year about this issue. He made it clear that even though the newspaper never lied, by ensuring certain things were never said in print, they molded the public narrative. It was a sin of omission."

Lucy nodded in understanding. "I suppose it would be like talking about how a police officer shot a teenager on the streets, and leaving out the fact that the teenager was aiming a gun at him."

"Exactly," Rivka affirmed. "Anyway, in the days just before Mendel died, he was particularly upset. He wouldn't talk about it, even to me. And then… and then he was dead."

"And you think he was murdered because…?"

Rivka picked up a manila folder from the desk and handed it to Levi. "That's the medical examiner's report. They said he was poisoned, though they labeled the manner of death as undetermined." She took in a deep shuddering breath. "But later, the manner was changed to suicide based on the testimony of someone who had to be lying."

Levi recalled what Lucy had told him about the claim of an affair. He wasn't going to push that for the moment. He flipped through the folder. It also contained a police report, with some names redacted.

"You mentioned a break-in," he said. "Tell me about that."

Rivka hid her face and began sobbing. Menachem patted her shoulder, and Lucy moved closer to her and handed her a tissue from a nearby dispenser.

Her uncle responded for her. "It happened during Mendel's funeral. Someone broke in and tossed this office, and touched nothing else in the house. Whoever did it had to know we were all gone for the funeral."

Levi thought of the ornate silver menorah and all the other valuable items he'd seen downstairs. "What was in here worth taking and ignoring the rest of the house?"

"We don't know." Rivka wiped her face, looking both distraught and embarrassed. "They took all the books off the shelves, emptied his drawers, and the only thing I know of that was missing was his work notebook."

"They stole his laptop?"

"No, a spiral notebook. Mendel preferred writing things longhand. I know it was on his desk, where he always had it. But it was gone."

Levi surveyed the office. There was something definitely not right about this. What could possibly be so important in a reporter's notes that they'd break in to steal them?

Levi stepped over to the mahogany desk and pulled open one of the drawers. It was full of empty file folders. The notebook had been lying in plain sight on top of the desk, yet the intruder had seemingly gone to the trouble of ransacking the drawers and shelves as well.

"Do you know what he kept in these drawers?" he asked.

"Not specifically," Rivka said. "When we cleaned up, we just put things back where it felt like they belonged."

He exchanged a glance with Lucy. They were both almost

certainly thinking the same thing. Not just a notebook was missing.

On top of the desk was a book with Hebrew writing. Levi thumbed through its pages of unintelligible script and stopped when he discovered a yellow sticky note. There were seven names written on the paper, with an arrow pointing to some of the Hebrew print in the book.

He turned the book toward Menachem and Rivka. "What does it say in the section the arrow is pointing to?"

Menachem leaned forward and squinted through his thick glasses. "Ah, this chapter of the Bible would be what you call Proverbs. This section says, 'A false witness shall not be unpunished, and he that speaks lies shall not escape.'"

Rivka smiled. "That would be just like Mendel. He'd find a passage with layers of meaning to him."

Levi drummed his fingers on the desk. He wasn't sure what to make of all this. But the least he could do was track down whoever had given the testimonial and learn about the truth of the affair.

He removed the sticky note from the book and noticed that it had more writing on the back, in Hebrew. He showed it to Rivka. "What does this say?"

She leaned forward, and her face grew pale. "It says, 'It's the Nazis.'"

AUTHOR'S NOTE

Well, that's the end of *The Inside Man*, and I sincerely hope you enjoyed it.

Since this is book two of a series, I'll presume that I've introduced myself to you before and won't make you suffer through that sort of tedium again.

However, I did want to talk a bit about my contract with you, the reader.

I write to entertain.

That truly is my first and primary goal. Because, for most people, that's what they want out of a novel.

That's certainly what I always wanted. Story first, always.

Now, don't get me wrong, there are all sorts of perfectly valid reasons to be reading, and in fact, I get a huge kick out of it when people tell me that they kept on having to look things up to see if they were real, and being shocked to learn that they were.

For me, I do take pride in trying to give people entertainment, while attempting to stay as true to the science and technology as possible. And if the novel is inspired by real events in some way, like this one, I try to provide verifiable excerpts that allow readers a bit more insight into the facts of the subjects covered in the story.

When my stories contain topics that have possible controversy or ones with potentially polarizing opinions associated with them (e.g. GMO) I never take a position as the author. I let the characters play out their roles and make no advocacies. However, I do endeavor to lay out the facts as they exist for the reader to ultimately draw their own conclusions.

So far, I've covered broken arrow incidents (See *Perimeter* for that), the potential disasters of uncontrolled genetic modification (*Darwin's Cipher*), and in this novel, child sex trafficking.

Some have called my choices eclectic, unexpected, but the vast majority of feedback I've received to date has been positive. So, thank you for that. Posting reviews is, of course, the easiest way to let me and others know what you thought of this novel or any of my work. Word of mouth is precious to us poor authors.

However, even though I enjoy writing about events, history, science especially, my primary goal always circles back to entertaining.

I do hope you enjoyed this story, and I hope you'll continue to join me in the future stories yet to come.

Mike Rothman
March 29, 2019

ADDENDUM

I took an unusual approach with this novel in that I started with testimony given in front of a Senate subcommittee from a person named Tim Ballard. We're very used to reading novels, especially thrillers, that blur fact with fiction, often making it hard to know where one ends and the other begins.

Well, let's just say that the excerpts I listed are word-for-word true testimony, and I made sure to include footnotes for any data that was used.

I've always lived by the motto of trust, but verify, and I want to make it easy on you, the reader, to do the same.

I chose not to excerpt more of Tim's testimony, because frankly, some of it is particularly intense. However, I did use some of the facts from his testimony in this story.

And since I did use his testimony, it would be unfair for me to not at least mention Operation Underground Railroad, a nonprofit that Tim founded whose goal it is to rescue victims of child sex trafficking. See https://ourrescue.org for more information.

ADDENDUM

Even though this title is very much a mainstream thriller, I couldn't help but include nods toward science in one form or another. Given that, I feel somewhat compelled to either explain some of the science or maybe give a bit more detail than the story otherwise demanded.

Obviously, my goal in this addendum isn't to give you a crash course on college-level science, but instead give you enough information or keywords so that you have the data necessary to do more research, if you're interested.

Levi's hat:

I actually introduced the concept of Levi's rather useful hat in *Perimeter*, but let me take a moment to talk a bit about the science behind this.

For those who need a reminder, this hat has tiny metal posts on the inside liner that give its wearer a little directional tingle when someone is staring at them. In other words, you put this hat on, and when you walk through a crowd, you'll be able to feel if someone is watching you, and from which direction.

It does sound a bit like science fiction, but the technology that would be needed to create such a thing is definitely in our grasp. Sure, some might argue it would be bulky or have some other complaint, but it's definitely possible to construct.

In fact, for me to explain, let me grab a small caption from *Perimeter*, where I think I did a pretty good job of trying to explain things at a layman's level.

ADDENDUM

Denny unclipped the hat from the belt and showed Levi the film-like electronics encircling the hat's lining. "So, you've seen how at night, when a light shines into an animal's eyes, you see an eerie glow reflecting off of them, right?"

Levi nodded.

"Well, humans don't have that same reflective property, at least not to that extent. For our retina to reflect light, we need something brighter. You've seen what happens when there's a camera flash."

"You mean that red-eye effect?"

"Exactly." Denny pointed at a series of tiny tube-like projections that barely poked through the lining of the mesh cap. "What I have here is something that's a bit nuts, because if you could see the light, your head would probably look like it was a 360-degree flashlight it was so bright."

"What do you mean?"

Denny pressed his lips together. "Okay, so we normally can only see light at certain wavelengths. Let me start simple for a moment. We probably all learned in school about ROY G BIV, the colors of the rainbow starting at red and ending at violet. That corresponds to light at wavelengths of roughly 700 to 350 nanometers. The bigger the wavelength, the closer to red, the shorter, the closer to violet. That's what our human eye can detect. But that's not the limit of the light that exists. For instance, that hat is sending out a bunch of light in every direction at roughly 1550 nanometers. Deep into the infrared spectrum. Each of the tiny lasers in there sucks up a good amount of power, and even though you aren't feeling it, the laser's aim is tilting up and down at about twenty times a second.

"So what you have is basically a hat that's projecting light that nobody can see in all directions. It's strong enough to hit *things and bounce off. That's where my electronic filters comes in. I'm heavily filtering what comes back and trying to alert you only if I've detected a signal bouncing back that seems to be following you."*

"Does it work from a distance?"

"It should be good out to about a hundred yards. Anything more than that, I'm currently squelching, because the reflection gets dicey."

Levi removed the belt, and Denny put both items back in the case.

"So, let me get this straight," Levi said. "I wear that, and it spits light out that nobody can see in every direction. If someone's looking at me, the light is going to bounce back, and the hat has sensors that will alert me."

So, even though there may not be a commercial product that you can buy that does what this hat does, it wouldn't surprise me in the least if there were such things available for those with certain clandestine needs.

Denny's Dry Suit:

We've all seen in the movies where the good guy (or maybe the bad guy) is trying to enter a highly-secure room and a drip of sweat sets off all sorts of alarms. That isn't quite what Levi was dealing with, but it gives you a flavor of the type of problem second story folks (thieves) might have to deal with in an advanced security setting.

Of course, dealing with heat signatures is a whole new level of difficulty. There actually have been movies that demonstrated

ADDENDUM

something like Denny's dry suit. One in particular comes to mind. It's the microchip scene in *The Saint*, with Val Kilmer.

In that movie, Val Kilmer finds himself trying to break into a vault to steal a microchip, but to even get near the vault, he has to pass through a series of thermal detectors. This is actually a great scene in that it's actually tough to make a human body suddenly not have a heat signature. For a movie, *The Saint* did pretty well. The suit the actor was wearing did at least give an homage to covering all the skin and face. However, it missed a few details, which is inevitable for a movie. If you're coming in from a cold climate into a warm one, no matter how good your thermal controls are, you won't be able to immediately match the warm temperature. These things take time.

An example of a common issue would be condensation.

Think about it. When you have a cold beverage, your glass will quickly get wet as the water in the air condenses onto the cold surface of the glass. It would be almost a certainty that our actor's vision would be fogged up before the suit readjusts the temperature.

For Levi, he didn't need something that did pretty well, he needed something that was rock solid.

Luckily, the scenario Levi faced was quite different than what Val Kilmer faced. The premise of any suit that's advertised to match the surrounding temperature has a few difficulties it needs to overcome. The first being that the body inside it is constantly producing heat. So, to counteract that heat, it needs to be able to resist that influence.

The only real way to do that is to have excellent heat conductivity. In this case, the dry suit needs to be able to conduct thermal energy efficiently and constantly, without any of that excess thermal energy being detected.

To accomplish it, you'd need to be able to circulate cooling or heating (depending on the need) at a constant rate so that every exposed surface has the same temperature. The easiest way to do it is with a circulating (heated or cooled) fluid, almost like how an air condition works.

However, if you're like Levi, and trying to match the temperature of the outside, let's say near freezing, you don't want your skin to be freezing.

What to do?

That's when you need to have several distinct layers. You'd need an outer layer that has the ability to keep things at whatever external temperature you want, but you also need another circulating layer that keeps you from freezing to death. And in truth, you'd want a third layer in between the prior two to act as insulation, to lessen the effect that each circulating layer has on the other.

So, we now have a dry suit, with three layers, two of which have some kind of independent pump that circulates a fluid to help normalize the temperatures. And remember, each of these circu-

ADDENDUM

lating layers would in essence be hollow—they'd need space for the fluid to flow.

So, even though making such a dry suit would be quite an undertaking, it's certainly possible. And likely bulky.

For all I know, they may actually sell such things, but at worst, we know people like Denny will be around to supply our clandestine forces with all sorts of interesting goodies.

Who knows what new invention Denny will come up with next?

ABOUT THE AUTHOR

I am an Army brat, a polyglot, and the first person in my family born in the United States. This heavily influenced my youth by instilling a love of reading and a burning curiosity about the world and all of the things within it. As an adult, my love of travel and adventure has allowed me to explore many unimaginable locations, and these places sometimes creep into the stories I write.

I hope you've found this story entertaining.

- Mike Rothman

You can find my blog at: www.michaelarothman.com
I'm also on Facebook at: www.facebook.com/MichaelARothman
And on Twitter: @MichaelARothman

Printed by BoD"in Norderstedt, Germany